PUTTING OUT
THE LIGHTS

Also by this author

Maggie Magee and the Last Magician
Village Life
The Jethart House
The Time Walkers
A Most Peculiar Hotel
Fields Of Stone
Tiggie
The Pineapple King Of Jarrow
Uncle Freddie & The Prince Of Wales

PUTTING OUT THE LIGHTS

*An Episode in the War
Between Good & Evil*

Alex Ferguson

ISBN: 978-0-244-09469-0

PublishNation
www.publishnation.co.uk

ALEX FERGUSON is a national award-winning writer with Silver and Gold Awards from the Writers' Guild. He worked with Corin and Vanessa Redgrave to write three successful plays for Moving Theatre. THE FLAG was performed at Battersea and CASEMENT at the Riverside. He has contributed to a number of television series and built a successful reputation in radio and theatre drama. His comic radio series ran for six years on Radio Four. He created and ran the youth theatre company, Bold As Brass, on Tyneside for ten years which climaxed in a wonderful run at the Jermyn Street Theatre with DO YOU SEE WHAT I SEE? In 2016 he wrote the feature film, BLISS! which has been chosen for screening by four International Film Festivals in the United Kingdom, Europe and the United States. Tiring of chasing actors to perform, he sat down to write books and filled a shelf on Kindle.

In March 2018, Alex Ferguson was admitted to Trusteeship of the Customs House Theatre Trust for his services to the Arts.

Millions face their demons every day. And count themselves cowards when they are heroes. Thousands perish, believing they are alone, not seeing the hands outstretched. But millions fight their demons, never surrender, and die fighting. The demons are not omnipotent, otherwise the battle would have been lost millennia ago and Mankind's brief reign, at best, a memory.

CHAPTER ONE

"I'm not with them.
I've come to set you free. "

Walter Ashcroft awoke into a sour Monday morning. Washing, shaving, dressing didn't change his mood. There was little more than a scraping of sugar in the bag and the instant coffee tasted as foul as ever. The midnight encounter with the prostitute had been both expensive and disappointing. Flushed with vodka and lager, he had been too fearful of going back to her flat and dragged the woman into a mews. Too excited, he had ejaculated before he could penetrate her. She had laughed at him and when he refused to pay, she squeezed his vulnerable parts in an iron grip. Walter paid up.

His umbrella wouldn't open properly and so he walked through the rain, carrying a furled umbrella to Epping underground. The platform was as crowded as ever. Walter knew then he hated the whole human race and hated Mr. Turnbridge of Turnbridge, Simpson and Tennyson with heart and soul. Every day spent with Turnbridge was a further day in Hell.

The three schoolboys were there as they were every day, standing before him at the exact spot the carriage door would open. The boys were laughing. The tall boy was telling a funny story. When his gaze swept over Walter, the boy didn't see him. Anger boiled in Walter. There was such an air of assurance about the boy, Walter decided to teach him a lesson. As the train pulled out of the tunnel, Walter gave the boy a sharp poke with his umbrella. The boy vanished under the wheels of the train. In the tumult and confusion, Walter Ashcroft walked home. As he passed the neglected garden in Elthem Terrace, he threw the umbrella into the nettles.

When he reached home, he made and drank another cup of coffee without sugar. He struggled to understand why he had done what he did and found no answer. Walter added the cup to the clutter on the

1

draining board. Then he dialled 999 to confess that he had killed the boy at Epping tube station.

"I only meant to give him a little poke."

"We all have our bad days, sir. Just relax. We'll be with you, soon as we can, to sort it out."

"Thank you. I'll leave the front door open."

An older man was mounting the steps to Walter's front door, but turned about at the rising whine of the police siren. He crossed to the farther pavement. A police car stopped outside Walter's door and two policemen entered the house. Ten minutes later the front door opened. Walter and the two policemen emerged. Putting Walter into the rear seat, the policemen drove away. The watcher took out a mobile phone and rang a number. The phone was answered.

"Too late to save either of them," the watcher complained, "Not bloody good enough."

The family and school were devastated. Walter had killed a uniquely gifted boy who was universally liked and admired. His mother told the local newspaper, "We always felt, his father and I, that Jacob would grow up to change the world. Do I wish it had been Patrick or Sean that maniac killed? No, in all honesty, I cannot. But I would like to ask his murderer why our only child has been taken from us."

* * * *

Seated at the table in the cell, his meal untouched before him, Walter Ashcroft became aware there was a tall thin man in a ginger wig standing behind him.

Walter complained, "Why don't you leave me alone? I've told you everything."

He started to rise.

"Relax, Walter," said the stranger, "I'm not with them. I've come to set you free,"

The voice was reassuring and the smile was genuine. Walter sat down again.

The stranger pulled Walter's head back and cut his throat with a razor blade. It was done so speedily, with practised skill, that Walter

Ashcroft never had time to protest his own death. The blood gushed over the table, covering the dried-up meal with an unusual gravy. The stranger put the razor blade into Walter's dying hand. He took one look about the cell and walked through the locked door.

* * * *

The first time Sheena Galloway saw Daniel Fallon, she was breathless from walking up the endless stairs to the top landing of the Hugh Gaitskill tower block. Neither would have guessed the pain and sorrow they would share nor how close they would come to dying together.

Sheena was breathless because although the lift worked, she found the stink of urine unbearable. On the familiar landing, she found a stocky, unshaven man of medium height with greying hair. Sheena judged him to be in his early sixties. He was dressed in leather jacket, jeans and trainers. There were several large cardboard boxes on the landing. The flat door was open. Sheena put down her carrier bag and picked up a box. She carried it into the sitting room and dropped it beside similar boxes. She was surprised at her own impulse.

When she returned to the landing, the stranger said, "Thank you. That was an unexpected kindness."

Tired blue eyes in a fatigued face. She smiled at him and saw him respond; a lightening of his shoulders.

"What's in the box? Metal Mickey?"

"Mostly books."

"Shouldn't you take them back to the library?"

The stranger smiled. She extended a hand. They shook hands formally.

"Sheena Galloway. We live across the landing."

"Daniel Fallon. Just moving in."

"Welcome to Gallin, Daniel."

Sheena walked across the landing and sought the key from her handbag. She heard the stranger move another box, but didn't turn around. Her impulse to pick up and carry the box continued to surprise her.

* * * *

Sheena dropped her bag on grandmother's hallstand that cluttered the tiny hallway. She hung up her coat and checked herself in the mirror. Midnight hair could do with cutting. Dark eyes. Chipped tooth. Same old face.

"You don't look a day over thirty."

The voice from the sitting room called, "Whose you talking to?"

"Your angel daughter, Mam!"

Lorraine and Morris came to hug her, calling out her name. Her mother and her friend, Hilda Stobart, sat in the best chairs smoking, hypnotised by the jumbo television. Baby Marianne bounced up and down in her playpen, excited to see her big sister, shouting shee-shee.

Lorraine asked, "Wha'd'y'call a line of men eating burgers while waiting for their turn at the barber's?"

Sheena groaned, "Oh, Lorraine! Where'd'y'get them from?"

"D'y'give up?"

"Put me out of my misery."

"A burgerqueue!"

Sheena laughed and admitted, "Yeah! Funny! Why don't you pick on your Mam?"

"She says, not listening."

Sheena picked up the remote and switched off the children who laughed. She also switched off the television sound.

"Mam, this telly's too big for this room. You're gona blind us."

"That's right! Take away me bit pleasure. See what I have to purrup with, Hilda?"

Hilda said nothing. Sheena kept her patience and tried again.

"Mam, I thought we agreed you only smoke on the balcony?"

"We cannot miss wa Neighbours, can wi?"

Sheena broke up a Mars bar and shared it between her siblings.

"Haven't you been to work today?"

Hilda decided, "I'll be getting meself away then."

"Don't let Princess Diana drive yi out. Yi've as much right to be here as anybody."

"She doesn't live here," Sheena challenged.

"Are wiz clubbing the-night, Ginnie?"

"I'll sneak out while her Royal Highness is enjoying a dump."

Hilda giggled uncertainly. When she was gone, Sheena said, "D'y'not feel ashamed to talk like that in front of the little ones?"

"Leastways we has a sense of humour."

Sheena repeated the question.

"Have you been to work today?"

"You forget yasel sometimes, Sheen. Ya Mam suffers a nervous condition. That nice doctor Zoomi, or whatever, told iss. Me narves is not connected prop'ly."

"Something's not connected properly."

Lorraine and Morris looked to Sheena and tried not to laugh. Marianne was too busy with her Mars bar. Sheena emptied her carrier bag into the fridge freezer.

"If you don't do days, Billy's not gona give you no nights, Mam."

"That's his loss!"

"No, Mam, that's our loss."

As an afterthought, she asked Lorraine, "You and Morris been to school today?"

"Mam slept in."

"She says we'll catch up tomorrow anyways," Morris offered.

"That's what she used to say to me. It doesn't work like that."

Mrs. Galloway recovered the remote.

Sheena heated baked beans and toasted bread for her siblings. "D'y'want some, Mam?"

"Not too many. Don't want to be blowing off all night."

"Then you won't want ice cream?"

Sheena fed Marianne as she ate. Peace descended.

"You seen him? The old feller?"

"Yes, I saw him."

"Gona tell him?"

"We mind our own business, Mam."

She cleaned the plate into Marianne's eager mouth and wiped the baby's face with her bib.

"What will it be for dessert, darling? Strawberry ice cream or cream ice strawberry?"

5

Marianne chortled with delight and Sheena smiled at her happiness. Life is really simple.

Sheena's mobile burst into an unintelligible rap to which Marianne responded, threatening to upset the highchair. When Sheena silenced the racket, the baby protested loudly.

"Marianne, shush, shush!"

Sheena listened and her mother offered, "If it's."

Sheena flapped her to silence, saying, "I just got in. She's been glued to the lavvy all day. Okay! I'll be in half seven. Half seven! Give iss time to wash me face!"

She closed the phone.

"That's another lie I've told for you, Mam!"

"Well, I can't believe what yi just said!"

"Next time I'll say, sat on her arse all day with her all-time mate, Hilda, watching telly."

As she rinsed the dishes, Sheena warned her mother.

"You go clubbing with Hilda tonight, get Jenny in to baby-sit. I'll pay her. Don't leave the little ones on their own. Don't go near the Steamer. And don't bring Hilda into the house when you come back. Some of us would like to sleep."

"Yi should come with iss."

"Clubbing with me Mam? Don't yi think that's a bit sad?"

"Brighten yi up. Make yi less crabby."

* * * *

Daniel cut the tape on the box. The bottle was wrapped in a towel. He went out onto the balcony carrying his drink. Below was the shabby shopping centre he had first seen when he arrived.

Decorating the decaying concrete entrance was a montage of three skinny-legged Ganymedes posing as sturdy fishermen dragging ashore a heavy net of fish from the briny deep. A closer look showed the net to be stuffed with crisp packets, newspapers, cardboard and unidentified detritus.

As Daniel fumbled for money, the taxi driver asked, "Sure this where yi want to be, mate?"

"Hugh Gaitskill tower block?"

"Aye!"

As Daniel gathered his bag, the driver questioned, "Yiz not from round here."

Daniel shook his head.

"Sight nicer places than this."

"I'll be alright."

"Yi need a ride. Yi've got the card."

"Will do!"

There was a stack of familiar cardboard boxes in the lobby. A teenager was prising open the top box, watched by a younger boy.

"Leave that alone!"

"Yeah? Why would I do that?"

Daniel looked at the older boy. The teenager saw something he didn't want to see. Reluctantly, they retreated up the stairs.

Daniel pressed the button for the lift. The doors opened. He breathed a sigh of relief. He loaded two boxes into the lift before the doors closed. Daniel pressed the button frantically. A hundred years later the lift returned. He was surprised to find his boxes intact. Learning his lesson, he blocked the lift door with a box and loaded his belongings into the lift.

Daniel unloaded the boxes onto the top landing. When he opened the door to the penthouse flat he was surprised to find he had been gifted with furniture. In the sitting room was a nineteen-sixties cocktail cabinet. It played a waltz when Daniel opened it. The shelves were empty. There were no bookcases.

The bedroom too was furnished. Three walls offered Victorian paintings of ships under sail. The bed was ready for occupation. The linen was clean and freshly ironed. The bedside clock ticked on.

On the kitchen table there was a plastic carrier bag. Daniel investigated cautiously. He laid out a sliced loaf, a tub of BettaButta, a packet of milk, a jar of Nescafe, a packet of bacon, a box of eggs, a bottle of olive oil, a bag of sugar, a Mars bar and a till receipt. He found a smile creeping onto his face.

"The girl across the landing!"

He surveyed the pristine bathroom. The snowy surfaces sparkled. The empty drawers of the bathroom cabinets opened and closed smoothly. The fan hummed soothingly. Switching off the light, closing the door, he recited, "Remember, thou too art mortal, Caesar!"

Moving the boxes into the flat was exhausting. He was surprised when a young woman came up the stairs and carried a box into the flat. Late teenage? Intelligent face. Generous mouth. Dark eyes. Difficult to read. She came out of the flat and he had said, "Thank you. That was an unexpected kindness."

She smiled and he couldn't help responding. He struggled to find anything to say.

Daniel sipped his drink, looking down into the gathering twilight. As a child he had always found this time of day depressing. The day was dying and with it, the hope that something good would come of the day. On the flat roof of the supermarket, feral teenagers were scampering like rats hunting mischief.

Lights were coming on in the streets below. As far as he could see into the darkening horizon, the daylight was fading and the oncoming darkness was defeating the street lamps.

Suddenly, he was sitting on a familiar doorstep, feeling so sad he was weeping openly; to be discovered by his mother and sister returning home. To be taunted by his sister and comforted by his mother. He had feared they were lost in the darkness and would never come home again.

* * * *

Sheena parked the shabby Seat in the back lane behind the Paddle Steamer pub and walked around to the front street.

Alec Skinner sat in his armchair by the front door. Even within Sheena's time this wreck was not the man Alec Skinner had once been. Nowadays he was not allowed in any pub, but Billy Younger had allowed Sheena to set up the old armchair outside the pub.

Alec offered his empty glass and Sheena took it.

"Yi know I shouldn't!"

Sheena entered the noise and lights of the pub. Billy looked at her and shook his head. Sheena went back out and gave Alec his glass of ale.

"Bless yi, darlin!"

The pub was busy, noisy and warm. Mirrors and lighting added to the false bonhomie. The ceiling was decorated with, if not the flags of all nations, most of them. Familiar faces filled the stools along the bar. The alcoves beyond were filled with the same lovers as the night before. Nothing had changed. Sheena was greeted with a cheer. She was a popular barmaid.

Late in the evening, Jessie came from the kitchen and tugged her elbow. Sheena nodded and continued to serve. When she was free, she went to her locker in the corridor by the kitchen and retrieved a frozen curry box. It promised a gourmet treat for two. The couple illustrated on the box were delighted with their choice. Standing in the yard was the man known as Squeaker.

"Took ya time, didn't yi?"

"I'm serving. Can't just walk away."

"Let's have it."

Squeaker took the box illustrated with juicy prawns and steaming rice. Sheena accepted an Aldi carrier bag.

"Next time, divvent keep iss hanging about."

She stowed the carrier bag in her locker and went back to work. When the last drinkers shuffled out reluctantly, shepherded by Billy, Sheena went for her handbag. There was no Aldi carrier in her locker.

"Good night, Sheena!!"

"Good night, Billy!"

The full moon gazed upon the empty terrace street. Alec Skinner was asleep. Sheena put his glass safely behind his chair. She found his blanket and tucked him up as best she could. She covered him in the plastic sheet and pulled his woolly hat down over his ears. She stood regarding what was once a strong, handsome face. The wind blew cold off the river.

"Good night, Alec," Sheena said aloud.

Alec Skinner said nothing. Sheena went home.

* * * *

Daniel unpacked his clothes. The drawers were lined with clean brown paper. His suit looked very lonely in the wardrobe. Daniel filled the cocktail cabinet with books. The waltz invaded his head. He found himself humming it. The remaining boxes he stored in the second bedroom.

He set an occasional table where he could look out the balcony door and opened his laptop. When he sat in the chair it was comforting; an island of familiarity in an ocean of indifference.

He said aloud, "I must ask the girl across the landing about the last tenant."

The image of Vermeer's The Girl with the Pearl Earring filled his head accompanied by a maddening Viennese waltz. The Girl across the Landing?

Daniel was drawn from his chair to watch the nine o'clock ferry pass beyond the shabby shopping centre. He found it disturbingly alien. A giant box sprinkled with lights moved solemnly down river in almost complete silence. There was no longer, as from childhood memory, a man hailing the outbound steamer from Lloyd's jetty. Where are ye bound! Lying in bed on Bank Top he would hear the cry and echo it silently. He would wait for the reply, a magical name from far Cathay. Or a late collier bound for London. The giant ferry passed on into the darkness of the North Sea, leaving diminished lighthouses, red and green, in its wake. Daniel closed the balcony door and returned to the laptop.

Before going to bed, he leaned his stick by the front door and left the sitting room and bedroom doors open.

He was awakened by voices. The bedside alarm read one seventeen. Daniel went quietly through the living room to stand listening in the hallway. The voices of women in dispute. Two older voices and a younger voice he recognised as the girl across the landing. The argument was loud and unpleasant. He heard the girl speak calmly to defuse the situation. He heard her accuse, you left the little ones alone again, Mam. The older woman's voice was not conciliatory. Finally, one woman returned to the lift despite the other's insistence she stay and the argument was taken into the flat. Silence reigned, broken only by a distant rumble of thunder across the landing.

CHAPTER TWO

*"Whatever that was,
it wasn't about ice cream."*

Daniel Fallon emerged from the kitchen, balancing a plate of bacon, eggs and toast on his head and a mug of very hot coffee passed from hand to hand.

Behind him, someone laughed. He turned startled, juggling breakfast and coffee. Sheena smiled at him. He felt a surge of irritation that passed as swiftly as it arose.

"Sorry,"

Cautiously, Daniel laid his breakfast plate on the table.

"I must be getting old. I can't remember letting you in."

"There's a stick. D'y'need a stick to walk?"

"I can't remember letting you in."

Sheena hesitated.

"I've been looking after the flat."

"Then I owe you my clean and comfortable bed."

"All part of the service."

Daniel sat down. Sheena stood.

"You've got a lot of books. Have you read them all?"

Daniel indicated a chair and the girl sat down.

"Do you have a key?"

"No. Ours fits both doors."

Daniel wasn't sure he believed her.

"What can I do for you?"

Sheena smiled apologetically.

"If I could borrow some bread and milk for the little ones? Mam never got to the shops yesterday."

Checking the till receipt, Daniel laid out the grocery money.

"Thank you."

"No bother."

Daniel vanished into the kitchen. He returned with the carrier bag containing half the loaf and the milk.

"I've eaten the Mars bar."

Sheena laughed.

"You're not thinking I'm a silly old fool, are you?"

"You're not that old!"

"As long as we understand each other? Okay?"

He looked into her eyes and saw no evasion.

"Go burn some toast for your kids."

"They're not mine."

Sheena vanished and Daniel sat down to his breakfast.

* * * *

"You embarrass me, Mam! I do expect you to get bread and milk."

"I was having one of me bad days. Doctor Zoomi. The big black one? He said, Missis Galloway, ya gona have ya bad days and ya gud days."

"Book me in for a good day! If ever!"

Sheena buttered toast for Morris and Lorraine who was feeding Marianne.

"Who wants peanut butter? Stand on one leg if you want peanut butter!"

Morris and Lorraine laughed and stood on one leg. Marianne laughed because they laughed. Happiness is very simple. Sheena poured two glasses of milk and winced at how little remained.

"I'm taking them to school today, Mam. I can't trust you."

"Suit yourself. Did the old feller kick off?"

"No."

"Then yarrin there right enough! Waggle ya backside and the auld feller'll give yi anything ya heart desires."

Sheena looked to her mother

"Is this the advice you give Lorraine? Waggle ya backside?"

Sheena gave Marianne a toasted crust to chew on.

"Any more toast?"

"Only if you stand on one leg, Mam."

All of Mrs. Galloway's children found this highly amusing.

* * * *

Within the railings, the playground buzzed with life. As Sheena arrived at the gate with Lorraine and Morris, Mrs. Kaplan came out and blew three sharp blasts on a whistle. Obediently, if reluctantly, the children began to enter the school. Sheena released her siblings.

"Have a good day! Listen to the teacher. Okay?"

Lorraine said, "Will Mam get us today?"

Sheena hesitated.

"Don't wait forever. Walk home together."

They nodded agreement and followed their classmates.

Mrs. Kaplan, chivvying the stragglers, spotted Sheena.

"Have you a minute, Sheena?"

Conditioning spoke. "Yes, miss."

"Lorraine and Morris. Their attendance is very poor. They've not completed one week this term."

"Sorry. I hadn't realised."

"I was so disappointed when you left Harton at sixteen. Are they going the same way?"

When Sheena didn't respond, she continued, "What're you doing now?"

Reluctantly, Sheena responded, "Bar work. And a shop."

"You should be at University."

When Sheena had no answer, she continued, "Is that what you want for Lorraine and Morris? Bar work? Serving in a corner shop? Two very bright children? They're already missing out. And it won't get any better."

Sheena wanted to explain, but bit her tongue.

"You aren't responsible for this sorry situation. But you must do something about it."

Mrs. Kaplan regarded Sheena's downcast face.

"Have I been too sharp, Sheena? Too much the Wicked Witch of the West?"

Sheena found a smile.

"No, miss. You've always been my favourite teacher."

* * * *

The fish quay was almost deserted. Daniel Fallon bought an ice cream from the van on the quay. He hadn't wanted an ice cream. He had wanted to talk to the ice cream man. He turned out to be a fat man with long dirty hair. He had an unfortunate habit of wiping his nose on his grubby white sleeve as he perused the Sun newspaper. When Daniel rapped on the counter to attract his attention, he seemed resentful at being dragged away from the latest human tragedy.

"Ice cream?"

"No, I'll have the pork chop, mashed potato and kidney beans, please?"

The fat man ignored his customer, wiping ice cream into and onto a sugar cone. He passed it to Daniel.

"One twenty."

Daniel took a bench where he could watch the quay. The long quay that had once held a thousand fish boxes every day was cluttered with debris. There was a stack of crab pots that once would've been booted across the river to hoots of derision. There were only three scratchers at the quay. Scratcher was an apt name. They scratched for a living.

A car drew up at the ice cream van and a tall thin man got out to talk to the fat man. They both looked in Daniel's direction and he stared back. When the car departed, it turned about in a wide circle that brought the vehicle close to Daniel. The car stopped and the passenger regarded Daniel. His ginger hair blazed in the morning sun. The driver opened his window and threw out his cigarette stub. Daniel and the passenger stared at one another.

The ginger man rolled up his window and the car drove away.

Daniel said aloud, "Whatever that was, it wasn't about ice cream."

He was left feeling uneasy.

* * * *

Staring at the uncaring river, Daniel was suddenly back in the school library with Mr. Gray and the Sixth Form History group. Mr. Gray was an excellent and imaginative teacher. The History group comprised both Sixth Form years. In the Senior Sixth, there was a brilliant boy, Eric Johnson, who debated on equal terms with Mr. Gray.

The teacher would often pose a question to the group.

"To stir you from your postprandial slumbers, my slothful young friends, I offer you a question."

The slothful young friends attempted to appear less slothful.

"Why did Abraham Lincoln free the slaves?"

Every boy had an answer; the wrong answer.

"No, no, no! Lincoln had no ethical problem with slavery. He was a politician dealing with a conflict that wasn't yet decided. Think, gentlemen, think!"

One hand rose alone. It belonged to Eric Johnson. Daniel Fallon was proud to be his friend. It felt almost as if he were answering the question.

"Yes?"

"Cotton was the basis of the Southern economy, sir. Any disruption would be to the Union advantage."

"Exactly!"

The group looked to Eric in admiration. Eric grinned and shrugged his shoulders. He was a modest boy. Mr. Gray promenaded the library, struggling not to compliment Eric.

"Eric Johnson will go on to Cambridge or Oxford from our modest repository of knowledge. No one would dispute that. Beyond University, there is no knowing what he will achieve. But it will be remarkable."

The History group did not disagree. Daniel Fallon glowed with pride.

From the bench, Daniel could see the favoured spot on the open quay where Eric and he often fished together. Both their fathers worked in the same shipyard. Daniel's father was a blacksmith and Eric's father was a scaler. Arthur Fallon was a craftsman. Viktor Johansson spent his working life inside ships' boilers descaling the walls with a hammer and cold chisel. It might have been a punishment devised by the Devil himself.

On a sunny afternoon the boys crouched together with hand lines catching small coalfish. A man stopped to ask the usual question.

"Caught anything?"

Daniel indicated the fish lying on the haversack.

"Do you eat them?"

"The cat does."

"I would've thought fishing where there was so much fish?"

Eric answered politely.

"Not a lot of waste goes into the river. It goes to the fish meal factory. But there's enough to bring fish in."

The man was silent. Then Eric fell from the quay, head over heels and vanished into the entangled darkness below the quay. There was not a sound, barely a splash and the boy was gone, never to be seen again. It was all so unexpected. Eric fell silently, clutching his fishing line. Daniel stood up slowly, disbelieving what he had seen, staring down into the dark water. When he turned about, the man had gone. He presumed he had run for help. Daniel, shocked, sat down, his mind in turmoil, to wait. No help came.

* * * *

In the morning mist, Sheena led the ponies out to the paddock. She had learnt if she took the horses and ponies out together, the older pony, Baldrick, had a nasty habit of trying to bite the gelding. If she took the gelding and the mare out first, Baldrick would bite anyone within reach. Baldrick had a high opinion of himself. It was simpler to lead the ponies out first and no one was bitten.

Why the Fitzpatricks of Tillingworth House hadn't discovered this for themselves, Sheena didn't understand. Mr. Fitzpatrick had warned her all four were difficult to handle. Mr. Fitzpatrick who had a high opinion of himself was surprised to find Sheena had no problem. Sheena was similarly surprised to learn no one in the family showed any interest in riding. She didn't ask why because she valued the cash-in-hand she received every Friday from the housekeeper.

With the stable empty, Sheena raked, broomed and hosed. The task was not difficult. The only difficulty was the occasional visit from Mr. Fitzpatrick. At first, Sheena was puzzled why he didn't come when the horses were in the stable. Then she realised the man was always behind her in the narrow alleyway as she replenished the hay racks or checked the water flow. She was tempted to stab backwards with the broom handle, but restrained herself. There was something distinctly unpleasant about the man. Sheena never saw the daughters or their mother. The tack she cleaned was never used.

When the stable was spick and span, Sheena went to the paddock and rode both horses and ponies bareback. Baldrick was ridden first. Sheena ate her sandwich at noon and drove home to Gallin. In the evening another girl would come to lead ponies and horses back to the stable. Once a week, she curried and dandied horses and ponies.

Sheena parked the faithful Seat in the back lane of Frederick Street, scattering the pigeons. She walked through the backyard and tapped in the code. She walked through the stockroom, breathing a mixture of spices, sugar and tobacco. Mr. Singh was at the counter replenishing the Pick and Mix.

"Ah, Sheena! Punctual as ever!"

"I wouldn't want to miss a moment."

Mr. Singh signed off the till and Sheena signed on.

"How were the horses?"

"Neigh bother!"

Mr. Singh didn't catch the feeble joke, but nodded amiably. As Sheena buttoned her overall, he asked, "Tell me, Sheena. If it is not a rude thing to ask. How many jobs do you have?"

"Counting my Mam? Four. I just start early."

Mr. Singh shook his head.

"Why?"

Sheena considered the question.

"I'm saving up. I want to make choices in my life. For that you need money."

Mr. Singh regarded her solemn face.

"Would you consider becoming my daughter?"

They smiled in understanding.

"Any problem. Ring me, please. You know where I am."

"Eccleston Terrace?"

* * * *

The police questioning was endless despite his parents' protests. During the break, his father asked only one question.

"Did you do anything to harm Eric?"

"No, Dad, I didn't. He's my best friend."

There was silence except for the sucking of the straw as Daniel drank his orange drink.

Before the interview was renewed, his father stated, "My son did not harm his friend. I asked him and he would not lie to me."

He was ignored and the interview was resumed.

"What time did you arrive on the fish quay?"

His mother protested, "The same questions! What is the point in tormenting my son?"

The detective said, "I will continue to ask questions until I am satisfied with the answers."

CHAPTER THREE

"They murdered him,
but naebody believes me. "

"What time did you arrive on the quay?"

"About two o'clock."

"Having been a boy myself, I know you were excited at going fishing."

"Yes."

"When did you start quarrelling?"

"We didn't. I've told you."

"What did you quarrel about? Did Eric want the best place?"

"There's no 'best' place on the quay."

"There's always a best place. You had fished there before?"

"That's where we always fished."

"What's the biggest fish you or Eric has ever caught?"

Daniel considered the question. The detective waited patiently. He heard his mother move restlessly.

"The biggest fish we ever caught is the monkfish head that Eric caught."

"Monkfish head? Just the head?"

"Really scary coming up out of the water."

"I would think so. Were you jealous of Eric?"

"No. I helped him shake it off. It wasn't easy."

"The day of the accident. What were you fishing for?"

"Poodlers."

"Who had caught more? You or Eric?"

"I think I had four. Eric had seven."

"How're you so precise?"

"The man asked us if we'd caught anything."

"So, you were jealous of Eric?"

Daniel suddenly became angry and couldn't restrain himself.

"You keep asking me if I was jealous! Never! Never ever! Eric was brilliant. I was proud to be his friend. You're wrong!"

Daniel's mother interrupted to say, "My son worshipped Eric. He would never have hurt him."

The detective said, "Show me how you were fishing?"

Confused, Daniel asked, "How'd'y'mean?"

"Were you standing, sitting, kneeling?"

"Kneeling sometimes?"

"Show me."

"Show you?"

"Get down on the floor and show me how you were fishing from the quay."

Daniel got down on his knees.

"The quay has a big timber edge. About six inches high. We kneeled behind it."

Daniel demonstrated, looking up at the dark mountain of the detective.

"You couldn't sit like that forever."

"We'd sometimes sit back on our ankles."

"Like you would for somersaults?"

"Something like that."

"So, it was easy to push Eric over the quay?"

"No! I never! I would never do that to Eric!"

Daniel's father moved to protest, but his wife's hand restrained him.

"This man you say came up to you?"

"Yes?"

"Did you know him?"

Daniel shook his head.

"Had you seen him before?"

"No."

"What did he look like?"

"I really didn't look. I think he had spectacles?"

"Hair? No hair? Dark? Light?"

"I can't remember."

"He wasn't a quay worker?"

"No."

"What did he say?"

"Caught anything?"

"Did he kneel down to look at the fish?"

"No."

"Did he touch either of you?"

"No."

"Anything else?"

"Why were we there. Close to the trawlers. Eric explained."

"Then he pushed Eric off the quay?"

"If he did, I didn't see him do it."

"Why did you make up this story about the man?"

"I didn't make up anything."

"There never was any man. You're lying."

"He was there!"

Daniel, kneeling on the floor, found his arms trembling.

"Shall I tell you how I know you're lying?"

Daniel was silent.

"Because you're smart enough not to say the man kicked Eric off the quay."

All Daniel could find to say was, "You're wrong. I've told you the truth."

The detective raised his foot and pushed Daniel who fell over onto his face. His mother cried out.

His father decided, "This has gone on too long. My son has told you everything twice. Unless you charge him, we're going home."

The detective said, "Stay where you are. I'll be two minutes."

He left the interview room. There was nothing to say. The family waited in silence. The detective didn't return in two minutes. Daniel's father consulted his watch and looked to his wife. Daniel wanted to say how sorry he was. In his head, the image played continuously. Eric fell from the quay again and again, his mouth open in surprise, fishing line in hand.

When the detective opened the door, they were all startled. Without expression, he said, "You may go. Thank you for your assistance in this matter."

Daniel's father asked, "What's going on?"

The detective said, "I trust you have not been inconvenienced. If you have suffered any expense in attending, such as loss of earnings, please, ask for the appropriate form at Reception. Thank you for your assistance."

There was no one visible in Reception.

In the street, the rain fell as a blessing. Daniel's mother began to weep, but no one might notice because of the rain. His father had one damp arm about her thin shoulders while holding his son's hand too tightly as they walked home. Daniel did not complain.

* * * *

Mr. Singh's Minimart kept Sheena busy throughout the afternoon. She discouraged one potential shoplifter by adding two packets of bacon and two packets of salami to the cost of his kipper fillets in a bag.

"I haven't got no bacon. Nor salami!"

"Yes, you have! Up your shirt! You'd steal eggs but they break."

When he swore at her, Sheena said, "Don't be a bigger arsehole than you are. The cameras record everything."

When he tensed as if to run, she said, "I can lock the door from here. Then we get the blue lights."

The young man emptied his shirt onto the counter. He dumped the kipper fillets. Sheena escorted him to the door.

"Do tell your friends about us. We're open seven to eleven."

Customers in the shop breathed a sigh of relief and clapped. Sheena laughed. Later in the afternoon, an old man was seventeen pence short on his groceries.

"Call it a personal discount," Sheena decided and didn't forget to add seventeen pence to the till. She didn't glow with righteousness, but remembered the occasions when she was similarly embarrassed. And no one helped out.

After dealing with a flurry of schoolchildren, the shop fell quiet. The doorbell rang. A schoolgirl entered to take a basket and shop for her mother. Sheena knew the child. Kimberly McLeod, eleven, a bright, sparky, pretty girl who livened up any dull afternoon. They first became friends when Kimberley made her a gift of the book she had written. Stories of the adventures of her rabbit, Gulliver. Sheena read the neatly stitched pages and marvelled at the warmth and originality.

Sheena watched her comparing prices, reading ingredients and checking off her shopping list. She brought the basket to the counter.

"Hi, Kimbo! What news of the Rialto?"

When Sheena had first used the quotation as a greeting, Kimberley had asked what the Rialto was. To Sheena's astonishment, the girl had found the following lines.

"Why, yet it lives there uncheck'd that Antonio hath a ship of rich lading wrecked on the narrow seas."

It was now their private code of greeting.

"Found everything?"

"Not much difference between one tin of baked beans and another, is there?"

"Beans is beans and pees is private."

Kimberly smiled. Sheena put items through the till.

"Sheena, would you like to know something you don't know?"

"Something I don't know is really what I like to know."

"I won the Spelling Bee today!"

Kimberly's face shone with pride.

"Excellent! I was quite good at spelling, but I never won a Spelling Bee."

"You can test me if you like."

Sheena laughed.

"No! Serious! Go on! Try me!"

Sheena thought for a moment.

"Spell Mississippi."

"Easy! M I double S, I double S. I double P I."

"Well done!"

"Too easy. Try me again."

Sheena raked around in her mind.

"Rumpelstiltskin. Spell it."

Kimberly had no trouble spelling the word correctly.

"Wrong!" declared Sheena.

The girl looked puzzled.

"I asked you to spell it," Sheena explained, "It! Not Rumpelstiltskin."

Puzzlement vanished into a smile.

"Sorry! Bad joke!"

"But I did spell Rumpelstiltskin correctly?"

"Yes, you did, genius!"

Sheena paused, all items totalled.

"Anything else?"

Kimberly's smile vanished.

"I have to get cigarettes."

She fixed appealing eyes on Sheena.

"You could lose me my job, Kimbo. Give Mister Singh a load of trouble."

Sheena knew what it was like to go home without what was demanded.

"Please! They're not for me."

"I know they're not."

The shop was empty. Sheena turned to the tobacco lockup and took a packet of cigarettes. She rang them up separately on the till. She looked to the child and saw such gratitude in her face.

"If he does something really bad, you must tell me. Promise?"

The girl nodded.

"It'll be alright. Mam always hides the really sharp knives under the couch cushions when he's home."

Sheena slipped the cigarettes into the carrier bag and returned the change to the child.

Mam always hides the really sharp knives under the couch cushions when he's home.

"Thank you, Sheena."

On the way to the door, she stopped and returned to the till.

Sheena asked, "What's the dirt, Squirt?"

"The Final of the North Gallin Schools Spelling Bee is at six thirty p.m., Saturday, the twenty-third. Followed by the presentation of the Cup and individual certificates."

"You read the poster."

"It's at the Town Hall. Would you like to come?"

"Me? I'd be delighted. Thank you very much for inviting me."

Kimberly smiled her angelic smile and turned away. At the door, she smiled again.

"Thank you, Sheena!"

As the door closed, Sheena said aloud, "I wonder if your Mam or Dad'll be there."

Mr. Singh's daughter, Adish, arrived at five. They exchanged a little gossip. Adish was infatuated with a certain pop star of whom her father disapproved. Sheena was her natural confidante. Sheena took a basket to buy items including bread and milk. She added extra for the old man across the landing.

* * * *

Daniel walked up Brickbank Stairs coming out in an alley by a pub in Percy Street. Outside the pub, a man was sitting in an old armchair. There was something about the alkie that was familiar. He turned a watery gaze on Daniel who stopped and regarded the man in the chair. The skull was beginning to show through the skin, but there was still intelligence in the eyes. He wore a bow tie without a collar. The shirt was dark with stains. His jacket didn't match the trousers. Long dirty hair strayed from the woolly cap. His boots had metal toecaps and were laced with twine. The broken knuckles read GOOD BYE.

"I knows I knows yi, just cannot recall ya name."

"What happened to you, Alec?"

"What's ya name?"

"What happened to you, Alec?"

The man in the armchair looked confused.

"I don't remember."

"Last time we met you were owner and skipper of the Arbroath Lady. Neatest oak beam trawler ever sailed out of Gallin."

"That right?"

"Your wife was Jenny Fittis. Beautiful lady. Now what was the name of your lad?"

"Bobby."

"That's right. Bobby. Robert Andrew Skinner. Ten years old and First Mate of the Lady. Bright as a button."

The silence was painful.

"Where's Bobby now, Alec?"

Daniel read the pain in the befuddled eyes.

"Can yi keep ya gob shut?"

"You know me, Alec."

"They murdered him, but naebody believes me."

"Who murdered him?"

Alec wagged his empty glass at Daniel.

"What'm I supposed to do with this?"

Daniel took the glass.

The pub was quiet with a handful of afternoon drinkers. Daniel put the glass on the long bar. The barman, a big man in his fifties, came to say, "Yi don't have to do this."

Daniel answered, "Oh, yes, I do."

"Why'd'yi think that?"

"Could be me sat out there."

The barman nodded understanding.

"Make his a Guinness. I'll have a pint of your best."

"Guinness?" Alec asked wonderingly, surveying midnight and snow in his glass.

"Very feeding. Knew a Royal Marine sergeant once that swallowed a gallon a day. Thrived on it. 'Til it killed him."

Alec laughed his broken laugh and Daniel turned to the pub.

Alec said, "I knows you now, Danny."

Daniel went into the pub to enjoy his drink. Nobody bothered him. He was left in peace to identify most of the flags that adorned the ceiling. When he left, the barman raised a hand in salute and Alec Skinner held out his glass.

"You're asking a blind man, Alec."

Alec laughed.

"Mebbes see yi timmora, Danny Fallon?"

* * * *

On his way home, he stopped at a supermarket to buy groceries. He added a six-pack of lagers and Mars bars.

"Sweet tooth," he explained to the girl at the checkout. She wasn't interested but helped the old man pack his carrier bags, rescuing the doughnuts from under the lager.

From the street, he could see the towers of Sodom and Gomorrah, but it turned out to be a longer walk than he anticipated. He was grateful the lift worked. As it rose unsteadily, apparently powered by urine, Daniel quoted, "'Where Sodom and Gomorrah reared their domes and towers that solemn sea now floods the plain, in whose bitter waters no living thing exists.' And I can't remember any more. But thank you, Mister Gray! And Mark Twain!"

The tragedy of Eric Johnson's death destroyed Mr. Gray. The memory was savage for Daniel as the lift jolted to a stop. He lingered on the landing, surprised by the pain.

Mr. Gray was never the same again. There was no life in his lessons. He read from his bulging folder in a dull monotone and the History group struggled to take notes. There were no historical jokes. No competitions to invent Last Words for historical characters. No intriguing questions for Eric to answer. At the end of term, Mr. Gray resigned. He was a lifelong ornithologist. In the Spring his body was found at the foot of South Gallin cliffs. The last sounds he heard were the laments of the nesting kittiwakes.

There was no funeral. Eric's body was never found. The Fallons attended the Memorial Service. They were boycotted, sitting in an empty pew. No one acknowledged their presence. In school, Daniel was invisible to fellow students.

One evening, walking home from school, Daniel was ambushed and badly beaten while Irene, Eric's older sister, enjoyed his agony. His left leg was fractured and his front teeth were broken. His schoolbooks and school bag were set alight and his blazer added to the fire. Irene took revenge by repeatedly kicking the boy in the head. She was so enjoying this savagery that she had to be restrained by her friends lest she killed Daniel. His parents did not bring charges despite Eric's sister and friends boasting of what they had done.

When Daniel was released from Intensive Care and could sit up in his hospital bed, he asked his father, "Why didn't you press charges against Irene and her pack of morons? They might've killed me."

Daniel thought his father wasn't going to answer.

"Irene in prison. What would that do for Eric's parents? Their only son's been killed. How would we feel if it was you? Those poor people don't know who to blame."

"You think I killed Eric?"

"We know you didn't kill him."

Daniel took a deep breath.

"I want to leave school."

"No. You'll stay and take your exams."

"You don't know what it's like, Dad! Nobody speaks to me. The teachers hate me."

His father almost smiled.

"You don't know what it's like, son. I walk through the gate every morning with Viktor Johansson. He never looks at me or says a word. There are other men who would like to beat me up, but they don't. They know I'd give them worse than they'd give me. But it's no bloody picnic."

"But I'm not strong like you, Dad!"

"You need a different sort of strength. You have that in bucket loads, son. Strength of mind."

His mother said, "Nothing can bring Eric back. It's a tragedy. But you did nothing wrong."

Daniel knew something was very wrong, but it was years before he began to understand.

CHAPTER FOUR

"It's been used as a teapot stand."

Daniel put away his groceries. He selected a Mars bar from the packet and took a large bite. He settled down at his laptop and began to type rapidly.

He became aware Sheena was reading over his shoulder. He snapped the laptop shut.

Sheena said, "It wasn't that interesting anyway."

"You have got to stop walking in on me, Sheena! I'm an old man with a dodgy heart."

The girl carried bread and milk into the kitchen.

"It just seems daft knocking on your door."

She returned to Daniel saying, "Your hair's too long. I'll cut it for you. You could look quite distinguished."

"You're changing the subject again."

"I'm returning your bread and milk."

"Thank you. Please help yourself in the morning."

Sheena froze. The air in the sitting room was arctic.

"Did you just call me a scrounger, Mister Fallon?"

"No, no! I'm sorry. I just meant."

"Why bring the stuff back if you're only going to borrow it tomorrow morning?"

"Something like that," Daniel admitted, "Sorry!"

Sheena smiled and Daniel surrendered.

"If you need anything, just take it."

"Who you writing to?"

"Nobody of concern to you."

Sheena lingered and Daniel asked, "May I offer you a drink?"

"Yes, please."

"Lager?"

"Sounds good, Bud!"

When Daniel went into the kitchen, Sheena picked up the book on his armchair. She took a quick nibble at the Mars bar.

"Dark Minds. Any good?"

Daniel called, "A study of why people perform evil acts."

Sheena put the book down quickly. She took a second nibble at the Mars bar.

"So, d'y'know why?"

"To put out the lights."

"Sounds a right laugh."

Daniel returned with two cans. Sheena accepted the drink and sat down.

"Thank you."

Daniel sat down to say, "Tell me about the departed tenant."

Sheena was slow to respond.

"Why d'y'want to know?"

"I'd just like to know. Did he take his television set with him? That seems to be the only thing missing."

"It was a portable. He took it with him."

Daniel nodded.

"An old gentleman. Educated. Deaf in one ear. With him being a bit deaf, I used to let meself in. Didn't bother him. Very pleasant man. Polite. I did the cleaning for him."

"Sounds ideal."

"One day he says to me, 'Sheena, I've made up me mind. I'm going to live with me son in Canada.' I ask about the furniture. He said, I cannot afford t'shift it. I'm leaving it for the next tenant."

"That was very good of him. Almost saintly."

"So off he went."

"Where'd he go in Canada?"

"No idea."

"Weren't you interested in knowing where he was? This very pleasant, polite old gentleman, educated, deaf in one ear?"

"Not really."

"Did he not write?"

"Not so much as a postcard."

"There was me thinking he was on the run. Y'know? From the constabulary?"

Sheena said reprovingly, "He would be shocked to hear you say that."

"Sorry. What was this very pleasant, educated, deaf in one ear, old gentleman's name?"

"His name?"

"Yes. His name."

Sheena hesitated.

"Miller. Yes. Miller. Tom Miller."

Daniel raised his drink.

"Here's to Mister Tom Miller, very pleasant, educated, deaf in one ear, old gentleman, taking his television set to Canada."

"Expect his son would let him have it in his bedroom."

Daniel studied his lager can.

Sheena excused herself, "I'd best go see if Mam has killed any of the little ones yet."

She rose to go, but Daniel said, "Hang on! I have a present for them. And you."

He vanished into the kitchen as Sheena called, "You shouldn't have bothered!"

Daniel returned with the bag of Mars bars.

"I've had one. Five for your clan."

"Thank you! That's very kind."

"Did I get it right?"

"Spot on! Four kids and me. Mam, Lorraine, Morris and Marianne."

"No father?"

"What's a father?"

When Sheena departed, Daniel began a new e-mail.

"Remember Harelip? Kevin somebody. At school. Had it fixed, but they botched it. Any idea where he is? Thought if he was still in Gallin, I'd look him up. Just a thought."

Daniel corrected his spelling and signed off. His mind played the image of the boy, Harelip, inserting a straw into a frog's rectum and blowing up the poor creature like a balloon.

* * * *

Nobody acknowledged Sheena as she entered. The Galloways were hypnotised by the giant television.

"Look what Uncle Daniel sent yous."

Sheena held up the bag of Mars Bars. There was instant jubilation from Morris and Lorraine. Marianne banged her doll's head on the floor in excitement.

"Homework finished?"

"I had to help Morris."

"I hope 'helped' doesn't mean 'did it forrim'?"

"I just showed him how."

Sheena dropped two chocolate bars on two auburn heads and lifted Marianne up into her high chair.

"You weigh a ton, Twinkletoes! Too many Mars bars."

She tore the wrapper and began to feed pieces to the baby.

Her mother said, "That's it, is it? Yer Mam left out as per usual?"

"You're worse than a bairn, Mam!"

Sheena rattled the packet.

"Two bars! Did I get two for rotating my particular posterior?"

"I know what that means," Lorraine boasted.

"That's right! Torment ya Mam. If yee'd been through what I've been through with me narves."

"Doesn't say nothing on the packet about being good for your nerves."

Sheena asked, "Has our Mam been good today?"

Morris hesitated and Lorraine offered, "She's not been bad."

"Then she shall have her Mars bar!"

The children clapped and Sheena presented her mother with a chocolate bar.

"I telt yi, didn't I?"

"What?"

"That auld feller'll give yi anything. Just keep wagging it."

"Oh, Mam! Just kindness."

Peace descended. Sheena wrapped up half of Marianne's bar and put it away for another day. She fed the child her drink.

As the giant screen explained the benefits of smothering your face in expensive grease every night, Sheena admitted, "He was asking about the last tenant."

"So what did yi say?"

"I didn't know what to say."

"So, what did yi say?"

"I said he was an old man. Much like him. I thought that was easiest."

"Easiest than what?"

"Anything else I'd forget."

"So?"

"He wanted to know his name. I didn't know what to say. Then I had an inspiration."

"Yi said, I'm busting forra pee. Ta-ra! And scooted."

"I told him Miller."

"Why Miller?"

"It was on the lager can."

"What lager?"

"He give me a lager."

"And yi niver thought of bringing one back for ya Mam?"

Sheena shook her head sorrowfully.

"Are you really my mother?"

"I'll tell yi somethin for nothin, Sheen. If yi think he won't cotton on, ya dafter than yi look."

Nonplussed, Sheena asked, "How daft do I look?"

"Niver seen worse."

* * * *

Daniel awoke with a start. The clock said two thirty-seven. He lay listening. He heard a male voice. Then he heard Sheena protest. Without thought, he was out of bed and running. At the front door, he heard Sheena cry out. Daniel pulled the door open. Sheena was struggling with a young man, protesting, "Let go of me!"

When the door opened, the young man turned to Daniel. An oafish face. Shaven head. A hand fastened like a vice on the girl's wrist.

"Piss off, Grandad!"

Sheena cried, "This has nothing to do with you, Daniel!"

"Let her go!"

The young man let go Sheena's wrist and turned on Daniel.

"Ya gona wish yi'd never opened ya fricking face."

Daniel reached for his stick and stabbed him twice sharply in the groin. The young man screamed and fell to his knees. Sheena cried, dismayed, "Why'd you do that?"

"I'm not gona wait 'til he does it to me."

Daniel raised the pained face with the stick handle.

"That's not the way to win a lass, son. You have to be nice. Now bugger off!"

The young man shuffled off painfully down the stairs. Safe at a distance, he shouted obscenities.

Daniel called, "Good-night, sweet prince, may flights of angels sing thee to thy rest."

"You're expecting me to say thank you."

Daniel saw she was both angry and ashamed.

"No. I expected your father to come rushing out."

"It was nothing to do with you."

"So, I hear you in trouble, I do nothing? That where we are now?"

"He could've hurt you."

"So be it."

They stood together and apart, reluctant to say what couldn't be forgiven.

"Don't do it again."

"I can't promise that."

"Just don't."

"Can I ask why you'd bother with a toerag like that?"

"Safer to know them than not."

"That's sad."

Sheena was silent.

"Gavin's alright."

Daniel said nothing.

"Well, least I know now what the stick's for."

Sheena found the key and opened her door.

"Good night, Daniel."

"If you say so."

Daniel went back to bed. It took a long time for sleep to find him.

* * * *

The man switched on the lights in the stable. The horses and ponies looked expectantly towards the door. The man came forward silently to regard the stalls. The gelding whinnied and the man moved to it. He began to talk softly and stroke its long nose. The horse responded, pleased with unexpected attention. Baldrick called, but the visitor ignored him. He turned to the mare that moved restlessly when he began to stroke her. She relaxed when he breathed into her nostrils and stroked her neck. He talked softly and the mare responded.

The younger pony in the next stall pushed against the bars, rattling the hayrack. Baldrick, the older pony in the farther stall, began to call restlessly, impatient for attention. The visitor spent a long time with the younger pony. Anyone might have presumed she was his favourite. Out of his pocket he brought an apple.

When he used a knife to halve the fruit, the scent of apple filled the air. He gave half to the younger pony and began to eat the second piece. Baldrick whinnied loudly and struck at the stall gate. The man ignored this behaviour and gave his portion of apple to the younger pony. He produced a second apple. He cut the fruit and gave pieces to each of the horses. The old pony protested loudly and kicked at the stall gate.

The visitor approached Baldrick and the pony relaxed, anticipating attention. The man produced a length of rubber hose and began to beat the pony about the head. An onlooker might have noted he avoided cutting or marking the unfortunate creature. As the pony retreated, the visitor entered the stall and continued beating the frightened pony. The victim of this cruelty whinnied in fear and stumbled backwards. When he stopped, breathing heavily, Baldrick faced him, teeth showing, eyes wide, sweating. His tormenter retreated, whirling the length of hose above his head.

The hose began to make a sour, droning note as it circled. The pony became quite frantic. When the man exited the stall, the pony kicked at the gate with both hind legs. The louder he created this unpleasant drone, the wilder the pony became, unsettling its stable companions. The noise stopped. The man put out the lights. Baldric stood sweating, trembling in the darkness. His tormentor closed the stable door and walked away.

* * * *

Daniel had moved the table with his laptop. With the hallway door open, he could see the front door. Daniel typed slowly, deep in thought. He paused to sip his coffee, referring to the local newspaper. A key turned in the front door and Sheena entered.

"You've changed where you sit."

"Save me having a heart attack."

Sheena came to stand in front of the table.

Daniel offered, "I'm not sure we're speaking to one another."

"Brought you a present."

Sheena came around the small table and presented Daniel with a stained and shabby book. He accepted with caution, turning it over in his hands.

"It's been used as a teapot stand."

"How did you guess?"

"But I don't have a teapot."

Sheena was nonplussed.

"It's to read. A present. From me."

Looking into the engagingly honest face, Daniel was strangely moved. The Girl across the Landing was making peace.

"Go on! Open it?"

Daniel opened the battered copy of Ernest Hemingway's FOR WHOM THE BELL TOLLS. Property of North Gallin Public Library.

"D'y'like it?"

"Thank you very much. Very kind."

Sheena was disappointed.

"You've already read it, haven't yi?"

"Yes, but what makes it special is that you gave it to me."

The sun came out from the clouds.

"It's just a book."

"No man is an island. Therefore, never send to know for whom the bell tolls; it tolls for thee."

"Why did Frosty go and live in the middle of the Atlantic Ocean?"

Daniel Fallon looked blankly at the young woman.

"Because snowman is an island."

Daniel didn't know how to respond.

"My sister Lorraine told me that one."

He knew he'd been effectively rebuked for quoting John Donne.

"Smart girl. Lorraine."

"Miss Kaplan says they're both very clever."

"Miss Kaplan?"

"Lorraine's teacher. Deputy Head Teacher. Morris will be in her class next year."

"How did you do at school?"

"Ribble Road with Miss Kaplan was ace. Secondary some teachers didn't care if you were there or not. I went if it was English Lit or History, but otherwise I didn't bother too much. Mam didn't care."

"In an odd way that makes sense."

"Now before I have a heart attack, please, give me your key to my flat."

"I've told yi. I haven't got a key."

"I know you have."

"Just our key fits your door."

"Go away and leave me in peace."

"No need to be shirty, Gertie!"

Sheena stopped at the door to say, "Your e-mails are weird. 'Fourteen child deaths in the Gallins this past year.' No surprise there. That's living in Gallin. It's not Kensington and Chelsea."

CHAPTER FIVE

"Let's see how they get on without me."

The young man picked up the telephone and recited brightly, "Housing. How can I help you?"

The principal secretary answered, "Mister Rington wants to see you now."

"Mister Rington?"

"The Chief Executive Officer of North Gallin Housing department requires your presence at his door pronto. Can I make it any clearer for you, Mister Griffiths?"

Acid dripped from the receiver.

A pale Clive Griffiths rose slowly from his chair. Roberts aka Randy Ron smiled at him with malicious delight.

"I'll start the whip-round for ya leaving do, shall I?"

Rose Chambers complained, "How can you be so mean, Ron?"

"Easy! I've never liked the little prick."

"He's only been here a month."

"Month too long."

The old man whose name no one in the office remembered, advised, "Take a pad and biro with you, son. If you don't, he'll ask why not."

Clive Griffiths nodded dumbly and picked up a pad and biro. With Rose's encouragement in his ears, he headed for the lift.

"We won't see him again," Ron decided, "I'll have his monitor."

The young man was met by the principal secretary.

"He's not happy."

He was ushered into the Great Man's office.

"You're Griffiths, are you?"

"Yes, sir."

He made to sit down, but was rebuked.

"I didn't say, sit down."

"No, sir."

He remained standing.

"How long have you been with us?"

"A month, sir."

"Transferred from where?"

"South Gallin, sir."

A risible snort demonstrated what the Chief Executive of North Gallin thought of the competence of the South Gallin Housing department.

"And you know what to do when you're dealing with a red-tagged property?"

"Refer to my supervisor."

"Which you didn't do with regard to the penthouse flat of Gaitskill House."

Clive Griffiths stared blankly at Mr. Rington.

"Well?"

"But I did, sir. I took it to Missis Wells for advice."

"And?"

"She was on the telephone. I showed her the file and she drew a finger across her throat as if she were cutting her throat."

"Which you interpreted as?"

"Difficult let. If you can get any tenant to take the property, grab him or her."

"She meant exactly the opposite. She was telling you to steer clear of the penthouse at Gaitskill House."

The office was silent. The clack of the keyboard in the secretary's office was clearly audible.

"The absent tenant of that flat is Mister Tony Buckle. Does the name Tony Buckle mean anything to you?"

"No, sir."

"Sit down!"

Clive Griffiths sat down gratefully.

"He is at present on remand, having been refused bail in the matter of penetrating an unfortunate gentleman's rectum with a red-hot poker."

Clive Griffiths' bladder was overflowing. His legs trembled.

"Apparently he parked in a spot favoured by Mister Buckle."

Clive Griffiths swayed on the chair, struggling not to faint.

"When that unfortunate matter is cleared up and Mister Buckle is returned to the community without a stain on the woodwork, what do you think he will do to you and the tenant in his flat?"

The young man swallowed hard.

"I would readily apologise, sir. Most profusely!"

"A monkey does not shit on its own doorstep."

"I didn't know that, sir."

"Mister Buckle has been considerate enough to keep his business affairs clear of North Gallin. Our dismal population of Cs, Ds and Es are safer because Tony Buckle lives here."

Clive Griffiths whispered, "I didn't know. I'm very sorry, sir."

"What experience do you have of children?"

The young man shook his head.

"None at all. I've always been in Housing."

"And an excellent job you've made of it. Therefore, I am promoting you to Nursery Provision. Clear your desk. Out of here by four. Change your name. Move house. Good luck in your new posting! Any further questions?"

"Is it Mister Buckle's monkey, sir?"

"Goodbye!"

* * * *

When Sheena had gone, Daniel rummaged through his boxes until he retrieved eight small metal pieces. The Reverend Arthur Dunedin's monstrous volume, entitled How We Must Defeat The Scarlet Woman of Rome in the Kingdom Complete with Illustrations of Past and Present Popes, was easier to find, but heavier to carry. The central pages had been loosely cut to fit the frame. Sitting at his work table, Daniel painstakingly cleaned each piece and reassembled the Colt semi-automatic pistol. He filled the magazine from his bag containing pencils, biros and paint brushes. He checked the slide and safety. When he was satisfied, Daniel replaced the pistol in the centre of the Reverend Arthur Dunedin's clunking great book. He placed the volume in the centre of the tastefully tiled coffee table. An interesting conversation piece. If you wish to hide something, always put it in plain sight.

* * * *

When Jessie came to tug her sleeve, Sheena was talking to a young student who was pretending to write a thesis on North Gallin public houses. She excused herself, but noted his disappointment. Sheena guessed his thesis might better have been entitled a survey of North Gallin barmaids. There was nothing in her locker. Puzzled, she went out to the yard. Squeaker was standing in the shadows.

"Wha'd'y'want?"

"Come here!"

Sheena approached him reluctantly. His face was in shadow.

"There's nothing for yi."

"Take this."

A bundle was thrust into her hands. Although wrapped in a cloth the shape was unmistakable. Instinctively, Sheena thrust it back to him.

"I am not taking this!"

Squeaker grabbed her arm and squeezed. Sheena struggled.

"How'd yi fancy I opens ya gob from lughole to lughole?"

Sheena hesitated. Squeaker released her arm. He pressed the bundle back into her hands.

"Do what ya telt!"

Sheena pushed the bundle to the back of her locker. She sat on the toilet until the trembling passed. When she returned to the bar, the student and his thesis had vanished. Sheena retrieved her handbag from the locker when the Steamer closed. The pistol was unclaimed.

* * * *

Sheena shouted up the stairs.

"Come on, you two!"

Lorraine and Morris came flying down the stairs as Daniel stepped out of the lift.

Daniel said, "The lift's quicker."

Lorraine replied, "Sheena won't let iss use the lift."

41

"Why not?"

"Somebody might get in."

"So?"

"You can't trust everybody."

They walked out together to where Sheena stood by the Seat.

"Get in!"

The children scrambled into the car.

"I've never seen you harassed before."

"I need to get them to school on time and I need to get to work."

Daniel hesitated and offered, "I could take them sometime. If they'd walk."

Sheena hesitated and Daniel laughed.

"As your sister says, you can't trust everybody."

"Where you going?"

"Get a paper."

Sheena got into the car and the Seat moved away.

The Seat stood at the traffic lights and Lorraine asked, "Why are you and Marianne brown and we're not?"

Sheena stalled the car.

Morris said, "Yes! Why're we not brown?"

The lights changed and the car behind hooted. Sheena restarted the car and drove on.

"You've never mentioned it afore."

Lorraine offered, "Mam used t'say you were baked too long. But we're not kids any more."

"We know all about human reproduction now," Morris assured Sheena.

"Marianne and I have a different father to you two. But it's not important. We're brothers and sisters sharing the same Mam. Does it bother you?"

Lorraine shook her head, saying, "We just want to be like you. Chocolate coloured. You're lovely and Marianne is going to be the same."

"Sweetheart," Sheena assured her, "I wish I had my magic mirror with me. You're going to be the most beautiful of the Galloways."

"What about me," Morris complained.

"Don't go out in daylight."

"She doesn't mean it," Lorraine assured him.

* * * *

The audience at Birmingham City Hall were unanimous in agreement with the judges. The applause was overwhelming. The Templar School string quartet was outright winner of the Edward Elgar Shield upon which was inscribed annually the name of every young musician of promise in the United Kingdom. Now four more names would be added to the Shield and the way to a successful professional future was open to the girls.

They stood under the lights together, clutching their instruments, savouring the moment. When their tutor, Eileen Galbraith, was introduced, the applause barely slackened, but reached a new climax when Kathleen O'Rourke was introduced. With bow and violin in hand, she bowed modestly to the audience, face alight with excitement. The applause was well deserved for Kathleen's performance was matchless. She gestured towards her tutor and the audience responded.

On the motorway, the tired girls dozed in the minibus as Eileen Galbraith drove. Glancing back at her charges, slumbering together, a nest of innocence, Eileen found an itch of irritation that grew slowly into a burning anger as the miles rolled by. The girls would've been nothing without her dedication. She said aloud, "I could do the same with any girl who can hold an instrument the right way up."

She was surprised she had spoken aloud and bewildered at how angry she felt,

"I'm the one who's guided, persuaded, even driven them along and never a word of thanks."

This was untrue, as all the girls had thanked her fervently and frequently.

"And Kathleen! What can I say? Ungrateful little pig! She thinks she's so wonderful. I never had a less grateful pupil. Why should she be the chosen one? Not just local television, but national too! And I had to sit smiling and nodding while she tells the world how wonderful she is."

Somewhere in the darker reaches of her mind, Eileen knew that Kathleen O'Rourke was a modest, unspoilt young musician with a giant talent: the once in a lifetime pupil that every good teacher longs to serve.

"Well, let's see how they get on without me."

Eileen Galbraith stopped the minibus in the outside lane of the motorway and walked across the carriageway to the accompaniment of screeching brakes and shattering metal. She walked up the embankment and vanished without looking back. The tanker driver struggling to avoid the chaos struck the minibus a shattering blow. The minibus bounced off the central reservation and fell onto its side.

Then came an artillery barrage of destruction as vehicle after vehicle slammed into the growing calamity. The first flickering of fire was unnoticed until oil and fuel conjoined to create a monstrous furnace that set the roadway alight. Three of the girls died instantly. Kathleen lived long enough to cry out for her idol, her beloved tutor. The tanker, struck again and again from behind, reared up and fell onto the minibus.

It was six days into the aftermath of this road traffic incident in which fifty-seven persons died, that it was confirmed the Templar School string quartet and tutor had perished. A telephone rang in a quiet terraced house in North Gallin.

* * * *

Daniel Fallon closed down the microfiche machine. He was sitting in the data vault of the North Gallin Gazette. He rubbed tired eyes. The coffee was cold and his back was aching. He added a sentence to his notebook and twisted the rubber band about it. Rising, he caught the attention of the old man in charge of the vault.

"Did you find what you wanted, sir?"

"I think so."

"They're considering closing us down."

"That would be a grievous error."

"You'll put a word in the book?"

"With pleasure."

* * * *

Daniel found Alec Skinner in his armchair outside the Paddle Steamer, dozing in the sunlight. Daniel refilled his glass and woke him up. Alec grabbed the glass.

"D'y'never say thank you?"

"Piss on their charity. They buys me drink so's they tell their mates, I bought a glass for Alec Skinner. D'y'remember how he was like? Well, yi should see the poor bugger now."

Daniel came close and knelt by the chair.

"That's not me, Alec. We were marrers once. Remember?"

"So we was."

"I've looked up how Bobby died."

Daniel was prepared for an angry reaction, but Alec sipped his ale.

"Ten o'clock at night. Skinty moon. He fell between the quay and the Lady."

Daniel waited for a reaction from the alcoholic. Alec swallowed more ale.

"Who was with him?"

The noises of Percy Street faltered for a moment as if to allow Alec to speak.

"Where were you?"

Alec shrugged thin shoulders.

"Who was with him?"

Alec shook his head.

"Why was he there?"

The broken man shrugged his shoulders.

"Why you doing this to me, Danny?"

"Because you said he was murdered."

Daniel saw Alec was crying, wiping tears with a dirty neckerchief. A man was watching from across the street. Daniel felt a sudden anger at the intrusion.

"Okay, Alec, let it go. But there's something you know."

He straightened up.

"You say thank you, I'll get you a Guinness."

"Thank you, Danny," said the man in the chair.

CHAPTER SIX

"Who was that you were talking to?"

Sheena parked the faithful Seat and walked around to the front door of the Steamer. Alec was asleep, his chin on his chest. Then she looked again and saw the shirt and trousers were scarlet. She took hold of his shoulder and the head fell away displaying the gaping wound in his neck. His throat had been cut almost from ear to ear. Sheena suppressed a scream. She checked the body for a knife or razor. There was neither. She let go of Alec. The body fell forward, head onto his knees. Sheena looked about to see if anyone had noticed. She went into the pub. Billy was serving a customer.

"What's up, Sheena?"

"Something's happened to Alec."

She collapsed trembling on a stool. Billy went to the door and returned to the telephone. Sheena summoned the courage to go back out to Alec. She covered the body with his blanket. Sheena stayed with the body until the police and ambulance arrived. There were no sirens. Alec and the police vanished almost simultaneously.

A bewildered Sheena asked the sergeant, "Is that it? Aren't you going to ask me anything?"

The policeman looked at her blankly and got into the car. Sheena went into the pub and sat on a stool. Billy put a measure of whisky in front of her. Sheena ignored it.

"Where'd you think he got the razor?"

Sheena gaped open-mouthed.

"What?"

"Well, who'd hurt Alec?"

Sheena hadn't expected to find a razor. She tried to remember without success, a razor in Alec's hands or in his lap. She checked the armchair, lifting out the cushion, sticking her hand down the back and sides into sticky blood and anonymous litter. She checked the gutters and the waste bin.

Billy came to refresh her glass and saw it was untouched.

Sheena said, "Thank you, Billy, but I'm alright."

As he turned away, she asked, "Do the police have the razor?"

Billy shrugged and went to take an order. He returned to Sheena.

"I know you cared about him. But he was an alkie. You don't know what they'll do. Alec had had enough. He was crying when he was talking to Daniel Fallon yesterday."

"I can't work tonight, Billy," Sheena decided.

"Nay bother."

* * * *

Daniel Fallon was reading the Gazette, notebook at hand, when Sheena burst into the flat.

"I'll get you an axe for Christmas," Daniel offered.

"What did you say to Alec?"

"What did I say?"

"Alec Skinner. He lives in a chair outside the Steamer."

"We were talking old times. I knew him a long time ago."

"He's killed himself! Did you give him the razor?"

Daniel was openly shocked.

"You killed him!"

"Whoa! Slow down! Alec is dead?"

"You killed him. You left him crying. I should've known you were trouble when you come."

"Sit down, Sheena."

"No, thanks."

"Please, sit down."

Reluctantly Sheena sat down.

"Would you like a drink?"

Sheena shook her head.

"Who found him first?"

"I did."

"Did you see a razor?"

Sheena shook her head.

"It would've been in or by his hand. In his lap. At his feet. Rarely does a suicide throw it away."

"I didn't see anything."

"He might've stuffed it down the side of the chair."

"I checked the chair."

"When a suicide succeeds in cutting himself he loses interest in the blade."

"The police came and took the body away. They never mentioned a razor."

"Alec didn't have a razor."

"Wha'd'y'mean?"

"He was murdered."

Sheena repeated, "Murdered?"

Daniel rose and brought two glasses from the kitchen. He shared what was left of his whisky into the glasses and placed one before Sheena.

"I don't like whisky."

Daniel sat down and sipped from his glass.

"Nobody likes whisky. We force it down because it's medicinal."

Sheena wet her lip.

"I'm going to tell you a story. You won't believe me. But it's true."

Sheena made no response.

Has it ever concerned you that it's always the best and brightest children that die in accidents? That the feckless, the foolish, the greediest, the most unpleasant sail through unscathed?"

"Can't say I've ever thought about it. What's that to do with Alec Skinner?"

"Eric Johnson was the cleverest boy in the school. We all knew when he grew up, he'd be someone important, do something different. He was my best pal and I worshipped him. We were fishing from the quay, sitting on our ankles behind the baulk when Eric fell into the water. One moment he was there and the next he was lost forever."

Sheena was listening.

"There was a man standing behind us who'd asked the usual question . . . caught anything . . .if he pushed Eric over, I didn't see him do it."

"What has this to do with Alec?"

"I was teaching in a secondary school in Exeter. I had a student whose intelligence quotient was off the scale. The one in a lifetime student every good teacher longs to meet. I invited him to join me in the holidays planting Haldon forest. In my conceit, I thought a taste of hard labour would be a good experience for him."

Sheena said, "This is beginning to be really boring."

"I'm sorry. Stories worth listening to don't have a snappy punch line."

"Planting a forest, you carry a sack of spruce saplings and you follow a tractor, walking in the furrow. Ten paces, stick in a sapling, stamp it firmly and march on. I was working, two, three furrows from Anthony when his tractor stopped on the hill. The driver got down to have a piss. Anthony sat down by the furrow, grateful for a break. Wiping the sweat from my eyes, I saw someone at the tractor. Then the plough and tractor ran downhill and killed the boy. No one believed me when I said I saw someone at the tractor."

"What has that to do with Alec?

"Alec had a son, Bobby, twelve. You'd march a long way before you'd meet a boy as bright as Bobby. It seems the boy slipped between their trawler and the quay and died. A simple step or jump that Bobby had taken a thousand times. Alec had always been a drinker, but the death of his son finished him."

Sheena sat in silence and Daniel waited.

Sheena said, "I don't understand what you're telling me."

"Recently, a boy was killed by a tube train in London. The underground was as natural to that boy as the quay was to Bobby. You don't see a connection between these deaths?"

"Maybe an old man who has too much time on his hands?"

Daniel drew breath and committed himself.

"There is an evil presence that strives to kill every child who might change the future."

"I know them. They live on the dark side of the moon."

"And they succeed because people don't want to believe."

"And these children are being killed all over the country? No way! Unless you have an army. Don't the police interfere?"

"There is an evil presence that twists the minds of innocent people and persuades them to kill. On Haldon Hill something persuaded a tired, overheated man that the boy Anthony threatened his job or was a condescending snob. Whatever the reason, a pimple grew into a boil. That man freed the handbrake on the tractor."

"You were the one who talked to Alec and made him cry."

"Someone saw us talking and decided to kill Alec because he may tell me who killed his son."

Sheena stood up.

"I don't know why you're telling me this nonsense. Maybe you want to frighten me. Maybe to suck me in."

She paused and when Daniel struggled to shape an answer, she demanded, "Stay away from us! I won't bother you again."

"I'm telling you the truth. Perhaps I could've explained better."

"Just leave us alone."

Sheena left the flat, slamming the front door.

"You should know better, Daniel. People only want to know what they already know. Never tell them a different truth."

The telephone rang and Daniel answered.

"Yes?"

Daniel listened and then said, "I'm coming."

He went into the bedroom and packed an overnight bag. The only change to his routine was to find and strap on a shoulder holster. In the sitting room, he added the pistol. Switching off the kitchen appliances, Daniel made his way to the front door. There was no one on the landing. Daniel closed the door quietly and chose the stairs rather than the lift.

* * * *

"Yes, I'm coming!" Sheena assured Kimberley, "I've never been to a Spelling Bee before. I wouldn't miss it for all the chewing gum in Chicago."

The child laughed and Sheena noted the slight movement of the lips as she assimilated the phrase: chewing gum in Chicago.

This is a bright kid. How long before the phrase is her own?

From their first acquaintance, Sheena found if she quoted a book title or character, Kimberley would find it.

The child was very excited, spinning like a top in the little shop, her face alight, every limb sparking.

Sheena said, "Kimbo, slow down! You're making me dizzy. D'y'want to do well tonight?"

Kimberley stopped and nodded.

"I want to win, but I don't mind if I don't. I just don't want to make a fool of myself."

"You'd never do that. But what you must do now is find somewhere quiet. Your bedroom? And just relax. Store up the energy you're going to need later."

Kimberley nodded judiciously.

"Will your Mam and Dad be there?"

"I think Dad's busy."

"Well, I'll be there to cheer you on."

Casting about for something to encourage the child, Sheena took a bottle from the shelf.

"A present from me."

"Energy drinks aren't good for you."

"This is different. No caffeine. It's got glucose. Feeds the brain. Sip it during the Spelling Bee."

"Thank you!"

"Now buzz off and relax! I'll see you later. I'll be the one shouting Kimbo, Kimbo!"

The child laughed and Sheena kimboed her out of the shop to the surprise of the older lady coming in.

Sheena paid for Kimberley's drink and bought one for herself. She found she was excited at the prospect of the Spelling Bee.

* * * *

The evening began with the Mayor making a short speech. The television personality who would run the quiz was introduced and he explained the rules.

"Ladies and gentlemen, the rules are simple enough even for me to understand. There will be three rounds of spelling challenges for

51

the teams. At the end of each round, the team with the lowest score will retire. When we have a winning team, the three members of that team will play for First, Second and Third place."

The teams were introduced and seated. Kimberley gave no sign of looking for anyone in the audience. Her team members, boy and girl, appeared to be in new school blazers. Kimberley was clutching her glucose drink.

Sheena's knuckles were white when Kimberley's trio stood up to answer. Kimberley answered clearly and correctly every word. The boy stumbled on one word. At the end of the first round, Kimberly's team was second. Sheena was cheering silently. The television celebrity did an excellent job making sure the retiring team was not humiliated.

In the second round, both the boy and girl of Kimberley's team did poorly. Kimberley didn't falter and made no mistakes. When the umpires agreed on the final score, a tempest of relief shook the chandeliers in one area of the hall. Kimberley's team survived by one point. The television celebrity comforted and supported the retiring team. They left the stage smiling.

In the third round, Kimberley tripped up and Sheena's heart stopped. It was the boy who rescued the team. It seemed his speciality was scientific terms. When the round ended, the atmosphere was electric. Kimberley seemed shaken. The trio sat huddled together, awaiting the result. The celebrity reported a draw. By the time the uproar had died away, the umpires had found an answer.

The celebrity announced, "The panel has decided upon a tie-breaker. One member from each of the teams will step up to spell five words each. The winner of the tie-break will be declared the winning team."

Sheena could not bear to look. When she did so, Kimberley was standing at the podium with a boy of the other team.

"This is not a penalty shoot-out," the celebrity warned, "To help your children, you must keep silent. Absolutely silent."

It was the most painful silence Sheena had ever endured. At the first word, Kimberley hesitated so long Sheena was in agony. Kimberley answered correctly. The boy spelt the first three words precisely and without hesitation. On the fourth question, Kimberley asked to hear the word again. The silence seemed interminable. Sheena couldn't breathe. Kimberley mis-spelled the word.

The audience struggled to keep silent. The boy repeated his word and without hesitation, mis-spelled it. It took time for the clamour to die down. Sheena noted Kimberley and the boy exchanged rueful grins.

The celebrity announced, "The contestants share three successes. This is the final round of five."

In the eye of a cyclone there is dead calm. Nothing disturbed the silence. Sheena gripped her left hand with her right as if she would break every bone. Kimberley listened to the word and spelt it correctly. It evidently shook the boy who made a hesitant beginning and then mis-spelled the word. The applause was ear-splitting.

The contest for First, Second and Third places was an anticlimax. Kimberley McLeod won First place, the boy won Second place and the girl won Third. The celebrity employed his magic and three proud children stood to be applauded, grasping their trophies.

Proud parents reclaimed their children and came to join the celebrity, the Mayor and the referee and umpires for photographs. No one came to claim Kimberley. The audience dispersed slowly.

Sheena made her way through the lingerers towards the official party and stopped. A tall thin man was talking to the child. She saw him smile, a charming smile, and Kimberley responded. Sheena found herself frozen, watching them. The stranger said something and Kimberley laughed. He took out a notebook and seemed to ask the child questions which she answered readily. Anyone watching might have assumed a journalist was taking notes for a local paper. For no reason, but instinct, Sheena knew something was not right. Intuition said, danger. Without reason, Sheena knew this man was wrong. Something about physical attitude, the faded raincoat, ginger hair, the smile that didn't fit the face. To Sheena it seemed his wardrobe was from a dressing up basket.

The stranger exchanged farewells with Kimberley and moved towards the Hall doors. Sheena was torn between going to the child and following the raincoat. When she dodged between chattering groups and stepped out into the marble corridor, the man had vanished. The empty corridor stretched into the far distance in both directions. Sheena knew then she was not mistaken.

She returned to the hall. Kimberley was talking to the Mayor. Her face lit up when she saw Sheena.

"Sheena, this is the Mayor!" she announced, "Sheena's my sister. She's called after a singer our Mam was mad about so it's not her fault."

Before Sheena had a chance to draw breath, the Mayor said, "I'm sorry your mother isn't well. Such a pity to have missed your sister's wonderful performance this evening."

Sheena played up, responding, "We'll tell her all about it, won't we, Kimbo?"

They walked down the marble staircase to the front door of the Town Hall in silence. Kimberley clutched her trophy. When they were out in the cold air of the street, the child offered, "Sorry!"

Sheena said, "Don't be! If you want me to be your sister, it's a position I'm willing to fulfil."

Kimberley glowed and skipped a pace or two.

"Who was that you were talking to?"

CHAPTER SEVEN

"I don't think Mum will be too upset."

Guillaume said, "We believe it is the same creature. There's a pattern of behaviour we've seen before."

Daniel and the black man were sitting in the car outside the tower block. Groundsmen were working on a site for a trampoline. The apparatus stood to one side of the children's playground. Daniel scanned the tower block with binoculars and focused on the balconies of the sixth floor.

"Sixth floor. They are neighbours. The boy is an A star student. Year nine. The Hampden School."

Daniel passed the binoculars to Guillaume, who commented, "The Bright Star Scholarship Trust has made a difference. We can now approach schools and identify promising children. But this is the first time we've got a line on this creature. Our watcher noticed on three separate occasions, there was someone else watching. She took photographs. Photographs that are blurred."

"Some form of radiation?"

"This creature may be able to influence minds, but it has no dress sense. That's what caught the watcher's attention. On the first occasion, a dress shirt with jeans. On the second, a very old hacking jacket and sandals. On the third, wellingtons, shorts and a football scarf. Ginger hair that must be a wig. A very dangerous creature."

The radio on Guillaume's knee crackled.

"Tell me."

A voice said, "Suspect has entered lift."

"Do not follow. Wait."

"Understood."

Daniel said, "Are they armed?"

"They have a taser."

Daniel was uneasy.

"They know the danger. Both have suffered."

Guillaume hit the radio button.

"It's begun. Be alert everyone, please."

"What's the story?" Daniel asked.

"The neighbour's grandson didn't get a place at the Hampden. This creature has picked and picked at the sore until the old man cannot think of anything but this 'injustice'."

They exited the car to watch the sixth floor. The workmen on the playground were taking a breather, sitting on the trampoline. The children, tiring of watching the workmen, had returned to the swings and jungle gym. It was a tranquil summer day on a pleasant Council estate in Salisbury. Guillaume was glued to the binoculars. There was movement on the sixth floor.

"He's inviting the boy across to his balcony. He's done this often enough. The boy's on the wall."

As Bobby Skinner went from the quay to the trawler into the dark water.

Guillaume called, "This is it! Go!"

There was a moment of disbelief.

Daniel shouted, "My God, he's pushed him off!"

The boy's scream of terror split the air. Daniel began to run, but Guillaume didn't move. Four workmen held the trampoline and the boy bounced six feet in the air.

Guillaume spoke into the radio.

"Well done! Fish in the net! Be ready for the lift."

Daniel complained, "Why didn't you tell me?"

"What would you have done?"

Daniel admitted, "Nothing."

"So, you see," said Guillaume, "We fight back."

A woman's voice spoke from the radio.

"I'm in the flat. Stopped him swallowing tablets. Don't know how many he's already taken."

"Ring for an ambulance and then get out of there."

Guillaume hit the button.

"Any movement on the lift?"

Silence.

"Ben, are you there?"

They ran together. There was silence in a lobby lit by the summer sun. The lift door stood open, constantly trying to close, frustrated by some obstacle. There were two dead men preventing the lift door from closing. Daniel stopped stricken. Guillaume knelt by the bodies. The heads of both men had been twisted back to front in mockery.

* * * *

In the car, Kimberley fizzed like a Catherine wheel with excitement. When she began to relax, Sheena asked, "Who were you talking to?"

"I think he was from the Gazette."

"Did he say he was?"

Kimberley hesitated.

"I can't remember."

"What sort of questions did he ask?"

"My name and address. He wrote them down."

"Then he must be from the Gazette."

"What I liked at school. What my hobbies were."

"What did you tell him?"

"I told him I liked Reading and History best. That I liked Maths, but I didn't like Geography because Missis Hopkins isn't very nice. He laughed at that."

"He was really interested, wasn't he?"

"He asked if I liked swimming which I do and what would I have liked as a prize. A special prize. I said a bicycle because the library is really far to walk sometimes. But I didn't expect that."

"Didn't he ask you about your Mam and Dad?"

Kimberley was reluctant to answer.

"Oh, yes, he did! He was surprised they weren't there, but I told him, Dad had to go out and Mam wasn't very well. He said he hoped Mam would be better soon. He was very nice."

"He does sound very nice."

"He had a lovely smile."

"Did he say he'd be seeing you again."

"No. But he took my photograph. D'y'think there'll be a piece in the Gazette?"

"Come in on Monday and we'll see."

Kimberley's smile lit the interior of the car.

Sheena drove Kimberley home and watched until she was in the lobby of Clement Atlee House. Then she drove her faithful Seat home. She switched off the engine and sat for some minutes in thought. Holding a handkerchief to her nose, she ascended in the lift. She checked her siblings had been fed and warned her mother not to go out leaving them alone. She washed, made up her face, changed her clothes and went off to the Steamer. The pistol was still in her locker. She was tempted to drop it in the waste bin, but didn't.

When she came home, breathless on the landing, Sheena hesitated and then made up her mind. She knocked loudly on Daniel Fallon's door. Not receiving an answer, she hammered again. Aloud, she said, "So what if he's in bed!"

She found her key and opened the door. The flat was in darkness. The sitting room and kitchen were too tidy. The bed was made up and unused. Sheena checked the wardrobe. Daniel's suit was gone. She felt alone and afraid. If he had gone forever, there was no reason why he need tell the girl across the landing. Suddenly, she missed his sturdy presence. She heard the lift arrive and her heart lifted. Then she heard the familiar prattle of her mother and Hilda. She intercepted the pair as her mother opened their door.

"Mam, you left them alone again!"

"Tha old enough t'look after each other. I certainly was."

"An eleven month baby? And her Mam's out clubbing?"

"And what about yee? Coming out of an old man's flat this time o'night! I'd say no more if I was you!"

The women cackled and vanished. Sheena heard the television begin to boom. She stood alone on the landing.

* * * *

Sheena didn't go to bed, but waited up to ambush her mother. When she heard Hilda's final noisy departure, Sheena caught her mother in the sitting room.

"Sit down, Mam!"

"I've no time for ya nonsense this time of night. Me bladder's tight as a drum."

Sheena turned off the television. "I said, sit down! I need to talk to you. If you leave the little ones again, I'll report you."

"I've a right to a life of me own!"

"You have a responsibility for ya bairns."

"What harm has come to them? Safe behind a locked door. In the top flat."

"Mam, out there are evil men who would harm them. Kill them is the kindest thing they would do. I don't even want to think about it. They'd only need to get a sniff they're on their own."

"Ya talking daft."

"If you leave them again, I'll report you. Yi'll be found unfit."

"And ya sisters and brother will go into Care?"

"No, they won't. They'll be with me. And we'll be out of Gallin."

"Yi've never thought much of your Mam, have yi?"

"Well, think on this. Hilda's here often enough to be a lodger. I don't like it."

Sheena regarded her mother; dragged up in an ignorant home where education was despised, married at sixteen to escape, but abandoned and abused by a succession of men who left a remembrance behind; Sheena, Lorraine, Morris and Marianne.

"Let's go to bed, Mam."

* * * *

It was raining in the morning and the children fought to get into the car. As they belted up, Sheena said, "I think I like rain. Yesterday I had to fight to stop you escaping. Today you're fighting to get in."

The children laughed and the day was brighter for Sheena.

The first traffic lights were red. As they waited for the lights to change, Sheena said, "I went to the Gallin Schools Spelling Bee competition Saturday. It was more exciting than you'd think. I bit my nails down to the knuckle. Why haven't you ever mentioned it?"

Lorraine said, "Miss Kaplan was keen, but Mister Piggott said no."

"We have good spellers in our class," added Morris.

"Who's Mister Piggott?"

"He's our Headmaster," Lorraine offered reluctantly, "He's just not interested in anything."

"But Miss Kaplan's the Deputy Head now?"

"She's not the Headmaster."

The lights changed and Sheena drove on.

Lorraine asked, "Why did you go to the Spelling Bee?"

"A girl who comes into the shop invited me. Called Kimberley. She won."

Morris said, "I bet Lorraine could beat her."

Lorraine said, "We've got a joke for you."

"I'm ready to have my ribs tickled."

Morris announced, "Doctor, doctor, every time I drink a cup of tea, I get a stabbing pain in me eye."

"Have you tried taking out the spoon?"

Sheena laughed out loud. Happiness is a very simple thing. Lorraine and Morris high-fived each other.

* * * *

Ronald Bishop smiled because he had been trained to do so. An only child in an unsmiling household, he had learned one smiled to influence possible customers. As his mother's sole companion, he had followed in her footsteps as she let out the holiday bungalows.

His mother opened the front doors with a smile and offered glimpses of bathrooms with a smile. She smiled as she opened bedroom doors to young couples whereupon the young woman sometimes blushed or giggled. But she smiled most proudly as she displayed the unyielding breakers of the iron Northumbrian shore, two hundred yards from the neat row of holiday bungalows. Somehow, she conveyed the impression she owned this awesome slice of sandy basalt.

Ronald hated all visitors. When he was perhaps five years old, he had asked his mother, "Why do these people come here?"

His mother kissed him and replied, "So we can take their money from them."

He was astounded.

"They pay you money, Mammy, to stay in our houses?"

"It's not cheap," his mother replied.

"But it's always raining."

"Never tell anyone that."

He had to be satisfied with this answer.

Ronald hated all visitors and in particular, the families. If he had ever been asked why he did, he might've said because they were happy. There was one particular family, the Forsytes who came every July, regular as clockwork. Mother, son Julian and daughter Eileen came in an older car on Friday. Father arrived every Saturday morning in a sports car. They had London voices and to Ronald's eyes, were immensely rich.

The boy Julian made fun of Ronald's Northumbrian burr. Eileen was quiet and Ronald collected shells with her. He was never invited by Mr. Forsyte to join them on trips to the Farne Islands. In this fashion, they grew up alongside each other until they came no more. Ronald smiled on through the years.

He even smiled through his mother's funeral which others thought odd. The routine changed not a tittle. Ronald smiled as his mother had done when showing the bungalows.

Then the next generation of the Forsyte family returned. The mother and son came by Volvo and the father, like his father before him, arrived on Saturday morning in a Lexus.

The boy of nine, James, a quiet child, was more interested in rock pools than mockery. His questions amazed Ronald; questions about the shore, the geology and the history of Northumbria. He used a camera skilfully and filled notebooks with sketches and notes.

Ronald found him very different to his father who seemed to have learnt nothing in the past years. He had taken up shooting and hung his trophies on the laundry windmill. Ronald overheard a blazing row on the first morning when James refused to go shooting with his father. Ronald withdrew discreetly, unnoticed.

He found himself drawn to James who seemed happy to talk. They would sit on the bench outside the bungalow when Ronald made his daily round to check everything was well with his tenants. Sometimes the boy's mother would bring them out a soft drink.

Ronald said, "Your mother's nice, James. Very kind."

The boy nodded thoughtfully, sucking on his straw.

"I suspect she's not too keen on your Dad going shooting."

The pheasants swung on the laundry windmill and the boy laughed, choking on his drink.

"She says, take no notice. I asked, what're we going to do with all those dead birds. Mum said, well, I'm not cooking them."

Ronald laughed which was something he didn't often do.

"He says you have to hang pheasants for two weeks. I asked Mum what happens when we go home."

"And she said?"

The boy had a natural flair for story telling. He held the pause long enough for Ronald to nudge, "And?"

"She said, those poor maggoty birds are not going in our car."

Ronald felt a rare regret that the family would be going home in a fortnight.

"Ronald," the boy asked, "would you like to come to the Farnes with us tomorrow?"

They sailed out of the harbour at Seahouses in bright sunshine, aboard the Glad Tidings, onto a sea as smooth as a millpond: Mr. and Mrs. Forsyte, James and Ronald. James chatted to the helmsman. Mr. Forsyte stared into his electronic gizmo ignoring the wonders about him.

Ronald would've enjoyed talking to Mrs. Forsyte. Instead a tourist, buried in foul weather gear, insisted on questioning him about the seabirds. Ronald who was struggling with the faintest pangs of seasickness and angered at Mr. Forsyte's behaviour, felt an irritation he failed to shake off. He did not wish to be rude to the visitor with his continual questions, but the trickle of irritation began to grow.

The thought that grew from a whisper was the certainty that James would become as his father. The boat passed below the clamour of the cliffs. The shrieks of the seabirds became an ear-splitting cacophony. Mr. Forsyte never raised his head. Ronald knew this must be ended before the boy became corrupted by his parent. As they disembarked at the first landing, Ronald knew he must kill James to save James.

The child took his hand as his mother decided to stay aboard the Glad Tidings. She smiled the ill-assorted trio away and they climbed the rocky path following their fellow pilgrims.

Ronald's head boiled with confusion; voices cried against and voices urged him onwards. James and Ronald stood on the edge of the cormorant gully that slipped away down to the boiling tide. James was excited at the birds and nests so close. For no reason Ronald recited, "The cormorant or shag lays its eggs in a paper bag."

James laughed and Ronald joined in. It was the happiest day of his life. Everything was clear to him now. He released the boy's grip and laid a hand on his thin shoulder. Looking around, Ronald saw their party had begun to move on with the warden. Ronald called, "Mister Forsyte! Come and see this! Please!"

Mr. Forsyte reluctantly came to join Ronald and his son.

"What is it?"

"Look! See! In the cranny!"

Mr. Forsyte bent to peer into the abyss.

"I can't see what you're on about!"

"There!" cried Ronald and pushed James' father into the cormorant gully. Mr. Forsyte screamed as he fell. The cormorants screamed too. His head struck the rocks and the body vanished into the rising breaker.

Ronald smiled to say, "You're free now, James!"

"I don't think Mum will be too upset," the boy replied.

They walked on together to join the warden.

CHAPTER EIGHT

*"How would you like to
join the losing side?"*

Sheena awoke from a sound sleep. She knew the rising of the lift.
Too often the creaking drone had brought violence into her home.
The clock read two forty-seven. Sheena slipped out of bed and took
her dressing gown. She passed silently to the front door. The lift
hesitated as it always did at the floor below. Sheena felt sick.
Cautiously, she undid the bolt, opened the deadlock, but not the
chain. With her hand on the lock, she waited for the lift. The last man
her mother had coupled with, promising everlasting love, was a brute
when drunk. How such a creature could have created sweet Marianne
left her baffled.

The lift stopped. Sheena opened the door a fraction to see who
was riding the lift. She tore open the door and flew across the landing
to hug Daniel Fallon, much to his surprise.

"Sorry! I just—."

When she recovered her composure, she saw how exhausted he
was; tired blue eyes, unshaven face, a shadow of sadness.

"Should you be hugging me?"

"I was just surprised to see you."

"No more surprised than me."

"I was beginning to think you weren't ever coming back."

Daniel smiled.

"The last thing I remember."

Sheena interrupted, "You should never remember the last thing."

Daniel asked, cautiously, "So, are we on speaking terms?"

"I really do need to speak to you."

"I really do need to sleep."

Disappointed, Sheena asked, "Soon?"

"Soonest," said Daniel, "Go back to bed."

"Yes, sir!"

She watched him open his door, raise a hand in salutation and vanish. Sheena bolted and relocked her door. Lying in bed, she was surprised how happy she was Daniel Fallon had returned.

* * * *

Mid-week was always quiet in the charity shop in Percy Street. Thursday, Friday, Saturday were busier days as teenagers sought the clothes older generations had discarded. Margaret Robson and Sandra Foulkes often shared a smile at what the girls bought.

Only twice had the doorbell rung on this particular Wednesday afternoon. Margaret had let Sandra go at three. She'd worked all day sorting and separating contributions in the back room; a job that Margaret didn't particularly enjoy. The shop would close at four.

No sooner had Margaret put the kettle on than the bell rang. If she had been asked to describe in one word the tall man who came into the shop, she would've said, 'scarecrow'. Whereas customers made a beeline for the clothes racks, this man came to the counter. Margaret approached cautiously. The ginger hair was most certainly a wig.

Margaret asked, "Can I help you, sir?"

To her relief, the customer gave a generous smile. Her apprehension vanished.

"I'm hoping you may be able to help me."

"I will if I can."

Margaret waited for him to explain. Instead, he strode to the door and pushed the bolt home.

Margaret cried out, "What're you doing, sir!"

The man in the ginger wig returned to the counter where Margaret had seized a glass rolling pin from the shelf behind her.

"Don't you dare come any nearer!"

"Fear not, dear lady! I mean you no harm!"

"Well, you certainly frit me!"

"My apologies! My sincere apologies! I was merely choosing a degree of privacy."

He smiled again and there was a childish innocence to his smile that charmed Margaret Robson.

"I have been told," the customer continued, "that I am very badly dressed. I wish you to help me find appropriate clothing."

Margaret decided not to lie to this man.

"You look like a scarecrow. If I'm being honest."

"I don't want to scare crows. I wish to scare no one."

Margaret found two good suits that would fit his angular size, pinstripe blue, clerical grey. She was a good judge of size. She chose three shirts, white, blue and stripes. She tried not to wince at his sandals and overgrown toenails. She found three pairs of solid brogues of different sizes.

"I don't think you need a tie, do you?"

He looked perplexed.

"Most men don't wear a tie nowadays."

He was reassured, but stood there as a child waiting to be told what to do next. Margaret indicated the changing room.

"Try on the clothes in there."

She hung the coat hangers on the rail and dropped a pair of socks on the bench.

"Choose what you want," adding, "I can do you suit, shirt and shoes for fifteen pounds. The socks are free. Is that going to be a problem for you?"

The customer smiled, "No problem, dear lady. You have been most kind."

When he had drawn the curtain, Margaret suggested, "That wig is doing you no favours either."

She left her tea to brew when he called her. He was wearing the blue shirt and clerical grey. The change was remarkable. She saw in his eyes that he read her face.

"You look splendid. You could pass for the Mayor's tea party."

"That's not my intention."

"You're no longer a scarecrow."

"And you're sure about the wig?"

"Hairless is normal now. Young men shave their heads."

He seemed pleased. His shining egg of a head was no different to a hundred others.

Margaret moved to the till and struck up fifteen pounds. She stood expectant as he came to the counter.

"Are the shoes comfortable?"

"Very much so."

"The suit looks smart. Do you need a receipt?"

When he made no response, Margaret urged, "Fifteen pounds, please. The socks are free."

The tall thin man in clerical grey studied her thoughtfully.

"You did say it was no problem?"

"There is no problem, dear lady. I will kill you or you will allow me to leave this shop without harming a hair on your head."

Margaret Robson stood frozen with terror. She knew he was speaking the truth. The warm smile had become a shark's grimace. She pushed the till drawer shut, tore off the receipt and said, "Thank you very much, sir. Please come again. The Chapel of Our Lady welcomes your contribution."

The customer tucked the receipt into the top pocket of his new suit.

"You are a very nice lady. Thank you for your help."

He walked towards the door and stopped at the hat stand. He chose a panama, checked his appearance in the mirror, unbolted the door and exited. Margaret ran to the shop door to lock it. She went into the back room and made a fresh pot of tea. When she poured out a cup she found her hands were trembling.

She drank two cups of tea and then went to gather up the customer's discarded garments, mismatched coat and trousers, frilly dress shirt and sandals. Picking up the ginger wig she shuddered. Margaret put everything in a bin bag. About to add the bag to the rubbish, she changed her mind and pushed it into a spare locker.

She closed the shop and went to Confession. She caught Father Callaghan coming out of the box and saw the irritation in his face as he turned back to receive her. Margaret Robson explained to the Father that she had met and talked with the Devil, but he wasn't interested. Father Callaghan didn't believe in God or the Devil. He wanted to go home for his tea. He mumbled the necessary ritual, but Margaret Robson wasn't satisfied. She wondered if there was anything on the CCTV.

* * * *

Despite Daniel's promise to talk soonest, Sheena found the flat empty. Daniel had vanished with the dawn. Although disappointed, she was relieved to find his suit hanging in the wardrobe. There were voices at the door.

Lorraine called, "Are you taking us to school?"

"We're going to be late. And it'll be your fault," Morris complained.

On the landing were two fidgety children and her mother.

"Lying abed, is he?"

"Here we go, Joe!" Sheena announced brightly, ignoring her mother.

"Leave the door open. I'll take the old feller a cup of tea."

Sheena shut the flat door firmly.

In the car, Sheena was silent. Lorraine said, "What're you worried about, Sheen?"

Sheena woke from her reverie.

"Nothing. You can't go around with a big smile on your face all the time."

"You weren't resting your face. It's crumpled."

"You're too smart for me, Tweetie-pie!"

"Have you fallen for him?"

"Who? Daniel? No way! He's old enough to be your Great Grandfather."

"Have we got a Great Grandfather?"

Sheena was as surprised as Lorraine.

"I suppose we have. Never thought about it."

"You've never met him?"

Sheena shook her head.

Morris said, "Then we have a Great Grandmother. They come as a pair. Like fish and chips."

How ignorant we are! Don't we have photographs? Marriage certificates? We didn't come out of nowhere.

"One day," Lorraine said, "I'll be a Great Grandmother. What will they be then?"

Morris offered, "GG to the power of four."

"Too clever for me. Is your homework as good, Einstein?"

Sheena stopped the car outside the school. The last-minute panic wouldn't start for another twenty minutes. She didn't release the child locks as her brother tugged at the handle.

"Just listen a moment. I'm being serious."

Obediently, the children sat silent.

"Don't talk to strangers. Don't accept lifts. Don't get into cars because somebody says Mam sent them."

When they moved to protest, she ignored it.

"I know you've heard it all before. But kids keep on getting taken off the street. You're both old enough to know there are wicked men out there who would hurt you. Even kill you. You have to be aware. If Mam comes to get you, fine. If not, walk home together. Together! Do you understand?"

Lorraine and Morris nodded soberly.

"Has Mam been collecting you okay?"

Lorraine said, "She only missed once."

Sheena unlocked the doors.

"Work hard and win a place in the world."

She followed them out of the car and watched them vanish into the empty yard. A car drew in behind and parked. Mrs. Kaplan appeared and took a fat briefcase from the rear seat.

"Good morning, miss,"

"Good morning, Sheena!"

The teacher questioned, "The Galloways first into school? Gold star! They can come in with me."

Sheena hesitated before asking, "Is there ever anyone hanging around the children, miss?"

"Men, you mean?"

Sheena nodded.

"We try to be vigilant. Do you know something?"

"I'm not sure."

"Then I'm aware. Thank you."

* * * *

Sheena was mucking out the stable when Mr. Fitzpatrick appeared out of nowhere in riding gear.

"Good morning, sir!"

"Riding today! Let's say, saddled up, half an hour?"

"Yes, sir!"

Sheena abandoned the broom and went for the saddles.

"Behave yourselves and don't embarrass me!"

All four behaved impeccably and were standing obediently in the yard awaiting riders. Mr. Fitzpatrick and two teenage girls appeared in riding kit. The girls didn't speak to Sheena. She found them pale and lifeless. There wasn't the excitement and enthusiasm she had expected. They followed limply behind Mr. Fitzpatrick who exploded before he had crossed the yard.

"What the hell have you done, girl?"

A confused Sheena replied, "What you asked me to do, sir."

"I asked you to saddle that brute? I don't think so!"

He slashed at Baldrick with his riding whip causing the pony to shy.

"No, sir. Sorry, sir."

To save further mistreatment, Sheena led the pony back into the stable. When she emerged, the trio were clattering out of the yard. Sheena brought out the pony. She mounted and leaning forward said into the twitching ear, "Take no notice of that ghastly man, Baldrick. We'll take ourselves for a canter."

They progressed from the yard and turned away up towards Tillingworth Woods. From that elevation they would have good notice of the trio returning. The pony responded happily. As she rode, Sheena said aloud, "Why does that man hate you so much?"

* * * *

Daniel pretended not to notice that Sheena had entered the flat until she put four cans of lager on the tabletop. He stopped typing.

He asked, "Don't you think it would be nice if we behaved as other people do?"

"No. I like it the way we are."

Sheena came around the table to view the screen. Daniel closed the laptop.

"When're you going to give me your key?"

Sheena opened a lager can and offered it.

"I really do need to talk to you, Daniel."

Taking the drinks, they went to sit on the couch. Sheena pulled her tab and drank deeply. Daniel gestured his thanks.

"I had six, but two mysteriously disappeared."

Sheena made up her mind.

"I believe you, Daniel. About evil. Something is very wrong."

"What changed your mind?"

"I saw something."

She stopped and Daniel offered, "Take your time."

"There's a girl comes in the shop. A very clever girl. Kimberley McLeod. On Saturday she won the Gallin Spelling contest. She talked to a man who asked her all sorts of questions."

"Go on."

"That's all he did, but there was something wrong about him. Mebbe like someone pretending to be a Geordie, but you know they're not? D'y'understand?"

"I think so."

"It may be easier for a woman to see than a man. A woman can feel when someone's into someone. D'y'know what I mean?"

Daniel nodded.

Sheena began, "When I was in primary school. The Christmas concert. I was nervous of performing. This man teacher I'd never met before walked me around the building in the darkness to calm me down. He held my hand. I stayed well out of his way after that. But this man wasn't sexually interested in Kimberley. I asked her if he mentioned seeing her again. She said no. He asked his questions. Didn't bother to flatter her. There was something else. Something worse. Please don't laugh at me. That child was talking to the Devil. I'm sure of it."

They sat silent together until Daniel spoke.

"I told you how the boy Anthony died on Haldon Hill. I went back to teaching, but it wasn't the same. I avoided anywhere I might meet colleagues. I used dodgy pubs and one night, in this dump, I saw the science teacher, Chamberlain, in conversation with a character out of a Dickens' novel."

Sheena regarded Daniel quizzically.

"Uriah Heep was doing all the talking and Chamberlain was doing all the listening. I started taking an interest in his students."

Daniel remembered his lager and drank deeply. Sheena finished her can.

"I found a girl who was always hanging around Chamberlain, Audrey Hutchinson, a most serious student, exceedingly bright. A nerdy Keyhole Kate. Although she probably never read the Dandy in her life. One look at her eager face with granny glasses and you knew one day she might cure cancer."

Sheena added, "I hope you never describe me."

"One day as I supervised the free study area outside the labs I noticed her in the small workroom off the Chemistry lab. She was washing glassware in the sink at the far end. As I talked with a student, I saw Chamberlain speak to her and leave, opening the fume cupboards as he left. He closed the door and walked away. I was blind to what he'd done. But the student said, 'Sir, that door shouldn't be closed when the fume cupboards are open.'"

Sheena started to say something and stopped.

"When we opened the door, the girl was on the floor and the fumes were stifling. We carried her out and she was still breathing. I knew then."

"What does it all mean?"

"There is a demonic presence that persuades people to kill the brightest and best. Often complete strangers."

"So, what do we do?"

"This is an ancient struggle. The good guys against the bad guys. The angels against the demons. And the demons are winning. How would you like to join the losing side?"

"What could I do?"

"You would be a valuable asset. We have very few who can sense evil as you do. But you would be placing yourself and your family in danger."

Daniel regarded Sheena soberly.

"Think about it seriously before you decide. These creatures do not hesitate to kill."

CHAPTER NINE

"Unfortunately, we came to
the wrong address."

Sheena stopped to watch the Corporation workman lift Alec's armchair to his mate on the lorry. The man on the lorry added the chair to the rest of Gallin's rubbish. When the lorry drove away, Sheena could see the dry shadow where the chair had stood.

"Is that it? All that suffering ends in an old armchair thrown onto a lorry? That's it?"

She picked up Alec's broken glass and dropped the pieces into the waste bin.

She was passing through the bar to the acclamation of her fans, which always embarrassed her, when Billy said, "Don't take your coat off! Yi've an errand to do."

She followed him through to the back passage where he said, "That package in your locker."

"Not mine."

"Take it to this address."

He offered a piece of paper that Sheena accepted reluctantly.

"Do I have to?"

"Do us both a favour."

Sheena nodded.

"I owe you."

Sheena put the pistol into a carrier bag and covered it with potatoes and carrots. She told the puzzled cook, "Mission of mercy," added an onion and fled.

She drove out to the Bronx, which was undisputedly the worse Council estate on the Tyne. The prime contestant for the honour was the Alamo. She was grateful for the anonymity the old Seat provided. In the cul-de-sac there were no lights visible in any house. She worked out which house was number eleven as two houses still had numbers.

On what was once the front garden stood the burnt-out carcass of a caravan. Sheena took a deep breath and walked past. Her heart beat like a kettledrum. Nothing jumped out at her. At the door, she stood listening to the silence. Across the estate, a dog began to bark. Sheena jumped when a dog answered from a nearby garden. She tapped on the door. There was no answer. She rapped harder. A light came on in the house. There was someone behind the door. The light was extinguished.

A voice said, "Wha'd'y'want?"

"It's Sheena."

A bolt was released. The door opened. The smell from within was not inviting. A man stood in darkness. He opened the door farther and ordered, "Come in!"

Sheena shook her head.

"No way!"

The man grabbed her arm and dragged her in. He closed the door.

"Billy knows I'm here!"

The light was switched on, a bulb hanging on its cord. Sheena was standing in the wreck of a sitting room. As he snatched the carrier bag, Sheena recognised Squeaker, the man who came to the kitchen door of the Steamer.

"What's this shite?"

Squeaker was staring at the vegetables in the carrier bag. He turned upon her angrily.

"In the bottom."

He upended the carrier bag and caught the pistol. The vegetables drummed on the floor. He seemed much relieved. As Squeaker checked the gun, Sheena became slowly aware there was another presence in the dingy room. She could taste it, smell it, was aware of a presence so evil she began to feel very afraid. Sheena backed towards the door.

"I'm going now, okay? Billy'll be wondering."

Squeaker laughed sourly.

"He's allis had the hots fa' yee."

Sheena had a hand on the door. She knew what the smell was now. The man had soiled himself.

He's terrified!

Squeaker said, "Tell them I'm sorry."

Squeaker put the pistol to his head and pulled the trigger. His body fell to the floor. Sheena screamed. Her ears rang. There followed a silence that lasted forever until Sheena finally managed to open the door and pull it shut behind her. Into the wreckage of the caravan, she vomited until her stomach was empty. A car engine started farther up the cul-de-sac. A car drove past throwing light into the broken caravan. She waited until darkness and silence returned before moving. Sheena fumbled the key to the Seat, but finally opened the door. She sat in darkness until the trembling stopped and then drove to the Steamer.

Billy said, "Okay?"

Sheena replied, "No bother."

She hung up her coat and went to work. The patrons of the Steamer were pleased to see her.

* * * *

Sheena checked her siblings were sleeping and her mother dozed before the television. She was thinking, *this telly must light up the block like a lighthouse. The light that never fails twenty-four seven.*

She crossed the landing and opened Daniel's door. The flat was in darkness. She switched on the light and went to his bedroom. Sheena hesitated before opening the door. Daniel Fallon was sleeping peacefully.

She shook his shoulder and said, "Daniel! Wake up, Daniel!"

He awoke startled and stared at her.

"Sheena?"

Sheena sat on the edge of the bed.

"Don't get too comfortable."

"I need to talk to you."

"I need to sleep."

"I saw a man kill himself tonight."

"Let me get dressed."

Sheena fidgeted in the sitting room until Daniel appeared, looking like someone dragged through a Roman catacomb backwards. Sheena offered a comb.

"Tell me about it."

She tried not to explain about the Steamer, but finally admitted, "People bring stuff to the pub and other people collect it."

"Did you hold the gun?"

"It was wrapped up."

"So only this guy, Squeaker, handled it?"

Sheena shuddered, struggling with the image of the man's head exploding.

"Yes."

"So, Squeaker wanted the gun, but couldn't come to get it?"

"I suppose so."

Daniel sat in silent thought. Sheena waited.

"Let's take a look."

Sheena hesitated.

"I'm frightened.

"Stay in the car."

Daniel took his stick from beside the door.

"Rather have a shotgun," Sheena wished aloud.

They parked clear of the cul-de-sac. As Daniel moved to get out, Sheena offered, "I'll come with you."

"Let me see if it's been disturbed."

She watched his reassuring solidity vanish into the night.

A car approached and turned into the estate. Sheena crouched down in her seat until darkness returned. The Seat groaned, whimpered and grunted as it cooled. Another car passed. She was sure Daniel had run into trouble. Then she saw him in the rear-view mirror and he slid into the car.

"Sorry, Didn't want to come back the same way."

"Well?"

"Undisturbed. No pokenoses in the Bronx."

"Now what?"

"Want to come with me?"

The house was dark and silent. With his stick, Daniel broke the small window by the door. The stench in the house was almost unbearable. Sheena buried her nose in her scarf. Daniel closed the door and produced a torch. Squeaker lay where he fell, but Sheena was astonished by the size of the blood lake about his head.

"What's with the veg?"

"I brought it."

Daniel left it unquestioned, stepping over potatoes. The sitting room was dressed with mismatched, cast-away furniture. No one had tidied up the empty cans and fast food packaging.

"A waiting room in hell," Daniel commented, "It fits a pattern."

Sheena felt faint and held to the back of a chair.

"You want to wait outside?"

She shook her head. Sheena was determined not to show weakness. It might have been Daniel's presence, but she felt less afraid.

"I'm going upstairs."

Sheena's mouth said, "I'm coming."

The stench was worse as they went upstairs. The torch seemed to awaken flies. The first bedroom was empty but for a dirty mattress on the floor. The bathroom reeked of urine and human soil. There was no body in the bath: Sheena's unspoken nightmare. In the second bedroom, there were two corpses on the bed; a baby and a toddler of two or three. Someone had swaddled the baby in a shawl. They appeared to be sleeping. Sheena cried out and moved to pick up the baby, but Daniel stopped her.

"This is not our problem."

Sheena knew she would never forget those human fragments, abandoned after death, mouths open, crying for a mother who never came. She began to cry.

"Why did he do this?"

"Ask him when we go downstairs."

"But why? Why would he kill these innocents?"

"Squeaker misunderstood what the demon wanted. Quantity for quality."

They exited via the kitchen door and crossed three jungle gardens before they reached a road from whence they walked to the car.

Daniel drove back to where the tower blocks lit the night sky.

"If only we'd known earlier. The demon was living in that house and we missed him."

"I'm glad we missed him."

"They're seeking one particular child here in Gallin. A child, perhaps not yet born, who is very important. This is the child who will change the world. They are determined that will not happen again."

Sheena said, "Then we must stop them."

* * * *

Peace reigned in the Kaplan household on a certain Friday evening. On Saturday they were anticipating a visit to Lindisfarne. But on that Friday evening the Kaplans' world changed forever. Peter Kaplan was washing the dishes his wife had used to prepare dinner. Janet Kaplan was reading The Magic Pudding again, an Australian children's book, because she always read first any book she intended to read in school.

This had been her rule since her first teaching practise in a secondary school. At the end of a tiring, frightening day she had hoped to quiet the noisy students by reading to them. The phrase was innocuous; an innocent enquiry by a maidservant about a lady's missing muff.

"Have you seen my lady's muff? It is quite small, but I do believe it would accommodate a gentleman's hands."

Miss Kaplan lost control of the class and never regained it. Her days in that school were haunted by enquiries about the lady's muff, both in the classroom and the corridors. It seemed the whole school taunted her. *Have you seen my lady's muff, miss?* She gritted her teeth and completed the teaching practice. She knew why she had failed and a weaker person would've given up. The teaching profession would've lost an excellent teacher. She never made the same mistake again.

She stopped reading when she heard raised voices and went to the window. She called to her husband, "Just going to see what's up across the road. It's Ellie Martin. The pregnant girl?"

"Do you really think you should be interfering?"

There were two men in white coats trying to get a struggling Ellie Martin into a car. Janet Kaplan was alarmed. Ellie was very pregnant. But what disturbed her more was husband, Sean. He was watching the struggle, seemingly unconcerned.

"What's going on, Sean?"

"They say Ellie has to go with them."

"Who says?"

Ellie Martin appealed to Janet Kaplan.

"Help me, Janet, please! Please! I don't know why they're doing this!"

Janet Kaplan reached into the car to snatch the keys from the ignition. To the men, she said, "My husband is speaking to the police. If you release Ellie, I will give you the keys."

The two men gaped and looked to another car parked across the street. Janet Kaplan assumed they feared the approach of a police car.

"Don't think you can take the keys from me. I will drop them down the drain."

The car across the street drove away. The men reluctantly released Ellie Martin who ran to Janet Kaplan. She was surprised at the ferocity of her embrace.

"Thank you! I was so frightened."

Mrs. Kaplan dropped the keys into the car and shepherded the young woman across the road. The car drove away.

The two women stopped to look back at Sean who hadn't moved.

"Sean! What's wrong with you! Don't you care about your wife?"

Sean Martin followed the women into the Kaplan house. Peter Kaplan came from the kitchen carrying a tray of sardines on toast and a coffee pot.

Janet Kaplan persisted, "I still don't understand why you just accepted his word, Sean?"

"He had papers saying the Court had determined."

"Have you got the papers?"

"No. He just showed them to me. It was all so quick. I suppose I was just dumbfounded."

"So, you were quite happy they were taking Ellie?"

Janet Kaplan was beginning to dislike this young man.

"He said something about a secure environment."

Janet Kaplan turned to her husband.

"Two men arrive to."

Sean interrupted, "Three men. It was the tall thin man who did all the talking. Doctor somebody."

"I didn't see him."

"Once he'd explained, he went to the other car, leaving the nurses."

"What other car?" interrupted Janet Kaplan.

"There was another car."

Janet Kaplan exchanged glances with her husband.

"Well, Ellie isn't keen to go home, so we'll let her sleep."

Sean Martin rose hesitantly. The hall clock struck eight.

"If you say so, I won't disturb her."

"I'll ring when she wakes."

Watching the young man cross the road, Janet Kaplan commented, "I know I'm past my sell-by date, but I find that young man rather feeble."

Her husband offered no response, so she pressed further.

"If men in white coats came for me, would you let them take me, Peter?"

Her husband pondered his answer.

"Well? Would you?"

"Considering the trouble I had getting you, only over my dead body, would I let you go."

* * * *

The Kaplans were watching television when the doorbell rang. A tall thin man smiled at Janet Kaplan from the gravel.

"Forgive the intrusion. I've come to apologise for the unfortunate incident earlier."

Janet Kaplan called, "Peter!"

Her husband came to join her. The man wore a suit without a tie. Somehow the Panama hat seemed out of place. The hatband proclaimed Guantanamo Bay Holiday Company. The intruder lifted his hat in salute, displaying an ostrich egg head.

"Good evening, I'm Doctor Prendergast. I'm afraid there's been a terrible mistake in communication. We came to the Avenue rather than the Close. We were expecting to escort a sedated patient to the Clinic. All very discreet. Unfortunately, we came to the wrong address. Unforgivable!"

The smile was open, honest and reassuring. Janet Kaplan felt her husband relax, accepting the explanation. It made sense. The departure of a distressed patient had gone wrong.

"I trust you will accept my sincere apology."

"Thank you," Peter Kaplan said, "Apology accepted."

As the doctor turned to move away, Janet Kaplan suggested, "I'd rather you didn't disturb the Martins. Ellie was very distressed. She's sleeping. Her husband is sitting with her."

She stood firmly on her husband's foot.

"Of course," the doctor agreed, smiling, "I shan't disturb them. And your name? I'm sure the Director will wish to write to you, as he will to Missis Martin."

He produced a smile, a notebook and gold pen.

"Kaplan."

"Initials?"

"P and J."

The doctor glanced at the house number.

"Thank you. And again, my sincere apologies."

Safe behind their front door, Peter commented, "But Ellie's here."

"He doesn't have to know that."

Her husband regarded her curiously.

"What's going on, Janet?"

"I didn't believe a word he said."

"Why not?"

"It just felt wrong. Surely they would have used an ambulance?"

"But as the doctor said, it was meant to be discreet."

"And the hat?"

"He's making a statement."

They decided to let Ellie Martin remain undisturbed overnight. Janet Kaplan rang Sean to tell him so. She suspected he had been drinking.

CHAPTER TEN

*"Policemen are as easily
tempted as anyone else."*

Tom Moore was the most persistent reporter the North Gallin Gazette had ever hired. The editor, William Harvey, phrased it differently. He believed Tom was the biggest pain in the backside the Gazette had suffered in a hundred years. Not just because Tom Moore was his son-in-law and father of his one and only grandchild.

The editor of the North Gallin Gazette waved the reporter to silence and picked up his telephone.

"Where's my coffee, Louise? Okay, okay! May I have a cup of coffee, please, Louise? And whoever let this idiot into my office this time in the morning is fired, okay?"

He didn't wait for an answer, but dropped the receiver to face the man across his desk.

"Nobody cares about Squeaker. Or that poor woman and her two bairns. Nobody, Tom, absolutely nobody!"

"Do you know Squeaker's real name was Anthony Breckenridge?"

"Who cares?"

"That's the problem! We should care!"

"Well, nobody does!"

"Well, I care!"

"Drop it, Tom! Finish the Metro story. That's what our readers like. A heart-warming chuckle story of generous Geordie folk!"

Tom blew a raspberry.

"I take it you disagree. Nay bother! But you'll do your caring on your own time. Nancy will bin any expense chits from you."

"That's not fair!"

"I'm not paying for your pub crawling."

The reporter changed tack.

"You dropped my story of the alkie who used to sit outside the Steamer. Remember? Somebody cut his throat. Oh, dear me, never mind! A man is killed on Percy Street. And absolutely nobody cares!"

The telephone rang.

"Hoppit, Tom! Don't let me see you again today!"

Before he reached his desk, the reporter's mobile buzzed.

"Gazette. Moore."

He listened, drew breath and said, "You sure? That's terrible. Played footie with him Sunday. On my way."

He grabbed his anorak from the chair and announced to the office, "He wants to know where I've gone, I'm auditioning for X Factor."

* * * *

Ellie Martin was sobbing quietly in the sitting room. Peter and Janet Kaplan were standing together in the hallway.

"When I went in, he was hanging from the landing. Dead. He'd tied the vacuum cord around his neck and lodged the vacuum behind the rail. Then he must've jumped from the landing. He broke the banister rail. I don't want to go into detail, but he had soiled himself."

Across the road, an ambulance and two police cars stood, blue lights blinking. Those whose employment was to deal with tragedy came and went on endless errands.

Janet Kaplan suggested, "He must've been desperate to use the vacuum cord."

"But he had everything to live for. The baby's due any day."

The doorbell rang.

On the gravel stood a man who said, "Tom Moore. Gazette."

Peter Kaplan said, "Go away."

Peter made to close the door, but the reporter said, "Sean's my best mate. We lost on Sunday, but it wasn't that bad. He'd never kill himself."

Ellie Martin tumbled out of the sitting room into the reporter's arms.

"Oh, Tom! I'm so glad you're here!"

"I had to come, Ellie."

Peter and Janet Kaplan exchanged glances.

"Come on in," Janet surrendered.

With the expectant mother dozing on the couch, tears exhausted, the reporter crossed the road to where official activity had dwindled to a single constable outside the front door. Tom carried a mug of hot coffee. The Kaplans watched him talk to the constable as he sipped his drink.

* * * *

"It doesn't add up."

The Kaplans agreed.

They retired to the kitchen.

"No note. No explanation."

They sat in silence.

Tom continued, "Sean was really looking forward to the birth of his son. We all had to agree this blob was the finest baby ever conceived. Before the game, we joshed him about it. How his life would change. Diaper Daddy. No more lie-ins. No more sleep. Just daftness, but he enjoyed it. And he was mad about Ellie. Totally!"

This was contrary to Janet Kaplan's assessment of Sean Martin.

"On Sunday, his mind wasn't on the game. He let in six. He's not that bad a goalkeeper. We lost six three."

Janet Kaplan confessed, "I believe I've misjudged your friend."

She told the story of the attempted abduction.

"How you've described him is nothing like the way he behaved that evening."

Peter Kaplan asked, "Did he take any drugs?"

"No way! That wasn't Sean's style."

"I believe he was drugged," Janet decided.

"There was one odd thing the copper mentioned."

"Go on!"

"Sean tried to hang himself twice."

"No!"

"There was shit on the stairs. He failed the first time and went back up to try again."

Janet cried out in horror.

Peter said, "I can't believe anyone, however suicidal, would do that."

The reporter suggested, "Not unless someone was forcing him to do it."

At 4.30 a.m. Ellie Martin woke Janet Kaplan. But she was too far-gone in labour to be moved. At 7.45 a.m. a baby boy weighing six pounds three ounces entered this world in the Kaplans' spare bedroom.

* * * *

Outside the tower block was parked a large but shabby motor home. The children had lost interest, but Sheena walked around it. The cab was tidy. It bore a D for Deutschland and foreign number plates. Seeing Sheena's interest, two boys ran over to her.

"Well, Sherlock? What news from Baker Street?"

The boy replied, "Belongs to a black guy. He give everybody chewing gum."

"Did he say anything?"

"Don't swallow your gum."

Sheena walked slowly to Hugh Gaitskill House.

* * * *

On the second landing, Sheena found a sparrow. Frustrated by its inability to escape, it crouched in a corner.

"You're in trouble, daft dickiebird. Trapped. No way out. Sometimes feel the same meself."

The sparrow made little protest, shuffling sideways until she picked it up. She carried it down to the lobby. On the shabby grass she opened her hands. For a moment, the sparrow didn't move. They eyed one another.

"Good luck," Sheena whispered.

The sparrow flew away.

* * * *

Struggling past the worm-eaten mountain of Granny's hallstand, Sheena heard voices in the sitting room competing with the television. She stopped to identify the voices, Mam, Hilda and a scrawny woman whose name she couldn't remember. Bracing herself, she opened the door. All three were smoking. The television was advertising anti-smoking aids.

"And here's our Sheena," Mam carolled, "You remember Diana?"

The scrawny woman repeated, "Sheena," and Sheena answered, "Diana."

"Don't think I've ever telt yiz this, but the morning like when the radio says Diana wa dead, I was in a terrible state. I were pregnant with Sheena an' all."

"She thought it was you," Sheena continued, nodding at the scrawny woman, "Going on and on about you owing her twelve pounds seventy-five. How she'd never get it now."

Diana and Hilda laughed; Diana less enthusiastically.

"What're you like, Sheena! Owt forra laugh! No, no, I were heartbroken, honest. Let me tell you, miss, Diana and me shared a desk all the way from Dunne Street Infants."

"You and Princess Diana? Ya kidding!"

"You're too much sometimes, Sheen!"

"So, what're the Witches Three planning for tonight?"

"Big night at the 'Hambra! It's Dennis's Thirtieth."

"Who's Dennis?"

All three laughed at Sheena's ignorance.

"Dennis has only been dee jay at the 'Hambra' thirty years!"

"That's a life sentence. Did he murder somebody?"

"Diana's always had a thing about Dennis," Hilda added.

Diana giggled and slapped Hilda; three teenage girls hitting forty.

"Where are the little ones? IYou haven't sold them?"

"Jenny's got them."

"Have they had their tea?"

"D'y'have to ask?"

"Is Marianne clean?"
"I give her the Pampers."

* * * *

Lorraine answered the door.
"Wha'd'y'call a Roman with a cold?"
"No idea."
"Julius Sneezer," called Morris.
Jenny was feeding Marianne. Sheena was fond of this middle-aged woman who lived with and cared for her ageing mother.
"Mam dumped them on you?"
Jenny laughed.
"You get sick of them, Sheena, I'll have them for keeps."
"No chance."
To Lorraine and Morris, Sheena said, "Good day at school?"
Lorraine frowned to say, "Miss Kaplan wasn't there today. We had a supply teacher. Okay, but she's not Miss Kaplan."
"Miss Kaplan never went absent when I was in her class. What did you do to upset her?"
Morris said, "Wish I was in Miss Kaplan's. Miss Shortridge is always on at the boys."

* * * *

On the landing, Sheena was about to put her key in the lock when she changed her mind. She opened Daniel's door and stepped into the hallway. Music was playing quietly. As she opened the door into the sitting room she was surprised. A black man, greying hair, white polar-necked sweater and jeans was sitting at the little table, typing on a laptop. He stopped typing, looked up at her and removed his spectacles. Sheena didn't know what to say.
The black man said, "Ah! The girl across the landing! You must be Sheena!"
The voice was educated and free of accent.
"That's your mobile home out there."
"His name is Guillaume. He's a friend of mine."

Daniel, in tee shirt and jeans appeared from the bathroom scrubbing his hair with a towel.

Guillaume stood up, offering a hand, saying, "Guillaume Barousse."

Sheena took a dry, strong hand and replied, "Sheena Galloway."

Daniel said, "Guillaume is a particular friend."

The black man said, "What news of the Rialto?"

Sheena, surprised, reacted, "Why, yet it lives there uncheck'd that Antonio hath a ship of rich lading wrecked on the narrow seas."

"Forgive me," explained Guillaume, "It struck me as odd."

Sheena knew the black man had picked the words out of her head.

"Who is Kimberley?"

"A girl I know. A clever girl."

"But you're concerned for her."

"Yes."

Daniel said, "Now that you've introduced yourselves?"

Sheena offered, "The police have linked the deaths of Squeaker and the children to the death of a woman on the estate. A drug tragedy. They're not looking for anyone else. Apparently, Squeaker broke up with this woman, killed her, the children and then shot himself. Tragic domestic incident. According to the grapevine, Squeaker never knew this woman."

Guillaume said, "Policemen are as easily tempted as anyone else."

Daniel said, "Guillaume has come to offer our scholarship scheme to the Gallin schools."

"The Bright Star Scholarships. The richest people in the country have donated millions to enable the brightest children from the poorest backgrounds to have access to Universities."

Daniel offered, "People of means can help their own children. Bright Star is looking for the very brightest among the most disadvantaged."

"If the Head Teachers will help us identify them, we can track their progress and hopefully protect them. The primary condition is that no one is to know of the scholarship until entry to University."

"Is this on the level?"

Guillaume asserted, "Most certainly. It has the blessing of the Department of Education. We've already approved one hundred and ninety-seven scholarships and the schools have agreed on the need for discretion."

"That surprises me."

"They understand if the children are told they are special there will be problems."

They fell silent at voices on the landing.

"My mother and friends going out to act irresponsibly. They think they're fifteen. Tomorrow they'll feel like ninety. I'll have to be moving. I'm working the Steamer tonight."

Guillaume looked puzzled.

Daniel explained, "Paddle Steamer. It's a pub. Sheena works as a barmaid."

"I'd like to see this Paddle Steamer," suggested Guillaume.

* * * *

In the car, Sheena asked, "We know this demon is here. Hunting a particular child. How do we deal with demons?"

In the darkness Guillaume smiled.

"The first problem is that the human race has given up believing in demons. Which is a cause of celebration among demons. They have also given up believing in God's Grace so difficult to perceive through the fog of material possessions."

He paused to see if Sheena was listening. In her head she declared, *I'm listening* and the black man nodded.

"Demons use noise and display to intimidate, but their greatest asset is their ability to manipulate human emotions. We see this demonstrated daily in road rage. Where some incident so trivial provokes homicidal behaviour. However, demons are temporally vulnerable. They are not all-powerful. If they were, the war would've been lost centuries ago."

The car stopped for the traffic lights.

"Within our timeframe, they slowly weaken. As we would, living in a heavier gravity. Then comes the moment when they must leave to recuperate. It takes a deal of temporal power, for instance, for a demon to walk through a wall. One way to kill a demon is to physically restrain it until that point of return is lost. The demon will then die. This is very difficult to do and on occasions the interceptor will also die."

Sheena said, "I think I know what you mean about the fog of material possessions. Today I had a few words with a sparrow."

Daniel laughed without mockery and Guillaume said, "The greatest source of happiness is the natural world. To see the wonder of a leaf, to marvel at the flight of a bird, to stand in the rain and feel the water on your head, face, hands, to love and be loved."

Daniel said, "Let us out here. Don't want to arrive at the Steamer together."

Sheena stopped the car and the two men alighted. Sheena drove on to the public house.

She was piqued as the two men ignored her during the evening. Billy, recognising fresh faces, served them and chatted briefly. They melted into the clientele among men of their own age. When Sheena emerged from the pub into the quiet street, freshened by rain, she was disappointed they were not outside, waiting for a lift.

CHAPTER ELEVEN

"Kick him up the arse
and see if he has an answer. "

Lorraine found two tee shirts she liked and Morris discovered a coloured pencil set with only two pencils missing. Sheena was wary of buying anything for Marianne, but Our Lady's charity shop was a favourite destination on a Saturday afternoon.

"Where does all this come from?" Lorraine asked, regarding the Aladdin's cave of treasures in which they stood.

"People give things."

"But these shirts are next to new. Mebbes new."

"People buy them. They change their minds. Then we buy them and people not so lucky as us get to eat a hot meal at the church."

"I like that."

She pushed the tee shirts into Sheena's wire basket.

"I'm going to buy an old lady rhubarb and custard."

When Sheena protested, she called, "Only a book."

At the counter, Margaret Robson asked, "You in a hurry, Sheena?"

Beside her a teenage girl snipped labels and folded garments. Sheena looked around to note both Morris and Lorraine deep in the jungle of the discarded.

"Don't think so."

"Give me a minute when I'm free?"

Sheena, intrigued, agreed.

Sheena looked up from editing Morris's choice of films when Margaret called her name. Sandra was at the till. Margaret stood in the doorway of the back room.

"Unless it says PG or twelve don't bother," Sheena counselled Morris, "You won't be seeing it."

In the back room, she sat down with Margaret at the sorting table.

91

Margaret said, "I don't know who else to speak to."

She believes because I live in a tower block, I'm elbow to elbow with knock-off merchants.

"I'm listening."

The charity shop manager recounted the story of her frightening customer. As she finished, Margaret emptied the black sack on the table. Sheena fingered the ginger wig.

"I'm telling you the truth. He was absolutely terrifying. But I wouldn't be surprised if you didn't believe me."

Sheena looked into Margaret's anxious eyes.

"I believe you."

Margaret burst into tears. Sheena came around the table to comfort her. The woman was trembling.

"I've seen this man. He's dangerous, but I know the very men to handle him."

Sheena opened the box from her carrier bag and offered Margaret a large white handkerchief with a capital S at every corner. The charity shop manager dried her eyes.

Sheena spouted, "I can recommend that hankie. Top quality Belfast linen. An initial of your choice at every corner. Ideal for tears or snot. A splendid gift for Birthday or Yuletide. Or being frightened to death."

Margaret laughed and cried again.

"It's just the relief of knowing someone believes me."

Soberly, Sheena warned her, "If he should return for fresh clothes, don't ring the police. Do exactly what he tells you. Act just as you have done. He won't harm you long as you're useful to him. Welcome him. Give him what he wants. Just play along. Okay?"

Margaret Robson nodded, clutching her new handkerchief, a fine example of Belfast linen. Sheena looked about for a piece of paper and wrote down her mobile number.

"When he's gone, ring me. Promise?"

Margaret nodded, reading the number.

"I'm going to take his clothes. Okay?"

* * * *

Sheena bundled the clothes back into the sack. Daniel sat considering the ginger wig.

Guillaume said, "We know he's here and we know why. We know how he's dressed. Now we must find his den."

Sheena asked, "Is that important?"

"The easiest way to kill a demon is with fire. If we can locate his den, we can incinerate the creature."

"What about anyone else in the building?"

Daniel interrupted, saying, "I've met this creature twice. He was on the quay when Eric died. The other day he was in a car on the quay. He looked at me longer than one might expect. Did he know me?"

"He was at the Spelling Bee. I saw him talking to Kimberley. She was the winner. She comes into the shop where I work three afternoons. Very bright kid. I only have to mention something and Kimberley's on to it."

Sheena said, "Kimberley's in danger."

"Tell me more."

"Dysfunctional home. Father boozer. Think the mother's given up. Neither appeared at the biggest event in their daughter's life. Teams all turned out in new school uniforms. The star of the evening wore a second-hand blazer. The child is very vulnerable. A kind word might be enough to tip the balance."

"I'll ask Klara to assess the situation."

Sheena wrote down Kimberley's details on the paper Guillaume offered.

Daniel suggested, "I could spend time in the charity shop. Our friend may wish to spruce up his appearance."

"I have another task for you. If you agree. There was the death of a quartet from a Gallin school that didn't survive the ride home on the motorway from a Festival in Manchester. A tragic accident. But five people began their last journey in that minibus. Only four cremated corpses were recovered. The music tutor is missing."

"Intriguing," Daniel mused.

"Interested?"

"Very."

"Would the lady in the charity shop object if a male volunteer joined her?"

"Don't think so."

"Then you can introduce Branco."

"What do I do?"

"You go on being Sheena, the girl across the landing. Eyes and ears wide open."

Guillaume recognised Sheena's disappointment.

"Leave the rough stuff to others. You're a valuable asset. You smell evil. Eyes, ears and nose wide open. Okay?"

Sheena nodded.

* * * *

Peter Kaplan was not a stupid man. When his wife proposed that Ellie Martin and baby Sean Ellis should continue to live with them, sleeping in the spare bedroom, he didn't protest. Janet explained Ellie was afraid to return to the house across the road, was safer here and needed support. Ellie's parents had never liked Sean. Peter Kaplan nodded agreement. That Sean's mother was widowed and living with his elder brother in Australia, he accepted. The house across the road was for sale. Peter Kaplan knew his childless wife was living the Grandmother dream. It was almost real. Janet was the comforting presence at the birth of Sean Ellis Martin.

* * * *

Saturday was the ideal opportunity. Peter Kaplan had departed on a golf weekend. Ellie was upstairs with the baby. Janet Kaplan was washing cutlery at the kitchen sink. The doorbell rang. Nurses were visiting regularly. Janet went to answer the door still clutching cutlery in a tea towel. She turned away as she opened the door, but it was not a nurse who stepped into the hallway.

The fat man asked, "Have you seen my lady's muff, miss?"

Janet was totally surprised. The intruder punched her in the face and she staggered back. Blood began to flow.

He raised his fist and demanded, "Where's the baby?"

Janet's eyes betrayed her and he ran upstairs. Blood flooded her face and blouse.

The fat man came thundering down the stairs with the baby. Ellie was screaming. The baby was crying. The man reached for the door handle. Janet realised she was holding the carving knife. She plunged the big knife deep into the intruder's back, driving it home with both hands. Her victim screamed and fell backwards on to the blade. As he fell, Janet snatched the baby from his flailing arms. She watched him die on her hall floor. When an hysterical Ellie floundered down the stairs, she cried, "It's alright, Ellie! I have the baby!"

She surrendered Sean Ellis to his mother and flopped onto the hall chair. She could not control her trembling. Mother and baby subsided into silence on the stairs.

In a moment of irrational triumph, Janet Kaplan cried, "He didn't get the baby!"

Her voice sounded bubbly as her nose was still bleeding.

Ellie asked, "What do we do now?"

Janet was watching the snakes of blood sliding out from under the dead man. The baby was feeding gratefully from his mother.

Ellie said, "D'y'know Tony Buckle?"

Janet shook her head.

"Tony runs North Gallin."

Janet dimly remembered the name. She was fascinated by the blood snakes.

"Does he punch women and steal babies?"

"Never! He sorts things out for people. They go to him when they're in trouble. Sean must've upset somebody really big. Tony would sort it out. The police are useless."

The blood snake had almost reached Janet's foot.

"So?"

"I know the girl who lives next door to him. He brought her to school every morning in his Rolls. We thought she was his daughter. But nobody dared ask."

"What's her name?"

"Sheena Galloway."

Janet returned to reality.

"I know Sheena."

"We tell her. She'll tell Tony."

Janet mused, "Such a straightforward girl. You'd never guess."

"You're a teacher. You don't live in the real world."

"True," the teacher agreed, "I don't live in the real world. I have Sheena's phone number. I have her school records, but apparently, not the truth."

* * * *

Daniel Fallon identified the corpse.

"It's the man from the ice cream van."

"You know him?" asked Janet Kaplan.

"He sold me an ice cream cornet."

Ellie Martin appeared from the kitchen with a steaming bucket and mop. She mopped tentatively at the drying blood.

Janet Kaplan asked, "Why have you stopped me ringing the police?"

"The police will arrest you and Ellie. The baby will be taken into Care. A lengthy process will begin at the end of which the police will refuse to believe the truth. And you will be imprisoned for manslaughter. You must trust us. When this matter is resolved we will explain everything and you will not believe us. But it will be the truth."

Guillaume added, "If that's what you want, Missis Kaplan, we will withdraw and you may ring the police."

Ellie wanted to protest, but Daniel raised a hand to silence her.

Janet Kaplan appeared deep in thought and then said, "Very well! But I'm amazed we're treating this death in such a matter of fact fashion."

Her query was directed to Guillaume.

"You think we should weep for this man? The brute came to steal the baby. The monster that sent him would've killed the child. He has killed other children."

Ellie exclaimed, "Then how haven't you caught him?"

"Believe me, we're trying. And we will catch him, I promise."

Janet Kaplan persisted, saying, "But why Ellie's baby?"

"If necessary he will kill every baby in Gallin."

"But that's monstrous!"

"The very word. A monster. I assume you've heard of Herod?"

"Of course."

Janet Kaplan shook her head.

"I can't believe that."

"Do you have an affection for this child?"

"Yes."

"Then guard him well."

Daniel said, "The ambulance is here."

The doorbell rang. Janet Kaplan opened the door cautiously to admit two men in white coats.

"Shall we withdraw to the sitting room?" Guillaume suggested.

They sat in a strained silence broken only by the contented noises of the baby, Sean Ellis, in his mother's arms. When the front door closed the tension relaxed. They heard the ambulance drive away and returned to the hallway.

Ellie said, "Thank you."

Janet Kaplan offered, "I murdered a man, but that's it, is it? Keep calm and carry on?"

Ellie cried, "You didn't murder anyone. You saved my baby from being murdered."

Guillaume suggested, "Need I say more?"

In the car, Daniel commented, "This Kaplan woman is quite a warrior. Maybe I should talk to her again?"

"I have to be in London tonight. I'll be back next week. We'll talk to her together."

* * * *

Klara Schuster tapped politely on the door of 17, Clement Attlee House. No one answered the door. Klara rapped firmly on the door. There was movement within.

"Please open the door."

A child's voice asked, "Who are you?"

"Miss Schuster. Welfare. Please open the door."

The door opened on a chain. A child's face appeared to scrutinise the caller.

"If you're Welfare, I want to see your card."

Klara Schuster produced a wallet and flipped it open.

"I want to read it."

The child examined the card carefully.

"It's not a good likeness," Miss Schuster apologised.

The card was returned.

"Wha'd'y'want?"

"To talk to your Mum. Your father, if he's home. And you too, Kimberley."

The child removed the chain and opened the door.

The girl, Klara Schuster registered, was tall for eleven, pretty, bright eyed, clad in clean tee shirt and jeans.

Kimberley said, "You can sit down."

"Thank you."

Kimberley did not sit down.

The visitor noted the child was defensive and wary in her movements. On the timeworn sideboard, in pride of place, was a silver cup. There was a large silver frame with a photograph of Kimberley and the Mayor of North Gallin. There was also a similar frame bearing her award.

"Is that you winning the Spelling Bee?"

"Yes."

"You must be very proud."

Kimberley did not respond. The child was not easily flattered.

"Is your mother home?"

"Mam's in bed. She's not well."

"I'm sorry to hear that. Has she seen a doctor?"

"Yes. She has M.E."

"I don't understand what that is?"

Kimberley recited, "She's always in pain and always very tired. She's become very clumsy. She forgets things. Sometimes what she's saying. Moods up and down. You don't know how she'll be next. And she wakes us up at night. She's always got a headache."

Klara Schuster realised she was dealing with a clever child who had memorised material from the Internet.

"I'm sorry to hear that. It must make life difficult for you."

"She's me Mam."

"And you help her, best you can to keep the house tidy?"

Kimberley nodded.

"But you must let me see your mother. If only for a moment."

Klara Schuster was surprised when Kimberley didn't protest, but replied, "I'll see what she's like."

Kimberley vanished and Klara Schuster sat listening to the flat. As if it were hiding under the cushions of the shabby couch or leaking from the drawers of the sideboard, she became aware a shadow of utmost evil pervaded the room; as carbon monoxide might leak from a damaged heating boiler. Its presence was slight but unmistakable to someone as experienced as Klara Schuster. Something terrible was waiting to happen here.

Kimberley returned and the visitor rose.

"I'm sorry, but Mam's asleep. She didn't sleep last night, so, please, please, don't disturb her. I don't know how she'd behave if you did."

Klara Schuster knew she'd been outwitted by a very clever girl.

"Then I shan't disturb her. Your father? Where can I catch him?"

"He's a lorry driver. He has to work."

The visitor gestured at the book on the couch.

"Yours?"

Kimberley brightened.

"Yes. Anne Frank's Diary. I don't want to read it, but I must."

"I understand."

"I love reading best of all. More than anything."

"A man called John Bunyan wrote a wonderful book called Pilgrim's Progress in Bedford Gaol."

"I've heard of him."

"On occasions when he finished writing as the light died, he was surprised to find himself in gaol. Is it like that for you, Kimberley?"

Kimberley laughed.

"Yes! Just like that. I'm so deep in the book."

"John Bunyan wasn't really locked up, was he?"

Kimberley smiled.

"No."

"And they'll never imprison you either."

* * * *

Out on the scrub grass where children played in a world of their own making, Klara phoned Daniel Fallon.

"A very clever girl. If I hadn't been briefed, I might've believed her. Mother has ME. Father a lorry driver. She lies because despite everything they do, Kimberley loves them. I think he's been here. There are two expensive photograph frames. The Spelling Bee."

She stopped to listen to Daniel.

"No. The Gazette might've given the photograph, but not the silver frames. Soon someone's going to die in that flat. The place is poisoned. Evil awaits the moment to whisper into the right ear."

* * * *

On a sunny afternoon the boys crouched together behind the baulk on the quay. They were fishing for coalfish using hand lines as they had done so often before. A man stopped to ask the usual question.

"Caught anything?"

Daniel indicated the fish lying on the haversack.

"Do you eat them?"

"The cat does."

"I would've thought fishing so close to the trawlers?"

Eric answered politely.

"Not a lot of waste goes into the river. It goes to the fish meal factory. But there's enough to bring fish in."

The man said to Daniel, "Smartarse isn't he? Always has an answer. You're just his stooge. I bet he even tells you when to shit. But you hate him really, don't you?"

Daniel felt the rage within him explode.

"Kick him up the arse and see if he has an answer."

Daniel stood up and kicked his best friend. He saw the look of astonishment on Eric's face as he fell from the quay, head over heels and vanished into the entangled darkness below the quay. There was not a sound, barely a splash and Eric, clutching his fishing line, was gone, never to be seen again.

Daniel awoke screaming. He flung off the duvet and sat on the bed edge, trembling. His own words echoed in his head. I've met this creature twice. He was on the quay when Eric died. The other day he was in a car on the quay. He looked at me longer than one might expect. Does he know me?

"He knew me. The detective was right. I killed Eric. That creature wiped the memory. Why? I might be useful another day? So, I survived unlike so many poor bastards."

Daniel quit his bedroom and poured himself a whisky without water. He drank it and poured another. On the balcony, looking out over Gallin and the dark river, he found some sense of calm.

"I promise you, Eric, I will find and I will kill our monster. On my soul, I swear."

CHAPTER TWELVE

*"Yi cannot turn down someat
that's offered yi fa nothin'."*

Daniel Fallon stepped out of the lift as Sheena arrived on the landing.
They smiled at one another.
"I'll get you a Zimmer frame for Christmas."
"I'm merely conserving my energy."
"You're an old man who has to use the lift."
Sheena opened the Galloways' door and heard female laughter.
Daniel turned to his own flat.
"Daniel!"
"Yes?"
"Can I hide with you?"
A puzzled Daniel said, "Of course," and looked for an
explanation.
"That hideous bellow is my Mam's big mate, Hilda Stobart."
Spot on cue, Hilda laughed again and Sheena closed the door. She
shuddered theatrically.
Seated on the couch, with the lager can in her hand, Sheena
explained.
"Hilda's always in our place. Morning, noon and night. They're
riveted at the hip these days. Wasn't always like that."
Daniel asked, "I presume she has a flat of her own?"
"Fourth floor. Her husband, Ron, died on my birthday. I was
fourteen."
"And Hilda found a friend in your mother?"
"I suppose so."
Daniel said, "I've been to the Memorial Service at Saint Paul's
for the girls who died on the motorway. Kathleen O'Rourke was a
Gallin girl. From what was said, she was an outstanding violinist."
"Not every child who dies in an accident is deliberately killed."

"A man was removed from the service for shouting. I followed him home to talk. Mister Donovan is sane enough. His niece died in the minibus. He wanted a question answered and no one would listen to him."

"What question?"

"What happened to the tutor, Eileen Galbraith? There were four girls and their tutor in the minibus. Four incinerated corpses. No sign of the tutor."

"Maybe she escaped from the minibus and died on the motorway?"

"There were many casualties in the pile up, but no Eileen Galbraith."

Daniel crushed his can and dropped it into the wastebasket.

"The innocent person who has been manipulated to kill is overcome with horror when they realise what they've done. Almost all commit suicide before we can reach them."

The image of Squeaker putting the pistol to his head arose in Sheena's mind.

"Mister Donovan told me he had an anonymous phone call from a man who saw from the bridge, a woman walk away from the minibus. Crossing the motorway. He said that's what caused the pile up. What happened to her he didn't know. I believe that was Eileen Galbraith."

"And if she's still alive?"

"I need to find her."

"She could be anywhere."

"She must be somewhere she knows and is comfortable with."

* * * *

Chief Superintendent Gerald Taylor was the public face of the police in North and South Gallin. His friendly face was reassuring and when he emerged from a funeral service, his clear message of condemnation was almost as good as actually arresting and convicting the villains. He always had time for members of the public and pretended goodwill to journalists.

To Tom Moore, he said, "I've only agreed to talk to you so I can get the message over to you. I don't like you and if you get in the way, I'll walk over you."

"Are you threatening me, Superintendent?"

The setting was not Taylor's opulent office with comfortable chairs and hospitality cabinet. There were no photographs of a dashing, younger police officer. No portrait of Her Majesty behind an expensive chair. They were seated on plain chairs across a table bolted to the floor in Interview Room Three. The room had discreet cameras and microphones. Tom Moore took from his shoulder bag his notebook and biro.

"Please understand, if you waste police time you will be prosecuted. If you obstruct police officers in the course of their duty, you will be arrested and charged. Do I make myself clear?"

The journalist made a note while the policeman waited for an answer.

"The man known as Squeaker, Maggie Doughty and her two children died in suspicious circumstances. The investigation into their deaths has been closed. Four Gallin girls died on the motorway. No sign of their tutor, Eileen Galbraith. No investigation. An attempt was made to abduct my friend, Sean Martin's pregnant wife. Later, Sean apparently committed suicide."

A telephone on the desk rang. The Superintendent listened to a tinny voice and growled at intervals. Tom Moore waited for an answer. Finally, Gerald Taylor said, "That's confirmed. But Bradshaw mustn't touch it. Is that understood?"

The policeman counted them off on beefy fingers.

"One. Domestic tragedy. Drugs involved. Two. Motorway pileup. Tragedy. Three. Removal of psychotic patient from wrong address. Apologies. Your friend's suicide? Suicide."

The familiar friendly face smiled upon the reporter. Tom Moore wrote at some length in his notebook. He could read the irritation in the policeman's face.

"You're wrong," Tom Moore declared, "I know there's a connection between these events."

"You don't know. You invent. You want a story. Don't think we haven't noticed you like to target the police."

"Didn't you want to know about two drunken constables, one a sergeant forcing himself on a terrified rape victim, sexual harassment of women constables?"

The policeman said nothing.

"There is something very wrong happening in Gallin. Can't you smell it, Superintendent? All three incidents involve children. A baby, a toddler, four schoolgirls, an unborn baby."

"Do you remember some years ago the Satanic rituals scandal that turned out to be nothing at all?"

"But at least, they did investigate thoroughly! When the next child dies in Gallin, I'll be watching to see what you actually do. If you do nothing, I will make sure our readers know."

The journalist began to write in his notebook. A frustrated Superintendent attempted to snatch the journalist's notebook from across the table, but Moore was quicker.

He responded, reciting, "The Superintendent has attempted to snatch my notebook, but didn't succeed."

To Gerald Taylor, he continued, "I trust you have this interview recorded because I have."

"This interview is ended."

The Superintendent stormed from the Interview Room. Tom Moore took his time packing notebook and biro. When he went to the door he found it locked. He knocked and the face of a constable appeared in the glass. He unlocked the door.

"Thought you'd gone, sir. Lucky, I was here,"

"Thank you. Unfortunately, your Superintendent lost his temper."

A poor jibe, but I'm short of one-liners.

As he progressed through the building, he met not a friendly face. The young female constable in Reception ripped his visitor's tag away as she brought it over his head.

Caught off-guard, he cried, "Ow!"

"Sorry, sir. Just the usual police brutality."

* * * *

Margaret Robson loved having Branco Liefcutter working in the charity shop. He was strong and good-natured. He would undertake any job without protest and was a success with the customers. He would fold and pack anything. Margaret noted lady customers turned to Branco for advice as well as the men.

Most importantly, he overhauled the security system. He installed new cameras and an alarm system that silently phoned Sheena, Daniel and Branco.

"Who is the best fish and chip shop, boss?"

Margaret loved the way he called her boss. It seemed to come from him most naturally.

"Kristian's without a doubt. But that's on the quay."

"I have the motorbike. Used to ride in the Manx TT. I will lock the back door after me. I have the key."

Branco departed via the back door into the yard. Margaret heard the roar of the engine as she locked the front door and reversed the card. CLOSED FOR LUNCH. Margaret turned to find her nightmare re-enacted. The tall, thin, bald man in a suit and tieless shirt stood at the counter, smiling at her. Margaret fought not to soil herself. Sheena's words ran in her head.

If he should return for fresh clothes, don't ring the police. Do exactly what he tells you. Act just as you have done. He won't harm you, long as you're useful to him. Welcome him. Give him what he wants. Just play along. Okay?

The man was not alone. A smaller woman stood at his side, face pale and without makeup. She lacked expression and displayed no interest in her surroundings. She wore a dress she wouldn't have chosen for herself. Her hair was dirty and screwed back in a ponytail. Margaret was surprised to see the man was breathless and trembling.

The customer removed his Panama politely to say, "You may remember me from a previous visit?"

"Indeed, I do, sir! Your suit fits you very well. Are the brogues comfortable?"

Inside Margaret's head a terrified little girl was huddled in a corner, weeping.

"Ah, you remember! Splendid! I have you to thank for my good appearance."

He glanced at himself in the mirror. Margaret wondered how she could get to the counter and Branco's alarm.

"How can I help you?"

She moved as if to return to the counter, but he did not give way.

"My niece, Ursula. She has an important interview to attend. Perhaps you can find her suitable attire?"

"I'll do my best."

Margaret smiled at the woman who did not respond.

"An interview? A job in an office?"

"Yes," the tall man agreed, "A job in an office."

"Then you need a business suit. I think we may be able to help."

She went to the rack of new incomings that took her farther from the counter.

"A young woman has just become a mother. For the foreseeable future, she has no use for a business suit."

Margaret smiled at the woman.

"I'm a poet, but don't know it. No use for a business suit."

Neither of her customers smiled. She offered the suit to the woman who stared blankly at her.

The tall man put an arm about the woman and led her to the changing cubicle. He took the coat hanger from Margaret.

"Try on this suit. I suspect you'll look very smart."

He closed the curtain and turned to the charity shop manager.

"She is very shy. But one tries to do one's best for family."

Margaret knew today he was going to kill her.

Margaret moved to return to the counter, but he forestalled her.

"Tell me, please, how long should one wear a pair of socks?"

"A week? Or less. Unfortunately, men tend to wear socks until they rot on their feet."

"I think I need new socks."

"And a clean shirt," Margaret advised.

They moved to the sock tub that stood beside the counter.

"Socks are free," Margaret offered, "Please choose what you need."

"And hats? How long should I wear this hat?"

Margaret Robson was suddenly inspired.

"You don't want to wear it until it rots on your head, do you?"

The tall man looked alarmed and removed the Panama for inspection.

"I have just the hat for you," enthused Margaret, offering a bright yellow beret, "Brand new. The wrong size for the gentleman, unfortunately."

He stood admiring his new headgear in the long mirror. His head blazed like a beacon.

"I have been very fortunate to meet you, dear lady."

Margaret's blood ran cold.

As her customer rifled through the socks, Margaret heard the rear door lock turn. In desperation, she picked up an old Walkman from the counter and turned it on. It blasted forth some forgotten pop song. The man took it from her and turned it off.

"Not your taste?"

In the back room, she could see Branco moving silently towards the shop.

"I'll take two pairs if I may?"

"Be my guest. Would you like to look at the shirts?"

They turned together and were distracted by the woman, Ursula, emerging from the cubicle. She was completely transformed by the business suit. She showed no interest in their compliments.

"Her hair is dirty," said the tall man, "What is the best hair shop in Gallin?"

Margaret answered, "Cinderella. On the Parade."

Cinderella had gone out of business a year since. Perhaps Prince Charming had turned up?

She knew the demon would kill her today. She had served his purpose.

Margaret became aware Branco was standing in the doorway of the back room. She was anxious to keep talking while moving to stand by Ursula, admiring the suit.

"Will it be cash, sir? Or as last time, on your account. I can do the business suit for fifteen pounds. A bargain. Quality tailoring. The lady needs two white shirts and at least one tie. Navy blue perhaps? Your socks are free. But I would recommend you buy two shirts. I don't think twenty-five pounds is too much to ask. We are a charity but the charity exists to serve the old, sick and deprived of our community."

Margaret simply ran out of anything more to say. The tall man heard a floorboard creak behind him as Branco stepped into the shop. He half-turned to spit at Margaret when Branco fired the pistol. The demon's left eye vanished. For the first time in a lifetime, Margaret Robson screamed. The demon in the yellow beret rocked on his feet.

Her ears deafened, Margaret did not hear Branco fire again. The bullet struck the creature in the mouth. He spat splinters of teeth and blood. He fell to his knees, raising a hand as if to accuse the gunman. Then the demon and the woman in the business suit vanished. One moment they were there and then they weren't. A bundle of socks, blood and tooth fragments lay on the floor of the charity shop. Branco and Margaret were alone.

Margaret fell into Branco's arms as if she would never let him go.

"You were very brave, boss," Branco assured her, "And a very good salesperson. You sold it all to me."

Margaret laughed. A great burden lifted from her soul.

"Have you somewhere safe you can go until this game is played out?"

"I have a sister in Hawick."

"Hawick is very pleasant this time of year."

"Have you ever been there?"

"Shall we have lunch, boss?"

* * * *

Sheena and Marianne had spent a happy afternoon in the sunshine on the old tartan rug spread out on the grass. She was amazed at how Marianne was beginning to build sentences.

"Yes, sweetheart, boy on bike. Marianne say. Whoops! Boy not on bike. Boy lands on head. Plop!"

Sheena laughed and Marianne joined in. Sheena rolled her over and teased her.

"Marianne not on bike. Marianne on tatty old rug."

Sheena marvelled at how simple happiness was.

"Drink, Shee!"

"Please?"

The child made a fair attempt at please.

Sheena produced the bottle and what was left of the Digestive biscuit packet. A bird flew overhead. Sheena broke up a little of her biscuit and cast it onto the grass. As if it had been waiting for the biscuit, a sparrow alighted and started on the crumbs.

"Bird," cried Marianne who started to crawl towards the busy sparrow. Sheena grabbed her and held her back.

"The bird'll fly away if you bother him."

Marianne sat by her sister watching the sparrow. A second bird came to join the first. Marianne threw a piece of her biscuit that bounced off the rug, but didn't seem to worry the sparrows.

"It's got to be small pieces. See? Otherwise it'll be like getting hit with a brick."

Sheena watched her little sister's chubby fingers breaking up the biscuit.

"Not all of it!"

The protest was too late. The fragments fell on the rug. Sheena gave Marianne half a biscuit.

"To eat! You'll get the spuggies too fat to fly."

The sparrows advanced to the rug. Their benefactrix chuckled.

Then to Sheena's amazement, the first sparrow fluttered to alight on Marianne's shoe.

"Don't move!" Sheena whispered. The sparrow sat on the shoe toe and inspected the child. Marianne inspected the sparrow. Sheena was further surprised when the second sparrow came to perch on the other shoe. Marianne chuckled, but no one was disturbed.

"Well, I've never seen that before!"

A shadow fell over the biscuit eaters. The sparrows flew away. Mrs. Galloway and Hilda Stobart blocked the sunshine. They were both carrying double carrier bags in each hand. Marianne tried to explain about the sparrows but gave up when her mother ignored her.

"Yi should see what we've got!"

"Yi cannot go short of owt," Hilda asserted.

"Yi could've give iss a hand!"

"To rob the Food Bank? Have neither of you got any conscience? I suppose if you had, yi'd be straight to old John on the ground floor. His missis could do with it."

"Yi cannot turn down someat that's offered yi fa free."

"Mam, if they offered to cut off ya leg for free, yi'd grab the chance, would yi? I suppose yi would. Yi've already had your conscience amputated."

"Yi see what I has to put up with, Hilda? Miss High and Mighty!"

"Mam, I'm working! You should be working. We're managing well enough. And Hilda? Well, Ron's pension from the foundry isn't a poke in the eye."

"Where's Lorrie and Morrie then?"

"Lorraine and Morris are at Miss Kaplan's drama club. I'll collect them at half four, don't you worry."

"Are yi gona give iss a hand upstairs with the bags then?"

"Sorry, Mam. I'm not touching stolen goods."

As her mother gathered a blast of vitriol, Hilda said, "You two shouldn't be lying out in the sun anyways."

"Ignoring vitamin D. Why not?"

"D'yi really want to go black?"

"What!"

"Ya halfway there already, Sheena. Milk chocolate now, fair enough. But black chocolate tomorra? D'y'want a black bairn, Ginny? Cos that's what yi'll get if Marianne stays out here."

Sheena was startled at the surge of anger that swept her being. She was on her feet faster than she could think. Only by extreme will power did she hold back from attacking Hilda who flinched away, but clung to her carrier bags.

Sheena snatched the carrier bags from Hilda's hands and scattered the contents on the grass. Her mother cried out, but Sheena kicked wildly at tins and boxes. Children came whooping to snatch up the goodies. Christmas had come early. Sheena picked up a tin of beans and for one mad moment was about to break Hilda's face with it. She checked herself in time, throwing the tin to a boy. She could read the confusion and alarm in her mother's eyes.

It was only later she realised she would have seriously injured the woman, if she didn't kill her. She stood trembling with anger. In all the confusion she could hear Marianne laughing and clapping her hands. Sheena said calmly, "Mam, walk away now."

She watched their lumpen progress towards the tower block. Marianne said, "Hilda not good."

Sheena sat down beside her sister.

"Bad Hilda," Sheena responded.

"Shee good," Marianne agreed and chuckled.

111

CHAPTER THIRTEEN

"If I told you we were hunting a demon,
would yi believe me?"

Hilda wasn't at the flat when Sheena and Marianne came up in the lift. Her mother was watching television. Sheena went to settle the baby for a nap. Filling the mop bucket with hot water, adding disinfectant, she made as much noise as possible.

Sheena began to mop out the lift. As she worked she began to feel better: the exercise and the antiseptic aroma calming her anger. Scrubbing at the walls, she took the bucket into the lift and the doors closed. As the lift descended, she continued to clean the walls.

When the lift arrived in the lobby, the doors opened and Daniel Fallon smiled at her.

"Am I allowed in?"

"At least, you'll be able to breathe."

Sheena gave the walls an extra mopping. She was surprised how pleasant the lift had become.

"I'm guessing you're very angry and you're cleaning the lift rather than hurt somebody."

"No. I thought, why does Marianne have to travel in a stinking bog?"

"You've done a good job."

As they parted on the landing, Daniel said, "If you want to talk about anything, the doctor is in."

* * * *

Sheena checked Marianne was sleeping before she came back to the living room and switched off the television.

Sheena's mother declared, "Before yi say owt, you know Hilda adores Marianne. She cannot do enough forra. You know that."

"Why did yi just stand there?"

"She were only getting back at yi. You was rude enough. Yi made iss out to be robbers."

"Are you ashamed of us, Mam?"

"I don't know what yi mean."

"Marianne and me."

"Ya talking daft."

"You stood there while Hilda abused your daughters in the vilest way. Are you ashamed of us?"

"When did I say I were shamed of yi?"

"You want somebody to be ashamed of? Try our Dad. He was a boozer and a bully. And that's nowt to do with the colour of his skin. A boozer and a bully. He terrified and abused us. He beat you up. But still you let him back in the house."

Her mother said nothing. Sheena dropped the remote into her lap.

"I feel sorry for yi, Mam, I really do."

* * * *

Sheena parked the Seat clear of the school. Lorraine and Morris were fidgeting on the pavement. As she approached, she saw the man who had been standing at the school railing walk away. She had assumed he was another late parent.

Sheena apologised, "Sorry, I'm late."

Lorraine asked, "Have you heard about the race between the lettuce and the tomato, Sheena?"

"Don't think I have. Tell me."

Morris said, "The lettuce was a head"

"But the tomato was trying to ketchup."

Sheena laughed, "Very clever."

"Miss Kaplan wants us to do a comedy act at Christmas."

"You'll have them rolling in the aisles."

As they walked to the car, Sheena asked, "The man that was standing at the railings. Did he speak to you?"

"He asked about some girl we don't know."

Sheena considered the answer.

113

"Now on, stay in the yard until you see Mam or me. Okay? Fast traffic on this road. And you're dodging about on the pavement."

* * * *

There were two cans of lager on the little table. Sheena took one and settled into the chair she was beginning to think of as her own. Daniel wasn't surprised when he came from the bathroom.

"Feeling better?"

Sheena nodded and pulled the tag from her can.

"The creature paid another visit to the charity shop."

"Thank God, Branco was there!"

"He'd gone for fish and chips."

Sheena had nothing to say.

"He had a woman with him wanting clothes. The manager. What's her name?"

"Margaret Robson. She alright?"

"She's fine. A remarkable woman. Very brave. If we meet him again, he's wearing a bright yellow beret."

"That's Margaret! She'd sell boots to a ballerina."

"Branco returned. Margaret Robson distracted the creature. Branco drove them both back to Hell. The fish was delicious, but the chips were claggy from standing."

Sheena laughed.

"This creature enjoys walking through walls. Drains a great deal of energy. He was weakened and if Branco had been able to hold him he would be dead."

"And Branco with him?"

"Perhaps."

"I don't want you to die.""I've died, nearly died before. You don't understand. All of our people have suffered terribly. From losing a loved one or from killing a stranger. If they can kill a demon."

He left the sentence unfinished. When Sheena didn't respond, he continued, "This is a battle that was old before Moses' mother left him in the bulrushes. Before Herod pursued the children of Israel to find the child Jesus. Both changed the world, Moses and Jesus."

Daniel decided, "Enough of the lecture," and swallowed his lager. "Guillaume has released almost everyone to cover Gallin. To watch and listen. We know where every pregnant woman, every newborn is in Gallin and we are watching the hospitals. We also have our best noses here on the streets."

"A man was watching Lorraine and Morris today."

"Did he smell bad?"

"Walked away as soon as I appeared. But I'll be there again tomorrow."

Sheena looked at her watch.

"The Steamer calls. Can't disappoint my fans."

As she rose, Daniel asked, "Does harelip mean anything to you?"

Sheena shook her head.

Daniel's mind played the image of the boy Harelip cutting off the baby rabbit's ear.

"Is it important?"

"No. Just a thought."

* * * *

Ellie Martin was feeding her baby and Janet Kaplan was filling the washing machine when the doorbell rang. Peter Kaplan went to answer. Tom Moore gestured at the FOR SALE board.

"Where're you going? Somewhere nice?"

"None of your business," and calling, "It's that reporter."

"Come in, Tom," Ellie called from the sitting room.

Peter Kaplan said, "I wouldn't let you in."

Tom Moore followed Peter Kaplan into the sitting room.

"Do we have to have him in the house?"

Ellie protested, "He was Sean's best friend. And he's my friend."

Peter surrendered. Janet joined them from the kitchen.

"Do I have to give him a drink?"

"Let's hear what he has to say."

"He wants something."

"I don't want anything," the reporter protested.

Peter Kaplan said, "I don't believe you."

Under protest he poured three glasses of sherry. Ellie refused.

"Have you had any more trouble?"

"What more trouble could we have than attempted abduction, a doubtful suicide and my wife killing a man?"

To Tom Moore he challenged, "D'you think we're sleeping easily? You'll only make it worse."

He ignored the young man's protest.

"The last thing we need is you."

The journalist asked Ellie, "How did you get in touch with the people who helped you?"

Janet Kaplan saw Ellie's mouth open, but was too late to stop her.

"Sheena Galloway. She knows people."

"Address?"

"Hugh Gaitskill House."

Tom Moore rose.

"Thanks for the sherry. Believe me, I'm not writing up a story for the Gazette. You have my word."

Peter escorted him to the front door.

"Don't come back."

In the sitting room, Janet Kaplan protested, "You shouldn't have told him, Ellie."

"He surprised me."

"He surprised us all."

"But you heard him. He promised it's not for the paper."

Peter attempted a sour laugh.

"You believe him?"

Ellie turned to Janet who said nothing.

Janet Kaplan awoke from her nightmare screaming. Peter put on the bedside light and held her close. Her body trembled. They listened together to the silent house.

"Same bad dream?"

"You were offering me the knife."

She shuddered and continued.

"He came down the stairs. When he turned his head, it was you. You gave me such an evil smile, I screamed."

"I heard you," said Peter and kissed his wife's nose.

She surprised him by asking, "Do you love me?"

116

Peter was silent.

"Well, do you?"

"Every year I love you a little more. I marvel at my good fortune. Not only are you the smartest cookie on the block, but also the bravest. When you saw he had the baby you didn't hesitate. So, in answer to your question, I can truly say, yes, Janet Kaplan, clever clogs and gladiator, I love you."

"A simple yes or no would've done."

"Ellie's not very bright."

Janet considered the statement.

"She's very young. She's sweet. She adores her son. But Ellie won't be joining Mensa."

"Her house hasn't sold. I suppose a suicide in a house is a bit off-putting."

"It won't sell for the price she's asking."

"If and when we sell this house, is she expecting to come with us?"

Janet was quiet so long, Peter thought she'd fallen asleep.

"Baby Sean needs."

Peter interrupted to say, "He's not our grandson."

"He doesn't seem to have any interested grandparents."

"You haven't answered my question. Does Ellie think she and the baby are coming with us when we move?"

* * * *

When Sheena walked into the flat, Daniel Fallon said, "Splendid! Just when I need you!"

To which, Sheena replied, "Do you realise that's the first time you've ever been nice to me?"

"Don't sit down. We're going on a trip."

"Why me?"

"I'm hoping to meet a woman."

"You surprise me."

"Eileen Galbraith."

"The missing music tutor? She could be anywhere. If she's still alive."

As they drove away from Hugh Gaitskill House, Daniel said, "Guillaume has discovered where she used to be, regular as clockwork."

"Which is where?"

"When she was a child, her parents hired a bungalow every Summer. South of Beadnel."

"That doesn't say she'll be there."

"It's the best lead we have."

"But why there?"

"She'll be somewhere she feels safe. The bungalow is her special place."

I have no special place. Nowhere I feel safe.

"It's raining."

"All the better. Drives people indoors."

"I'm working at the Steamer tonight."

"I'll make sure you're back in time."

* * * *

It rained steadily all the way and Daniel wasn't talkative. Sheena tried twice and gave up. She was relieved when she spotted the board at the lane end that said HOLIDAY BUNGALOWS AVAILABLE. At the first field gate in the hedge, Daniel said, "Park here."

"It's raining."

Daniel undid his seat belt. Sheena parked the car in the gateway.

"What next?"

Sheena watched as Daniel took a pistol from a shoulder holster and checked the slide.

"We don't know what we're walking into," Daniel explained.

"Rain. Lots of rain. And dreary cardboard shacks."

"Stay in the car."

"If you think I'm letting you out on your own, you're mistaken. I have my umbrella."

When they exited the car, Sheena saw Daniel carried his heavy stick.

"If need be, please, use your stick."

Sheena followed Daniel down the lane in the shadow of the thick, wet hedge. They came to a bend that opened to a parking area and a line of six small bungalows. Beyond was the roaring North Sea. The bungalows weren't dreary, Sheena admitted to herself. They were painted in primary colours and looked well maintained. There were three cars on the parking area. Daniel produced a pair of binoculars and studied the bungalows. There was no sign of life.

"Rain's an advantage," Daniel judged, "Holidaymakers are out for the day. Or playing Monopoly."

"P'rhaps we could join them. I always win at Monopoly."

"I'd like you to walk along the bungalows looking for your Aunt Edie. If the board's right, there are empty bungalows. Skip any that appear empty. But remember which. I'm going to work along the back."

With more confidence than she felt, Sheena set out to enquire for her Aunt Edie. Daniel followed the line of the hedge and darted across to walk behind the bungalows. Each had a small kitchen window and a half-glazed back door. Daniel watched for movement within the back doors. The first two bungalows yielded no clues. From the third he heard an echo of music. Four and five were silent. From number six he heard voices. He returned to the hedge to await Sheena.

The first thing Sheena noticed was that all the bungalows had been refitted with double-glazed picture windows. The curtains were drawn at number one. Sheena saw no sign of life. The curtains of number two were withdrawn, but when Sheena approached the bungalow, the sitting room within was empty. There were young men in number three who came to the door amid deafening music to invite her in. She ignored them. Number four bore a notice on the window. TO LET DATES AVAILABLE. At number five, she thought she saw movement within the sitting room. But when she approached, she found no one visible. In number six, a family of four were playing a board game. They didn't notice her passing.

Sheena reported to Daniel what she had seen.

"We can ignore three, four and six. You think you saw movement in number five?"

"I'm not sure. It was the merest flicker."

119

"One, two, four and five."

"If I said, we're getting wet for nothing, would you shoot me?"

"If you were a holiday tenant and someone passed the front window, would you hide? Or would you want to know who was out there?"

Sheena loaded her umbrella with sand and rolled it tightly.

"Ready?"

Sheena started the engine and the Seat obediently drove down onto the car park. As if to encourage them, the rain dwindled and stopped as they walked towards the bungalows.

"Be casual," Daniel advised, "Smile. We're going to be invited in to have tea with your Aunt Edie."

The young men in number three came to the door to offer an invitation. Sheena, smiling, refused.

They passed number four with its notice of letting and approached number five. Standing outside number five, hesitating to knock, Sheena suddenly knew they were wrong.

She crossed to number four. Daniel joined her.

"I just know."

Daniel knocked on the door loudly. There was movement within.

Sheena called, "Aunt Edie, it's Sheena! Surprise!"

The door opened slowly. A small thin woman said, "You must be mistaken."

Sheena said, "No, I'm not! You're Eileen Galbraith!"

The woman tried to close the door, but Daniel pushed it open and they entered.

"We're not here to harm you. We're here to help you."

Sheena saw razor scratches on the woman's arms.

"Nobody's judging you. You're a victim. Let us help you."

Neither Daniel nor Sheena were prepared for the appearance of the demon. He manifested himself with his arm about the woman's neck. Her face reflected absolute fear.

"Move and I will break her neck."

Sheena saw the damage Branco had done. Below the yellow beret the face was a horror. The left eye was missing. There was a hole right through the head. The mouth was more horrific with broken teeth and a split tongue.

With a salivating lisp, he announced, "Thank you for your concern for this dear lady. But fear not, she is in good hands."

He squeezed the wretched woman's neck. She whimpered and reached appealingly towards Daniel.

Daniel said, "Don't hurt her."

"Do what I say and she will come to no harm."

Sheena could not contain herself.

"Haven't you done enough harm to her already?"

"Kneel. Both of you."

As they reluctantly complied, the creature snatched away Daniel's stick with his free hand. Holding the stick in the air, he said, "A simple stick, young woman? Yes?"

Sheena said nothing. The creature in the yellow beret shook the blade from its hiding place. Sheena gasped. The blade glowed in the twilight of the bungalow and grew in length and breadth as an opening leaf.

"I surprise you?"

"Nothing you do surprises me," Sheena admitted.

She noticed he was cautious in his handling of the sword. He held the handle, but avoided touching the blade. The creature released Eileen Galbraith who fell to the floor, gasping for breath. He held the sword now in two hands. It seemed to gain weight.

"Here is what I propose. I will behead the woman or your friend. You will choose which."

Sheena felt Daniel stir beside her. She was shocked to the very core of her being.

"Don't look at him!"

"You can't mean to do this."

"I mean what I say. This man. I do not know his name. They change their names as often as some men change their hats. Or this woman. She is not important to me. I will find another to carry out her task. One or the other will die. Which shall it be? Your choice."

Sheena was silent and shocked.

"If you do not choose, I will kill them both."

Daniel said, "He's playing with you. He will kill us anyway."

"I will not kill your woman. I will leave her to suffer the agony of the human conscience."

"Kill me," Sheena decided, "and let them go."

She bowed her head. Daniel cried out. An older man appeared in the doorway of the bungalow and said, "What are you people doing here?" But even as he challenged them, he was smiling.

Daniel launched himself at the demon bowling him over. He snatched the sword from failing hands and raised it to strike down at the creature, spitting and snarling, struggling to rise. With all his strength, Daniel struck with the sword. In vain. The blade buried itself in the wooden floor. Demon and woman were gone. Sheena found sanctuary in a chair. Daniel freed the sword and returned it to its wooden sheath.

Ronald Bishop said, "I don't want to believe what I saw. Tell me we're being filmed."

"If I told you it's for a film, would you believe me?"

"No," he said and smiled.

Sheena offered, "If I told you we were hunting a demon would you believe me?"

"That sounds more plausible."

Sheena's face displayed surprise.

Ronald smiled to say, "I have met a demon. Who else would sail on a summer's afternoon in full storm gear?"

Which statement was unintelligible to both Sheena and Daniel.

"Unless you are considering renting a bungalow, may I ask you to leave?"

* * * *

As they drove back to Gallin, Sheena asked, "Why is she still alive?"

"He has some use for her."

"Did you really expect to walk in and rescue her?"

"Foolishly, I did. Mea culpa. He was two steps ahead of us again."

As they neared the towers of Sodom and Gomorrah, Daniel asked, "How did you know we were at the wrong door?"

"I just knew."

"I think that creature told you."

Sheena was silent.

"Drive to the Steamer. I'll walk from there."

When they parked in the back lane behind the pub, Daniel moved to leave the car.

Sheena asked, "Show me the sword."

Daniel withdrew the sword from its hiding place. It glowed as it unfolded.

"How wonderful! It's a sword. It kills people. And yet so beautiful."

Hunted animals and horsemen galloped through a living forest to dissolve into an angry ocean with sailors struggling to bring their craft through the storm that became sunlit meadows where peace reigned.

"What does the writing say?"

The words glowed on the blade.

"Manus Dei sum," recited Daniel.

"Which means?"

"I am the hand of God."

Sheena said slowly, "Then would it let the demon strike off our heads?"

"Who knows? Would you want to risk it? After all, it's only a sword."

CHAPTER FOURTEEN

"I have terrible nightmares.
I'm frightened all the time.
I never used to be."

Before the images appeared, Daniel knew the nightmare was beginning to play yet again. As if he were seated in the cinema listening to the opening theme music. Then he was transposed to the action.

Only it wasn't Eric kneeling beside him, fishing line in hand, but a creature in a bright yellow beret with broken teeth and a hole where its left eye had been. Daniel could see the farther quay through the hole in its head. A dying fish flapped on the haversack between them.

"That's not true," said Daniel.

The creature laughed.

"Of course, it's true! You cosy up with Eric because you think it makes you look better. Look at me! Eric is a genius and I'm his best friend. Ipso facto, I'm clever too."

The lisp of the broken mouth gave the words a certain snakelike quality.

"You know what I'm telling you is the truth. You hate Eric with every atom of your being, don't you, Daniel?"

"Yes."

"Then kick the little shit into the river."

Eric became Eric and Daniel stood up.

"You okay?"

"Just cramp."

Daniel stretched one leg elaborately and then the other. He looked around to see no one was watching.

"Eric?"

The boy looked up at his friend. Daniel kicked him into the river. The boy fell silently, clutching his fishing line. He hit the water with barely a splash and vanished under the pilings of the quay. The silence was broken only by the calling of the gulls.

"That was easy, wasn't it?" said the creature with its arm about Daniel's shoulder, "I did expect more fuss."

They stood companionably looking down into the river. Daniel lived a terror beyond expression; he could neither scream nor weep.

"I will need you to kill the woman, Sheena. You lust after her, but you're too old. She would laugh at you. So, you will punish her rejection. Trust me! You will feel such relief when she dies."

Daniel awoke in such terror, he fell from the bed onto the floor. He wriggled under the bed where he lay for a long time before the trembling stopped and his intellect subdued his fear. He relaxed in the shower, but didn't return to bed. He went out onto the balcony with his whisky.

To the sleeping town, Daniel Fallon said aloud, "A nightmare is a nightmare. Nothing more."

He was dozing when the grey sky began to lighten and the traffic began.

At the laptop, he typed an account of the dream into an e-mail: his memory of the nightmare was vivid. He hesitated to confess his fear that he was compromised by the demon. Guillaume would draw his own conclusions from the e-mail. Daniel would be withdrawn from the conflict and vanish with a new identity. The e-mail was addressed and titled Most Urgent when Daniel changed his mind and deleted it.

He sat down with his breakfast to hear Sheena and the children leaving for school. He found her voice calming, but he'd forgotten how lively children were. Silence was alien to them. He heard Lorraine and Morris chant, "Look at my face and you see somebody. Look at my back and you see nobody. Who am I?"

"A demon," Daniel answered.

The trio clattered happily down the stairs and he didn't hear the answer.

But he knew now who had killed Alec Skinner's son, Bobby. It was the identity of the killer that Alec dared not say aloud. Harelip.

Kevin somebody. The only boy in his class Daniel loathed. He and his cronies trapped bumblebees in jam jars and set them out in the hot sun to time how long it took them to die. Daniel opened the jam jars and was beaten. No one interfered because Daniel had killed Eric Johnson and torturing harmless bumblebees was a scientific experiment.

* * * *

Tom Moore skipped down the steps of the venerable building that housed the North Gallin Gazette. His heart was singing. The story of the bicycle-riding parrot on the Metro, with his byline, had been top story of the week. It had been taken up by local television and Tom's amiable face had appeared alongside the parrot. He had been ambushed by the local presenter. Olly Oakes faced him with a miniature bicycle and dared him to race the parrot. How could Tom refuse? The parrot won easily and Tom fell off the bicycle twice. It was a great success.

Tom's editor, William Harvey, also his father-in-law, had hinted at the idea of a weekly column that would amuse the readership. There are moments in life when pygmies surmount the world. This was Tom Moore's moment of triumph.

He crossed the road to the car park as someone called, "Love the parrot, Tom!" He waved cheerily in response. There were two men standing by his car, an older, thickset man with a sour face and a young man with a shaven head and neck tattoos.

They stood back as he unlocked the car.

"You Tom Moore?" enquired the older man.

"Yes. You want the parrot's autograph? No problem."

Tom brought out two cards displaying the parrot and Tom, claw print and autograph. He offered them, smiling to the strangers.

"We may be doing some more stories like this. The world news just seems so terrible, doesn't it?"

The two men perused the cards and then to Tom's surprise, tore them up. They threw them into the air over his head.

"Shabby wedding!" the older man cried and the young man laughed.

"I don't understand," Tom admitted, "There was no need for that."

"Let me introduce myself," said the unsmiling stranger, "Until you interfered, I was a sergeant of police. Remember?"

Tom's stomach contracted.

"All I did was expose the truth. Nothing personal."

"Well, this is personal. Get in the car."

Tom Moore got into the rear seat and the ex-sergeant joined him. The young man with the neck tattoos slipped into the driver's seat. A black bag was forced over the reporter's head.

"Am I being kidnapped?"

"Shut up!"

The car moved out of the car park and turned right.

* * * *

The sun blessed Hugh Gaitskill House and surrounding concrete and grass. Sheena parked the Seat in the shadow of the motor home. Guillaume was working at a laptop and didn't look up as she walked by. Hilda was navigating Marianne's buggie out of the double doors of the tower. Hilda bent to speak to Marianne and the buggie moved off. Sheena almost ran to intercept them.

"Where you going, Hilda?"

Marianne called out to her sister and held up her arms.

"Why you so rude when yi speak to me, Sheena?"

Sheena knelt by the buggie blowing raspberries that always sent Marianne into fits of laughter.

"I asked where you were going with my sister? Is that rude?"

"Yi make it sound rude."

Sheena rose to say, "Sorry. Not intended."

Are you stealing my sister?

"Wa going up the shop for ya Mam's tabs."

"You could encourage her not to smoke. She listens to you."

"We's alwizz smoked."

She can't steal Marianne now she knows you've seen her.

A thought struck Sheena.

"D'y'leave Marianne outside when you're in the shop?"

Somebody could take her.

The hands grasping the buggie handle displayed muscular forearms. The knuckles whitened. Looking into the sharp face, Sheena saw a stranger.

"You has no idea, Sheena, has yi, how much I do for Marianne?"

Sheena could find nothing to say.

"If wi has your permission, wa going up the shop now. That right, darlin'?"

Sheena watched Hilda and the buggie continue up the path towards the parade of shops.

Marianne said Hilda bad. Sheena good. But that's a baby talking. Am I losing touch with reality? Trusting no one? Seeing demons everywhere? Will I end up in a loony bin? Hilda is not going to harm Marianne. Okay? Just calm down, Sheena.

Sheena walked up the stairs to compose her thoughts. Perhaps because she mopped out the lift regularly, landings and some flights of stairs were cleaner. It was just beyond the fifth floor that she stopped. She sniffed again, hoping she was wrong, but the taint was clear. The halitosis of Hell lingered on the stairs. When her heart slowed again and she felt less nauseous, she continued walking upwards. On the eighth floor, she found the scent. There was the faintest trace on the penultimate landing. Anyone less gifted than Sheena would not have become aware. She realised she was naïve in believing the tower was safe. That she walked on secure ground. That the enemy did not know where Daniel and she lived.

She walked into the flat where Daniel sat reading in his chair.

"That creature has been here. I smelt him on the stairs."

Daniel lowered his book to say, "You're sure?"

Sheena nodded.

"How fresh?"

"The stairs are cleaner now, but it's difficult to say. Certainly, in the last week."

"This is as good a battle ground as any."

"I don't want to be on a battle ground."

"When we first began I did warn you."

"I'm not thinking of me."

Sheena was silent.

"Mam? The little ones? What should I do?"

"The poster says. Keep calm and carry on."

"I'm frightened."

"Good! That's healthy."

"And then?"

"We will find the creature and kill him."

"You say that and yet you sit there, doing nothing."

Daniel put down his book.

"Something has upset you."

Sheena sat down in her chair,

"I don't know who to trust any more. I thought Hilda was abducting Marianne."

"Was she?"

"No. She was taking her up to the shop. She'll probably buy her an ice cream."

"You never buy me an ice cream."

"I worry about the little ones. I worry about you. I have terrible nightmares. I'm frightened all the time. I never used to be."

From the balcony, they could hear the lament of hungry seagulls.

"While I am sitting here doing nothing?"

Sheena interrupted to say, "I wish I hadn't said that."

"While I sit idle, Guillaume has an army of people out there, watching and listening. The noses, few enough, are out there doing what you do. To turn a familiar saying on its head. This demon has to be lucky every time. We have to be lucky only once."

"He knows where we are."

"Then perhaps, we have distracted him from killing a child."

Daniel rose from his chair.

"Isn't it time you bought me an ice cream?"

They walked down to the lobby. Sheena pretended not to be concerned for Marianne. Daniel opened the windows on landings eight and five. They walked out into sunshine to find Hilda sitting on the grass with the buggie.

"Lean on your stick. You'll look older."

"Am I not old enough?"

Marianne stopped drowning in ice cream to shout, "Sheena!"

Sheena said, "That's the first time she's done that. Generally, she says Shee-shee."

They walked over and Sheena made the introductions.

"Daniel, this is Hilda, our Mam's best friend. They're smoking themselves to death together. Hilda, this is the old man, Daniel Fallon, who lives across the landing."

Daniel said politely, "Nice to meet you, Hilda."

Sheena seized his arm, saying, "I know he's too old for me, but I don't care. He's everything I ever longed for."

Somewhat to Sheena's surprise, Hilda responded, "Just make sure he makes a will in ya favour, pet."

Daniel laughed. Marianne laughed. It was a sound Sheena loved almost as much as her chuckle.

"And this," said Sheena, kneeling down, "is the sweetest child in all the world. Marianne Galloway, the first woman to land on Mars."

"Hello, Marianne," Daniel smiled, "D'y'really want to go to Mars?"

The child regarded him soberly.

"Marianne, you can call him Uncle Daniel. Dan-yell."

"Pan-yel," said Marianne.

"Near enough. Uncle Paniel's taking me up to the shop for an ice cream. Another time, we'll take you and he can treat us both."

As they walked away, Sheena proposed, "You have a choice."

"I do?"

"Put your arm around my shoulder or hold my hand."

Daniel hesitated and offered, "If I must, I'll hold your hand."

"If you must?"

Sheena seized a strong, warm hand. She found it comforting.

"Everything you do surprises me, Sheena. But what is this all about?"

"Aggravating my mother."

"How long do I have to hold your hand?"

"That's not very gentlemanly!"

"How long?"

"As long as Hilda's watching."

When they came back, licking ice cream cornets, Hilda and Marianne had gone. As they sat down on the grass, the motorhome reversed from its parking slot. Guillaume waved as he drove past.

"He has all but two of the secondary schools signed up to the Bright Star programme. All the primary schools except one are with us. This will give us a constant flow of intelligence as to what happens to these children as they go through their school lives. Hopefully, we can react more quickly."

"Is Ribble Road Primary the school that's not joining in?"

"No idea. You'd have to ask Guillaume."

* * * *

On entering the flat, Sheena was surprised to be greeted by applause. The Galloways and Hilda clapped vigorously.

Her mother came to hug a bewildered Sheena.

"I knew yi wa listening, pet."

"Listening to what?"

"What I telt yi. Waggle ya bum. Niver fails."

Sheena couldn't think of anything to say. Biter bit?

Hilda offered, portentously, "They do say these marriages with a younger woman and an older man are the ones that last."

"How would yous bairns like to have an Uncle Daniel?" Mrs. Galloway asked.

The response was overwhelming. Sheena saw in their eyes a longing for stability and said nothing. She understood the yearning to be safe from violence and abuse.

CHAPTER FIFTEEN

"We may get bored,
but we're not going to die."

"Where we going?" Tom Moore asked.

The black bag over his head smelt sour. He felt nauseated. No one answered him.

"I don't know why you're doing this."

He heard his voice tremble.

"What I did any reporter would've done."

The ex-sergeant spoke.

"Not Micky Dennison."

The young man was shocked. The veteran reporter was his idol and his mentor. If asked who he'd like to be, it would be Micky Dennison.

He echoed, "No way! Not Micky. No way!"

The blow to his midriff took his breath away. His assailant had said too much.

"Shut ya gob! Or I'll shut it for yi."

They travelled in silence.

The car stopped.

"Don't move!"

The driver got out and opened the passenger door. The older man exited.

"Come on."

Tom Moore shuffled along the seat and was pulled from the car. He felt another hand seize his left arm and he was walked, stumbling, up a garden path. There was sunlight on his back. He walked on gravel and brushed past plants. He was bundled into a doorway and into what he sensed was a hallway. A door was opened and Tom Moore was pushed into what he guessed must be a sitting room.

"Why have you taken so long?"

A voice he knew as the ex-sergeant answered, "Sorry, sir. We had to wait for him. We couldn't go in and get him."

"Excuses disappoint me. I would rather you didn't disappoint me."

"No, sir. Sorry, sir!"

Tom Moore was surprised at the fear in the man's voice.

"Let me see him."

The bag was pulled roughly from his head. The reporter blinked, eyes adjusting to the twilight in the room. Beyond the curtains, the summer sun blessed the garden.

"Thomas Moore?"

"Yes."

The room was comfortably furnished. Someone loved her porcelain figurines. A man was sitting in an armchair, his face in shadow.

"You're the reporter who has been poking his nose where it's not wanted?"

"I work as a journalist, yes."

The inquisitor was wearing a bright yellow beret.

"I haven't invited you here to."

Tom Moore interrupted to say, "I wasn't invited, I was kidnapped."

The voice continued, "I didn't invite you here for conversation. I am going to teach you a lesson you will never forget."

Despite himself, Tom Moore flinched and the grip on his arms tightened. His interrogator laughed, a surprisingly melodious laugh.

"My dear man, I'm not going to hurt you. If I killed you the lesson would be wasted."

* * * *

When the reporter and his escort had left the house, the interrogator went into the kitchen. On the table were the empty blister packs of an opiod analgesic. There were three capsules lying among the empty packs. An elderly man was propped up on a kitchen chair. His eyes moved when he was approached.

"Still alive? You surprise me."

133

He gathered the stray capsules together, opened the unresisting mouth and dropped them in. He reached for the whisky bottle and poured a good volume into the throat. He returned the bottle to the table uncapped.

"You made me do this. You only had to obey!"

Lifting the head, he stared into his eyes.

"Goodbye."

He laid his hand upon the scrawny chest. The old man sighed and died.

The executioner looked around the kitchen. All seemed to be in order. He went upstairs and closed the doors to the bathroom and the second bedroom. In the master bedroom, an old woman lay in the bed. At the bedside was an uneaten breakfast on a tray. The woman was dead. Saliva and snot on the pillow by the bed told the story. He drew the curtains and at the bedroom door said, "Thank you for your hospitality. Most kind."

He closed the front door. The street was silent. The residents were either at work or enjoying coffee and biscuits after a morning's diligent hoovering. The creature walked away, the yellow beret burning bright in the hot summer sun.

* * * *

Donna Gilbert's baby was born on the stroke of midnight after a short labour. The boy weighed four pounds, seven ounces. He went from his mother's womb to an incubator, showing signs of jaundice. Donna Gilbert was fourteen.

Sharing coffee at three a.m., Klara Schuster explained to the midwife, Joan Reynolds, "She was living on the street. Came to our notice six months ago."

"She'd be thirteen?"

"Wouldn't settle at Audley House. Fostered out. Doing well. Gave no indication of being pregnant to her foster parents. Then, quite unexpectedly, she vanished."

"Taxi driver saw her under Willen Bridge. Stopped. Saw the problem and brought her here."

"Well done, him!"

"She's not Geordie. We're not even sure she's giving her right name."

A bell rang and the midwife stood up.

"Ask not for whom the bell tolls," she quoted.

Klara answered, "It tolls for thee."

They exchanged smiles and the midwife vanished. Klara went to inspect the newborn in the incubator. There was a definite tinge of yellow to his skin. He was very small with dark eyes and curly hair. Klara went to visit the other child, sleeping in the bed that the chart named as Donna Gilbert. The girl sharing the room was sleeping fitfully. Her baby had been stillborn. Klara tiptoed out and found a quiet corner to write her notes.

Donna waited until she was sure Klara had gone. Voices from the delivery room assured her the night staff was engaged. She searched the nursery until she found the incubator. Donna regarded her son for some minutes. His unfocussed eyes gazed at her. The young mother examined the incubator. A notice printed in black on yellow stated THIS INCUBATOR IS ALARMED.

Donna carried a chair to the incubator. She sat down and slipped her hands into the rubberised nursing entries. She held her son's tiny hand and stroked his foot and toes. The wristband seemed enormous.

The midwife, Joan Reynolds, taking a breather from the latest delivery, found Donna Gilbert's bed empty. She alerted Security that no patient and baby must be allowed to leave the hospital. Then she went to the nursery and found the missing mother sitting with her baby. Donna looked alarmed when Joan approached.

"Are you warm enough?"

The midwife was looking at the thin hospital nightdress.

"I'm okay."

Joan Reynolds retreated and cancelled the alert. She returned to the nursery with a robe she settled about the girl's shoulders. She lifted her feet into the slippers.

"Don't tell anyone I'm spoiling you. They'll all want mollycoddling."

Joan regarded her handiwork.

"When you're ready, go quietly back to bed. Okay?"

"Thank you."

The midwife returned to find how far the next member of the human race had tunnelled her way to freedom.

* * * *

The breeze cooled the beach of St. Catherine's Bay. Bounded by cliffs, it was a small bay favoured by locals who understood the currents that cycled the tide in and out There were several family parties sharing the beach. Relaxing under a beach umbrella were Mr. and Mrs. Moore, the grandparents of eight-year-old Mark Moore. Building a sand castle nearer the water's edge were the boy Mark and his mother, Lisa Moore. Mark's grandfather was dozing and his wife was reading.

It was the boy Mark who spotted his father coming down the stony path onto the beach. He abandoned the sand castle and his mother to run to embrace his father and question the package he carried. They came together to hug and kiss his mother, Lisa.

"Tom! I thought you were working?"

"Too good a day for work, sweetie. I thought I'd join you."

"How's the parrot, son?"

Tom Moore groaned.

"Not you too, Dad!"

"Everybody loved it, Tom," protested his mother.

"Dad has a present for me," Mark announced.

His arm about his wife, Tom and his parents watched the boy open the package.

The boy cried out in wonder, "It's a boat! You blow it up!"

"A dinghy," Tom corrected his son.

"I'm not sure I like this," Lisa said.

"Is it safe?" his mother asked.

"Of course, it is!" Tom assured the family.

His father was doubtful.

"I hope you know what you're doing, son."

Tom explained, "I'm not going to set him in a dinghy and watch him float out to sea."

"Don't even say that," Lisa shuddered.

"This steel stake I drive deep into the sand with this mallet. I fasten the end of this nylon rope to the stake and the other end to the eyelet of the dinghy. Then Mark can paddle about to his heart's content. Skipper of his own ship!"

The boy was wild with excitement and refused to let go of the paddle. His father and grandfather drove the stake deep into the sand. Lisa and her mother-in-law used the pump to blow up the dinghy. The rope was tied to the stake and dinghy. Mark's grandfather made sure the knots were sound. Then Mark climbed aboard his first command, face glowing, clutching his paddle.

To applause, he began to paddle out into the tide to the extent of the rope, twenty-five metres. Lisa, holding hands with Tom, watched anxiously. The grandparents similarly held their breath. The boy cried out with delight as he crested a placid wave. The adults relaxed. The boy paddled freely.

"Look at me!"

They looked at him.

"That's a wonderful present," Lisa agreed, "Who thought of that?"

"A friend," said Tom.

"I like to see boys behave like boys." his grandfather agreed.

"Long as we keep an eye on him," his grandmother cautioned.

Mark was still paddling happily when the adults decided it was time to head home. The tide was tugging at the rope, but the stake was unmoved.

"Five more minutes, Mark," his mother called.

Grandmother and Lisa were packing the remains of their picnic lunch. Grandfather Moore had folded the umbrella and windbreak and was carrying them up to the car. Tom was watching his son.

"Time to go!" called Lisa.

"Just five more minutes, Mum, please!"

Tom said, "I'll get him."

He waded out into the sea, neglectful of his new jeans. Mark stopped paddling. Tom reached the dinghy. He took out a knife and cut the rope.

"Dad! What're you doing?"

Tom pushed the dinghy seawards and turned back to the shore.

The tide carried the slight craft swiftly away. Mark's heart-chilling scream of "Mammy!" shocked the women and the old man. Tom marched ashore gathering up the rope.

Lisa screamed, "What've you done, Tom?"

Her husband looked at her blankly. His father dropped his burden and stumbled back down the path. The breeze caught the dinghy. Despite the child's frantic paddling, the craft began to move seaward.

When the child cried out for his mother, Branco Liefcutter was already sprinting through the shallows to dive into deeper water. He swam with frantic urgency after the dinghy.

Lisa cried, "Why has he done this?" as her parents-in-law reached her. Tom Moore slashed his wrist to the bone with the knife he'd used on the rope. Shocked by the torrent of blood pouring from the wound, he sat down in the shallows, the water turning red about his ankles. His father forestalled his attempt to cut his right wrist.

Tom Moore, in a mindless frenzy, stabbed his father twice in the back and side as the older man struggled to create a tourniquet on his wrist. Using a handkerchief and his club tie, Mr. Moore completed his task. The knife was deep in his back beyond reach. The fracas ended with the older man sitting astride the younger. He dialled and spoke to the police. Tom Moore wailed in despair. Mrs. Morgan struggled to stop Lisa from running into the sea.

Branco was unable to catch the dinghy. It was tantalisingly close; twenty, thirty metres away. Mark reached out imploringly. Branco was exhausted. The dinghy was now on the open sea. Then for a moment, the wind veered and the dinghy was blown towards Branco. He swam beyond exhaustion. With a supreme effort, he hauled himself aboard. He lay panting, struggling for breath.

Mark offered, "Are you alright?"

Branco grinned to say, "Never been better."

He sat up to say, "I know your name. You're Mark. My name is Branco."

He offered his ham of a hand and they shook hands politely.

"Are we going to die?" Mark asked.

He was struggling not to cry.

"No! We may get bored, but we're not going to die."

"Really?"

Mark was impressed by this abounding confidence.

"D'y'think I'd be here if there were any danger? You can manage fine by yourself. But I couldn't resist parading as a hero."

He knew he hadn't the strength to carry the boy back to land.

"So what do we do?"

"If we had needles and wool, I would teach you how to knit."

Mark almost laughed.

"Or maybe play games. I spy with my little eye?"

"The sea," Mark cried and actually laughed.

"Or we sit here telling stories waiting forl the lifeboat . Or the helicopter. Or best of all."

"Yes?" cried Mark.

"A pirate ship. And we join the pirates and off we go a-pirating. You can send your Mum and Dad a postcard from Jamaica."

"Are there still pirates?"

"You bet! I used to be Branco the Beastly!"

"Really?"

"I gave it up. My mother didn't like it."

Branco could feel the sea changing tempo. When they rode an unbroken wave, he said, "You see? Just like riding a horse? Should I tell you about how I used to be a wrangler?"

"What's a wrangler?"

"A wrangler is a man who tames wild horses. I found I could talk to horses and they would listen to me. People would bring me horses they couldn't ride. I would explain to the horse the way to deal with humans is to let them believe they're superior when we horses know they are not."

When the helicopter came from RAF Boulmer to pick them out of the sea, Mark was reluctant to leave until Branco promised to finish telling the story of the grey horse that found its way home from two hundred miles away. Branco finished the story in Wansbeck General Hospital where they were kept under observation for the night. Tom Moore was detained under Section Twelve of the Mental Health Act. Lisa and her mother-in-law spent eternity in AandE where the knife was removed from the older Mr. Moore's back and his stab wounds were treated.

CHAPTER SIXTEEN

*"That creature mustn't ever be
allowed near the girls again."*

Sheena parked around the corner from the school. A traffic warden
was working his way along Ribble Road making people's lives more
difficult. Yet who sees more of life on the street than the wardens?

She waited for him to catch up and asked, "Excuse me. This your
usual round?"

He seemed a stolid, sensible man.

"Any complaints must be."

Sheena interrupted to say, "D'y'ever see any men hanging about
the school?"

He stopped and looked at her.

"Have you bairns of your own?" asked Sheena. He nodded and
she continued, "Then yi know how Mams worry?"

He nodded again. A man of few words.

"You're our eyes on the street. Will yi look out for us as you pass
the school?"

She didn't wait for an answer, but seized his notebook and biro.
On a fresh page, she wrote her mobile number and name.

"Yi could save a child's life. It's that serious."

"If yous don't mention me name."

"It's a deal. Thank you."

* * * *

Her brother and sister were in the schoolyard. Lorraine was sitting
on the doorstep reading. Morris was bouncing a tennis ball against a
wall and striking the rebound with a cricket bat. Lorraine stood up
and they came towards her.

"Sorry, guys. If Miss Kaplan's still here, I need a word. Stay in the yard, please."

They went back to reading and playing one-man cricket.

Sheena entered the familiar corridor, smelling as ever of polish and people. She found Mrs. Kaplan in the classroom and tapped on the open door. The teacher looked up from the desk and smiled.

"Sheena! Come in!"

Sheena entered and stood before the desk.

"Grab a chair and bring it round."

Sheena found the largest chair and joined the teacher.

"You've come to tell me you want to go to University."

Sheena smiled.

"Rumour says you're leaving, miss."

"I think it's time to go."

"You'll be much missed."

"I'm not the only decent teacher."

"Just the only one Lorraine has, miss."

Silence.

Sheena tried, "I know things have happened that you may find difficult to explain."

"Such as attempted abduction, suicide, murder? Is that what you mean?"

"Has anyone tried to explain to you?"

"I don't need an explanation for criminal behaviour. In fact, I'd rather not know what the young man did to bring such appalling consequences on his wife and child. Never mind my husband and myself."

"He did nothing wrong."

"It doesn't seem so."

Sheena hesitated.

"I'd like to explain, miss, but I know you won't believe the truth."

Mrs. Kaplan smiled, "I've known you a long time, Sheena Galloway. Never once have you told me an untruth."

Sheena found herself blushing with embarrassment.

"Tell me and I'll decide whether to believe you."

Sheena drew a deep breath.

"There is an evil presence in Gallin that is killing children. But not only here."

Mrs. Kaplan didn't respond.

"This demon is seeking to find and kill the child in Gallin that will change the world if he or she lives. Like Herod, it doesn't know which child, but kills at random."

Mrs. Kaplan raised a hand.

"And how does this demon go about it?"

"It persuades an innocent to kill a child, manipulating emotions. It decided to kill Ellie's baby. You frustrated the latest attempt."

"Is anybody trying to stop this 'demon'?"

"Ordinary people who have suffered. Men and women such as yourself. Very often these victims, manipulated into killing, don't survive. They commit suicide once they realise what they've done."

"And this organisation? Does it have a leader?"

Sheena apologised, saying, "I'm not sure I should tell you any more, miss. Mebbes, I've told you too much already."

"Then why are you here today?"

"The children need you. You mustn't run away."

"We're not running away."

"When this demon catches up with you, wherever you are hiding, you will do what it wants. Because you will be alone and afraid."

"Nonsense!"

The tone carried little conviction.

"I'm afraid, miss. We're all afraid. But we're together."

Mrs. Kaplan was silent. They could hear the cleaner in the classroom next door.

"And that's the truth, miss."

"I'd like to meet the leader."

Morris interrupted, bursting into the classroom.

"That man's back. Lorraine's talking to him."

Sheena was already moving. Mrs. Kaplan was slower.

"In the yard?"

"Yes."

Sheena was already running down the corridor. Mrs. Kaplan and Morris scurried after.

When Sheena appeared at the school door, a man broke off from speaking with Lorraine and walked quickly away.

Sheena shouted, "Stop, please! I'd like a word with you!"

When she entered the yard, Sheena had closed the heavy school gate. By the time she got out onto the pavement, the man was nowhere to be seen. She turned back, disappointed.

Mrs. Kaplan said, "Average size. Decent suit. Losing his hair. Didn't see his face."

Lorraine added, "No moustache or nothing."

Morris offered, "I knew you'd want to know, miss."

"Well done, Morris!" applauded Mrs. Kaplan, "You have a good brother, Lorraine. Looking out for you."

"Did he give you anything?"

The child shook her head.

"What did he talk about?"

"It was sad really."

"What d'yi mean? Sad really?"

"He has a daughter, Melanie. My age. She's been sick a long time. Doesn't go to school. So, she has no friends. Melanie has a little puppy called Tiny, but that's not the same. So, her Daddy's looking for a friend for her. And I look like a nice girl. Maybe I could be her friend."

It seemed Lorraine liked being a nice girl.

I keep forgetting she's a child. She doesn't believe anyone would lie to her and hurt her. Too many girls grow up believing that. Too many girls are lied to and hurt.

"Go on!"

"Would I like to be a friend for Melanie? Spend an hour with her sometimes. It's alright because his wife is always there. He'd pick me up and bring me home. It was just really sad. Poor Melanie!"

Sheena looked to Mrs. Kaplan.

The teacher said, "How many times have you been told to stay away from strangers?"

"Lots, I suppose," Lorraine estimated.

"How many times not to go with strangers? Not to get into cars?"

Lorraine looked to Sheena who saw a troubled child.

Mrs. Kaplan said, "You've just broken every rule, Lorraine."

"But it's so sad. That poor girl. No friends. She's been ill so long."

Sheena stated, "There is no Melanie. No puppy called Tiny. No Mummy in attendance. No Daddy looking for a friend for his sick daughter."

"But he said."

Mrs. Kaplan interrupted.

"You're a clever girl, Lorraine. But you're a child. That man was going to take you somewhere and hurt you. Kill you. That's the blunt truth. Are you old enough to understand me?"

"Yes, miss."

"That wasn't a demon," Mrs. Kaplan stated, "Just a man. A vile and dangerous one."

* * * *

They sat together in the car for a long time. Morris had gone to play cricket with the boys on the green. A beautiful Summer's day was dying. With a certain irony Sheena noted that Lorraine's childhood was dying too. It was hurtful to know her simple view of the world was fading.

"So, I mustn't trust what anyone says to me?"

"You have to ask yourself, what do they want?"

"Doesn't this make life harder?"

"Makes life safer."

"He sounded so real."

"You should've asked for his telephone number. For Mam to speak to his wife and arrange a time for you to visit Melanie."

"I never thought of that."

"He wouldn't give you the number because there is no Melanie and no Mammy. You have to learn to test a man's lies and use them against him."

"How do you learn all this, Sheen?"

"The hard way. Maybe, I can save you a few hard knocks. Believe me, nice girl, this is only the first such chat we're going to have over the next few years."

Lorraine hugged and kissed her sister.

"Alright, alright! Don't go overboard!"

* * * *

Sheena didn't get her key in the lock before Morris jerked it open.
"What now!"

Morris burst out with, "Wa gona get a lorra money. Mam's on the phone now."

Sheena pushed the fish and chips into her brother's arms. Ginny Galloway was on the phone. Lorraine stood beside her, looking concerned. Marianne was bouncing up and down in her play pen.

"What you up to, Mam?"

"Wi've won a lorra money. Two hundred thousand pounds! Can you believe that?"

"No."

"All wi has to do is forward a thousand pounds for adminny thingies stuff. I'm just giving him the details. Such a nice man."

Sheena snatched the phone from her mother.

"You have been talking to a lady with dementia. May I ask who you represent?"

The connection was cut abruptly.

Lorraine said, "I told her she should ask for his telephone number, but she wouldn't."

"Mam, that was a scam! Nobody's ever going to give us money!"

Morris asked plaintively, "But we won the lottery!"

"No, we didn't! My God, we've got two morons in the family! That's not fair! One's enough!"

To her mother, she said, "Where were you going to get this thousand pounds from?"

"Out of the bank."

"We haven't got a thousand pounds."

"I'd pay it back out of the two hundred thousand pounds."

"Which you wouldn't get."

Sheena looked around the disappointed faces.

"Let's just eat our fish and chips and be grateful?"

* * * *

Walter Duns loved living in Rosebank Crescent. When he drove up the short drive into the garage, he said aloud, "I live at number five, Rosebank Crescent." It was a most salubrious address.

He regarded himself in the rear-view mirror. The hair was receding. A sign of maturity. The mole by his lower lip meant he had been marked by a Higher Authority. His mother had told him so. When mocked at school for having a bug on his face, he merely smiled. Little did they know he was special.

The Christmas when Uncle Eddie remarked the boy had eyes like pee holes in snow, he had been pleased, thinking of the gallant Arctic explorers. His cousin Kane had explained it wasn't a compliment. When the visitors had departed, taking an undue share of the Christmas cake with them, Walter retired to his bedroom.

He created a model of Uncle Eddie from Playdough and was considering where to place the pins when his mother interrupted him, walking into his bedroom without knocking. She sat down on his bed, narrowly missing squashing Uncle Eddie.

"Hasn't Kane grown, Walter? He's a fine boy!"

There was a certain wistfulness in her tone. Walter would never reach six feet.

"Your Aunt Phyllis has been promoted again! And Uncle Eddie was voted top player in his firm's football team. They won both the League and the Cup last season. It's a shame your father's never been interested."

Walter had once been dragged with his father to watch Uncle Eddie play football. They stood in silent misery on the frosty touchline. Walter never felt closer to his father. Commentary was provided by Aunt Phyllis.

"Course, he could've gone professional. Everybody said so. He could have been another Madonna."

To Walter's unskilled eye, Uncle Eddie's talent seemed to consist of running into and over anyone in his path. When his mother retreated, Walter knew where to place the pins. It was gratifying that on Easter Saturday, Uncle Eddie failed to run into and over a double decker bus. His right leg was amputated.

From the garage, Walter moved to check his garden gnomes. He exchanged a few words with each. Neighbours with their patronising smiles were unaware that each gnome was equipped with a movement sensor. Should anyone approach the house, the opening chords of the 1812 Overture would resonate within number five, Rosebank Crescent.

Putting his key into the lock, Walter said aloud, "Five Rosebank Crescent is my home."

He had had difficulty making friends at school. He was a clever boy, but no teacher made a pet of him. His apples were spurned which puzzled Walter as the song assured him; An apple for the teacher That seems the thing to do, Because I want to learn about romance from you.

His gifts at Christmas were regarded with suspicion and refused. They were expensive, but he was never caught stealing from the big shops in Newcastle. He was always careful to remove any price labels.

The only person who accepted his gifts was Raymond Uttercliffe, a boy in his class who lived in Rosebank Crescent. Walter was once invited to his home. When they sat down to look at a stamp album, Mrs. Uttercliffe insisted, "We must wash our hands first." Walter washed very quickly to return to the album before his friend, to steal Raymond's three cents Mozambique airmail. He was never invited again.

But the ambition to live in Rosebank Crescent was kindled. When this was finally achieved, Walter presented himself on the doorstep of Raymond Uttercliffe's home. Raymond was astonished. He hadn't seen Walter for decades. Out of politeness, Walter was invited in to meet Raymond's wife and three young daughters.

Four hours later, Raymond Uttercliffe bundled his wife and bewildered children into the car to get Walter out of the house. They drove to Newcastle for the family to enjoy an unexpected visit to the cinema. That night when they had bathed and put the children to bed, his wife said, "That creature mustn't ever be allowed near the girls again."

After suffering under siege for nearly six months, Raymond Uttercliffe and his family moved out of Rosebank Crescent leaving no forwarding address.

CHAPTER SEVENTEEN

Would you like to see a photograph
of my little darling?"

Mr. Singh had been very understanding of Sheena's need to collect the children from school. She now started work in the shop at twelve and signed off at four to Adish who came in an hour earlier. Adish didn't seem particularly pleased at the new arrangement. Sheena didn't remark on the fact that Adish often came in half an hour early to gossip to Sheena of her latest infatuation. But she did point out the girl would be free an hour sooner. Adish's mood changed. Life was still a mad scramble for Sheena, but she consoled herself that her savings account was growing.

* * * *

At the school, she found Morris and four boys playing cricket in the yard. There was no sign of Lorraine. Sheena's heart stopped, but Morris called, "She's with Miss Kaplan."

She heard their voices as she walked the corridor, but they stopped talking when she tapped on the open door. Mrs. Kaplan was guillotining sheets of coloured paper and Lorraine was folding the pieces.

"Ah, Sheena! Forgive me. I kidnapped your sister."

"That's alright, miss. You can keep her."

Lorraine protested, but Mrs. Kaplan smiled.

"She's been very helpful. And we've had an interesting chat. That right, Lorraine?"

"Yes, miss."

"And I've learned a joke. Would you like to hear it?"

"That's why I'm here."

Lorraine said, "Where do wasps go when they have a tummy ache?"

Mrs. Kaplan replied, "I don't know. Where do wasps go when they have a tummy ache?"

"The Waspital."

"I think it's time I took her home, miss."

They drove in a peaceful silence. Morris hugged his cricket bat. Lorraine wrote in her day book. Until Sheena couldn't endure the silence any longer.

"Wha'did you talk about with Miss Kaplan?"

"Nothing."

"You didn't talk about nothing."

"You weren't there."

"People don't talk about nothing. They say that when they don't want to tell their sister what they were talking about."

"That's a long sentence about nothing."

"Alright, you don't want to tell me."

Morris said, "I would tell you if you asked me."

"But you never have anything to tell," Lorraine objected.

They drove in silence until Lorraine put her day book and biro back into her shoulder bag.

"She just made me sad, that's all."

"How did she do that?"

Lorraine hesitated, looking anxiously at her sister.

Sheena asked, "What did she say?"

"She said you should be at University. Not serving in a pub. Or in a shop."

"It's my life."

"She said you would say that. But it's not your life. Bits of it belong to Mam and Morris and Marianne and me. And a bit belongs to Miss Kaplan. Why aren't you at University?"

"It's too complicated to explain."

"She said, I must go to University. And Morris. We mustn't get bogged down. We mustn't waste our lives."

"So, I'm wasting my life?"

Lorraine didn't know what to say.

Morris said, "We couldn't do without you."

149

"Oh! And Miss Kaplan said she's not leaving Ribble Road. It was just a silly rumour."

* * * *

The flat was empty. The television was dark and silent. It felt like an abandoned ship, drifting idly in the Sargasso Sea. Sheena knew Lorraine sensed it too. She smelt the faintest whisper of evil, but it faded. She knew he had been in the building. It would not be beyond reason if he had investigated the flat. Sheena put away her groceries. Morris switched on the television. Sheena switched it off.

Lorraine said, "Mam said she was going to Bingo with Hilda today."

"Marianne's a big fan of Bingo, is she?"

When she looked at their downcast faces she knew she had soured the day.

"Come here," she said and hugged them both, "I'm sorry. My day for playing Cruela de Vil. Sorry!"

She passed her hand over her face.

"Gone! There! She's gone! Sheena's back!"

* * * *

Sheena walked to the Community Centre. The bingo session was held in the big room. In the anteroom there were a dozen or more buggies and prams. Sheena opened the door quietly and slipped inside to watch the bingo.

Her mother, Hilda and two other women were seated at one of twenty-five tables. Marianne was seated on Hilda's lap. Her mother was excited. In the tawdry lighting of the bingo session, Sheena saw the pretty girl her mother once had been; the child of the dysfunctional family, shadowed always by the prospect of violence and abuse. Robbed of education. A limited choice of employment. Better choose a strong man and you'll always be safe. Unaware, the bully will inevitably abuse her. The world turns sour and a succession of unwanted children by uncaring men completes the cycle.

Ginny Galloway cried out wildly, standing up to wave her bingo card. Sheena guessed she had won, perhaps fifty pounds that would melt away tonight when Ginny and Hilda went clubbing. In the confusion, Sheena caught sight of the baby's bewildered face. She knew then she must escape these doldrums to save Marianne.

Marianne spotted her sister and started waving, babbling, trying to attract her mother's attention. The child was ignored in the excitement of the bingo win. Sheena blew a kiss to gain a smile and vanished.

* * * *

In the smaller bedroom, there was a single bed dressed for a child. The duvet pictured a life-size Barbie. The bedside table carried a Barbie lamp. The room was crowded with soft toys. Walter Duns went first to Melanie. She was lying, eyes closed, in her cot. At four feet long, she looked out of place in a full-size bed. Walter had constructed and furnished her bed himself. The woodwork was painted lead-free pink and the bedding was ethereal pink. A white stuffed puppy sat at the foot. The tape player attached to the railing of the cot foot was clicking impatiently. Walter reversed the tape. Melanie's favourite In Apple Blossom time filled the room. When he lifted the doll from the bed, her eyes opened.

"Hello, darling! Daddy's home."

He kissed her cold plastic brow. When he had bought her at the Sunday market, she had recited, "Mamma!" when raised from the horizontal. Walter had been unable to find a doll that said, "Dadda!" He had silenced Melanie with a screwdriver. He had also failed to have sex with the doll.

Melanie was wearing her favourite nightgown and knickers bearing images of Barbie. From the wardrobe that contained a surprising array of children's clothing, he selected a simple button-through dress and matching underwear.

"Lorraine will be coming to see us soon. I had a chat with her today. Such a lovely girl. I'm sure she'll become your very best friend, Melanie. What biscuits do you think she likes?"

He brushed her hair in rhythm with the music and arranged an Alice band. Approving of her appearance, he switched off the music and carried Melanie through to the sitting room.

He bent her legs into a sitting posture and placed her where she could watch the television.

"I'm going to have mushrooms on toast for tea. Hands up if you'd like some."

The doll did not move.

"Suit yourself."

The doll stared at the latest unfolding human catastrophe.

Walter returned from the kitchen with a tray, carrying his mushrooms on toast and tea. As he settled himself, he asked Melanie, "Perhaps we might have a sleepover when Lorraine comes? In the big bed? That would be fun, wouldn't it?"

The doll didn't agree or disagree, but stared impassively at the weeping, frightened faces of the latest refugee children. The presenter promised that a donation of three pounds would solve the insolvable.

"My God! But there's a beautiful child! Imagine what she'd look like if she were washed! Surely, they could do something by fostering them out? But anything practical they ignore. Makes you want to weep!"

They sat together, Walter and the doll that couldn't weep. He had solved that problem with a screwdriver too. As the camera displayed their tragedy, Walter appraised the lost children lustfully.

"These celebrities and their promises! Even in our humble circumstances, we'd be happy to take in a pair of sisters, wouldn't we, Melanie?"

With tea things cleared away, the pair settled to enjoy photographs of Lorraine stolen between the railings of Ribble Road School. Walter particularly enjoyed the pictures of Lorraine playing netball.

"Perhaps we could put up one of those hoops in the back garden? That would be a nice surprise for her. Later she may bring friends to play. Shouldn't be expensive."

* * * *

Sheena stepped out of the lift with a carrier bag from the chippie as Daniel came from his flat and locked the door. She sensed immediately he was troubled.

"Something wrong?"

Daniel hesitated to say, "Guillaume's not called in."

"Is that bad?"

"It's unusual. He's generally so punctual."

"Where did he go?"

"To a school to discuss Bright Star. Shouldn't have been a bother."

"This time of night?"

"Five fifteen was the appointment."

"The motorhome's downstairs."

"He'd take a taxi."

Sheena said, "I'm holding you up."

Daniel stepped into the lift.

"This lift smells of fish and chips."

When Sheena smiled, he added, "It must be nice to belong to a family."

The lift doors closed. Sheena keyed the door and entered the flat. The jubilation that engulfed her as she fed supper to the ravening pack formed the thought in her head.

It is nice to be part of a family. We shouldn't take it for granted.

* * * *

The Lens was a private photographic club for gentlemen who shared a particular taste. The membership was select and discreet. They would display photographs and sometimes show videos, but it was a perfectly respectable club for amateur photographers. There was never any rowdyism or drunkenness. From the street, no one would recognise 49, Salisbury Terrace, a late Georgian town house as a club. One would have to approach the front door to read the modest brass plaque that stated The Lens.

There were seven members in the club when Walter Duns arrived. He settled himself at the rear of the clubroom with his glass of

Amontillado. As a freelance photographer for the North Gallin Gazette, he preferred not to be in the limelight. He came in the hope that Ralph would have the photographs of Lorraine's head transferred to other children's bodies. The Internet was not a secure medium. Photographs by hand were safest.

The stranger said, "May I sit with you?"

Walter was surprised, but not discomforted by this approach.

"By all means."

The stranger was wearing a yellow beret, which intrigued Walter.

"Forgive me, but does your headgear have any particular meaning?"

The man did not appear to understand him.

"Is it a club beret? Signifying membership?"

"I understand it is most becoming. But one must be careful it does not rot on the head."

"No, indeed."

Walter appraised the stranger.

"If I may say so. The eye patch is quite rakish."

Combined with the yellow beret, the black eye patch was quite striking. Walter had to admit it gave the stranger an individual air.

"Thank you."

"May I ask? Was it an accident? Or?"

Despite beret and eye patch, he didn't have a military air. The stranger lifted the patch. Walter looked through his head to see the view of Lake Windermere on the opposite wall. The patch dropped and Walter regarded his sherry thoughtfully. He did not believe what he had seen.

"Would you care for another drink?" asked his new friend. Without waiting for an answer, he raised a hand to the barman. As they waited for the drinks, the stranger said, "Forgive me, I haven't introduced myself, Walter."

Before Walter could ask how he knew his name, the man said, "Rudyard Kipling, at your service."

A bewildered Walter replied, "An illustrious name."

"Thank you."

The drinks arrived. Walter swallowed half the glass before he realised it was vodka. His new friend followed his example.

"How is life with you, Walter, old chum?"

For no apparent reason, Walter felt the need to share his happiness. It may have been the alcohol or the friendly hand upon his sleeve, but he felt quite euphoric.

"Come on, Walter, admit it! You're in love!"

Walter was surprised and delighted at his interest.

"She's the sweetest girl you've ever seen. So beautiful. Takes your breath away. I talked with her earlier today. She said she loves me. Lorraine loves me! That's all I've ever wanted. Just to be loved. She's coming for a sleepover this weekend. In the big bed. One day, we'll run away together. Going somewhere no one will ever find us. And we'll love each other forever. Would you like to see a photograph of my little darling?"

"It would be an honour!"

Walter brought out the photograph of Lorraine. He was a good photographer. While Lorraine was smiling at a team mate on scoring, she appeared to be smiling into the lens. The waiter arrived with fresh drinks and Walter emptied his previous glass. Rudyard Kipling studied the photograph.

"Absolutely lovely," agreed his new friend.

Walter accepted the compliment gracefully.

"There was once another girl, but Lorraine is my soul mate."

The image of a rose bed replanted was hastily suppressed.

Rudyard Kipling sighed to say, "Unfortunately, I know this Lorraine. She is a heartless little tart. A greedy little bitch. I'm sorry, but she has been leading you up the garden path, old friend."

Walter was stunned. His heart stopped. All he knew was the great pain that overwhelmed him.

"I've seen her with other men. All she wants is your money. Greedy little trollop! She doesn't love you, Walter. Love you? She'd laugh at the notion. After all you've done for her too. How you've cared for her. Bought her anything and everything. Given your heart and soul to her. She makes fun of you to her friends. She boasts she has you kiss her arse. Love you? If you died, she'd dance on your grave before going off to the bank for your money!"

Walter felt his anger grow to overwhelm the pain. The anger exploded until every fibre of his being was aflame.

"That cheating little tart!"

Rudyard Kipling decided, "That cheating little tart must be punished. She doesn't deserve to live."

* * * *

As he expected, the school seemed abandoned. The taxi stopped and the driver awaited instructions. It was the same man Daniel had met on his arrival in Gallin. They sat in silence until the driver said, "It is a man we're looking for?"

"He should've been back by seven at the latest."

"Met a mate? Stopped for a drink?"

"He's very reliable."

Daniel started to exit the car.

"I'll take a look."

Daniel had almost circled the principal building when a large man in overalls stepped out in front of him.

"What you doing here?"

"I have a friend who had an appointment with the Head Teacher today. Five fifteen. He should've been back long before this. Older man. I was just checking he might've fallen. Had an accident."

"Never seen the Head here at five fifteen any day. Most of them beat the bell to their cars. Besides, he hasn't been here today. Meeting with the high and mighty. The cleaners never mentioned seeing anybody."

"So, the Head hasn't been here today?"

The caretaker shook his head.

The taxi driver said, "Take you back?"

"No. The Steamer, please."

Coming into Percy Street from the other direction, Daniel said, "Don't bother turning. Drop me here."

He exited onto the pavement.

"Hope your mate turns up."

"Thank you."

* * * *

As the taxi pulled away, Daniel stood for a moment looking at the Paddle Steamer public house on the opposite pavement. It was a classic, Victorian public house, dressed in green marble with gargoyles in profusion. Its stained-glass windows still bore the elegant inscriptions, SALOON BAR, PUBLIC BAR, LADIES' SALON and JUG and BOTTLE over a minor door. The hanging board displayed a majestic paddle steamer riding a bow wave, a plume of black smoke issuing from its tall funnel. The second floor, Sheena had told him, was the Function Room. The upper two storeys were the living quarters of Billy Younger and his wife. It belonged to an age when the Gallins, North and South, were rich and busy fishing ports.

The bar stools were occupied as usual. A pleasant older woman served Daniel a pint of Best and he ordered his supper. He retired to a small table in the bar corner and dialled Guillaume's mobile. The phone went straight to voice mail. Daniel struggled not to believe Guillaume was in trouble. An appointment with an absent Head Teacher. Cleaners who hadn't seen a stranger arriving for his appointment. A school that was silent and empty apart from a prowling caretaker. He rang Branco.

"Have you heard from Guillaume?"

"Not today."

"I think he's in trouble."

"Where are you?"

"Pub called the Paddle Steamer. Percy Street."

"I'll be there in half an hour."

Daniel finished his supper as a cheer along the bar announced the arrival of Sheena. She was surprised to see him as she passed along the bar to her locker. When she returned, Daniel was ignored. He sipped his ale and watched her work. He noted how she always had a smile and a few words for her customer. For a few fleeting moments, he or she had Sheena's full attention. She never talked over the customer's head to someone else. When she left to serve another, it was apologetically, as if she didn't wish to leave.

I confess I have a liking, an affection for Sheena. Something of human feeling is stirring within me This girl lights up wherever she is. These men feel better when they see her. The women don't feel threatened. Am I wrong to have an affection for her? Dangerous at any age, never mind, April and October. April and November? April and December?

Daniel was surprised to find Branco at his elbow. He sat down long enough to listen to Daniel telling what he knew. Then Branco was on his feet.

"Let's go!"

"Where're we going?"

"Talk to the caretaker."

"Why?"

"Because he won't be expecting us."

"I've already talked to him."

"He's a liar."

"How'd'y'know?"

"We know Guillaume went to that school today. The caretaker is a liar."

As they quit the bar, Daniel stopped to say to Sheena, "Guillaume may be in trouble."

"Try not to step into the same."

Her smile vanished as she watched them leave.

"Your Granda, is it?"

"More trouble than a bairn," replied Sheena, evading the question.

* * * *

There was a light downstairs in the caretaker's house.

Branco said, "I'll go to the back door."

"He's a big man."

"We only going to ask him a few questions."

"I'll give you five minutes, then I'll knock."

"Be nice," said Branco and vanished.

It seemed to Daniel to be the longest five minutes ever before he knocked on the door. He stepped back a pace as he heard footsteps approach the door.

The caretaker snarled, "Yes?" and then recognising Daniel, "What the hell d'yee want?"

Behind the caretaker, Branco materialised. He kicked him behind the knee and the big man fell down.

"Just to ask a few questions," Branco answered.

CHAPTER EIGHTEEN

"Mam, have you seen yourself in that nightie?"

Klara Schuster tapped on the open door of the staff kitchen. The midwife, Joan Reynolds, looked up from the boiling kettle and smiled.

"You smelt the coffee?"

"I'd be grateful for a cup."

Joan brought two mugs to the table.

"How's life?"

"Frantic."

"I was here for the quarterly meeting. So, I thought I'd ask about Donna and her baby,"

"Donna's put on a stone. Baby's just over eight pounds,"

"Good!"

"Now she's worrying we're making her fat."

"Oh! She's a teenager after all!"

"A boy turned up. Black lad. Called Joe."

"The baby's father?"

"When I asked, he just smiled and said, 'No, miss.' He'd stay twenty-four seven if we let him.'"

"Is she feeding the baby?"

"Poor lamb does her best, but we have to supplement her milk."

"What's next?"

"They have nowhere for her at the moment. So, she stays. She's no bother. She and Joe spend all day with the baby. They do everything. She listens and she's smart."

"And the baby's called?"

"Donna won't give him a name. When you ask why not, she says because."

"Because what?"

"Just because."

Klara closed her notebook. Joan said, "Something you should know. Recently, somebody gave that poor child a most vicious beating. I'm surprised the baby survived."

"Would it be this boy Joe?"

"No! Never! He absolutely adores her."

* * * *

Branco said, "It isn't smart not to answer our questions."

The big man's wrists were taped to the table in front of him. Branco had taped his legs to the chair.

"You're not the police."

"We're worse than the police. We're Nemesis."

Daniel stated, "Please answer our questions. Then we will part good friends. We have been very patient. But if you don't answer now, life will become unpleasant. Do you understand?"

"You can't touch me."

Branco said, "My friend will ask you the same question as before. If you don't answer truthfully, I will cut off the top joint of your little finger."

He tapped the nail with the knife blade.

"Who was here when our friend arrived at five fifteen?" Daniel asked.

The caretaker said, "He never come."

Branco put his blade to the top joint of the little finger and pressed down. The knife cut cleanly. The man screamed and stared in shock at Branco. Blood trickled across the table. He stared at the amputation. Branco flicked the fingertip aside.

Daniel repeated the question.

"Who was here when our friend arrived at five fifteen?"

The man looked to Daniel with pleading eyes.

"These people will kill me."

Branco cut off the second joint of the little finger. The victim screamed again and stared at Daniel in utter disbelief.

"You're bliddy savages!"

"Yes," agreed Daniel, sadly, "You have made us savages."

Branco asked, "Who was here?"

The caretaker pleaded with Branco, eyes glistening with tears.

"Please, if I told you, you wouldn't tell him, would you?"

Branco amputated the final joint of the little finger.

The caretaker screamed and wept, his eyes upon his mutilated hand, tears running down his face.

Branco consoled him with, "Now, I will take a whole finger each time you refuse to answer the question."

"Who was here?" asked Daniel.

Through snot and tears, he mumbled, "A tall man in a daft hat. Two men that was police, but now they's private detectives and a woman."

"Speak up!" Branco threatened.

Daniel said, "Describe them."

"The woman was small. Dark hair. Business suit,"

Daniel looked to Branco who nodded.

"The tall man?"

"Suit. Yellow beret. Eye patch. Bad teeth."

He hesitated to continue and Daniel said, "We know the other men."

"What happened?"

"I took the men to the Head's office and opened up for them."

"The woman?"

"She waited at the front door for your friend."

"And when he came?"

"She took him to the office."

"What did you do then?"

"Stayed out the way."

"What does the Head Teacher know?"

The caretaker shook his head.

"Nowt."

"Then?"

"Car come to the front. They got in and drove away."

"Our friend? The man in the yellow beret and woman?"

"Yes."

"Did he say anything? To the driver?"

"He said. The house. That's all I heard."

* * * *

Kimberley lay very still in bed listening. The reappearance of her father had terrified her. When she had returned from school, she smelt him on the landing before she opened the door. The flat stank of cannabis with an afterscent of alcohol. Her mother held up a warning finger. She hugged Kimberley and said quietly, "I'll ring ya Auntie and yi can go for a sleepover with Milly?"

Kimberley said, "I'm not going for any sleepover."

"You like Milly."

"But I love you."

They waited for the man to wake up. Kimberley tackled her homework at the table. She knew it wasn't done well. Her mind was buzzing with anxiety. Her mother sat in the chair waiting. Kimberley knew she had already worked out what she could offer the man to eat before he went out to the pub. After an eternity in a waiting room of hell, they heard him stirring.

Her mother tried to smile at Kimberley. They heard the toilet seat clatter and the toilet flush. When he came into the sitting room, Kimberley almost cried out. He had not shaved his face for some time yet he had shaved his head. She knew what was tattooed on his knuckles and why his head was scarred.

"Hello, Dad," Kimberley greeted him, standing up from her chair. Her knees were pressed back to stop her legs trembling. Her mother had risen too.

"I can smell that stinking rabbit."

"Gulliver's on the balcony. He doesn't come in here."

To his wife, he said, "Thought I told yi to get rid of it, Mel?"

"What can I get yi for tea, Jack? I've got a nice family pie from Dickson's. Can do you egg, chips and bacon, egg, chips, bacon and beans? Or a bacon sandwich?"

While he was mulling over his choices her mother said to Kimberley, "Get your Dad a drink, pet,"

She rose to obey.

"Ya gettin' big, Kimberley. How old yi now?"

She ignored him and her mother answered, "She's just eleven. Changes school next year."

At the refrigerator, Kimberley was tempted to give the can a good shake, but refrained. When she came back to the sitting room, she found he had pulled her mother onto his knee despite her protests. She cracked the can and handed it over. Her mother took the opportunity to escape.

"Right! Egg, bacon, beans and chips, it is!"

She sounded almost jolly and vanished into the kitchen. Kimberley returned to her homework.

"What yous doin'?"

"Homework."

"What kind?"

"The hard kind. Mathematics."

Her father stood up and came to the table.

"Well, let's see if yi can count this."

To her amazement, he scattered twenty-pound notes over her.

"Go on! Count!"

Kimberley counted.

"A hundred pounds!"

"Well, niver say I don't niver give ya nowt!"

"Thank you, Dad! Thank you very much!"

She came around the table to hug him, but felt nothing but surprise.

"Right! Back to your homework."

He watched her as he sipped the lager.

"How's yous doing at school then?"

"I do okay."

"Yi should be top of the class!"

"I am. But I don't go shooting off about it."

He was silent for some time and Kimberley pretended to work.

"And yi've turned out a right bonny lass."

When they heard a clash of plates from the kitchen, her father said, "Divvent mention dosh ti ya Mam."

"No, Dad."

Kimberley went into the kitchen to help bring in the meal. They sat together and ate happily enough. But two lagers later, his mood had changed and they were glad when he departed to go drinking with his mates.

Kimberley and her mother had retired to bed before her father returned. When he fell in the door of the flat, Kimberley almost cried out. She had used an old Geography text to create a wedge under her door, but she didn't feel safe. She heard her mother cry out, but the noise soon ceased.

Kimberley lay looking into the darkness. She said aloud, "When I grow up, I am not going to live like this. I would rather be dead. I really would. We will escape from here, Mam and me. Somehow. I don't know how, but we will."

Kimberley found the sound of her own voice reassuring. She lay sleepless, clutching five twenty-pound notes.

* * * *

Sheena had coaxed her mother out onto the green with Marianne to pass a surprisingly pleasant hour together. The sparrows came to visit Marianne, which astonished her mother and delighted Marianne. Inspired by the cheery presence of the sparrows, they played Two Little Dickybirds. Sheena biroed two little birds' heads on scraps of paper stuck with spit onto her index fingers. When Ginny and Sheena sang, *Fly away, Peter! Fly away, Paul!* the two dickybirds vanished behind Sheena's head, fingers tucked into her palms. Marianne couldn't find the dickybirds anywhere. She was astonished, eyes popping wide. She went around to search Sheena's hair and regarded her sister with awe.

"Again!" she cried, "Again!"

Sheena's phone rang and persisted. The sparrows flew away and a voice she didn't recognise said, "He's on his way to the school. I've just passed him. Okay?"

As the call ended, she recognised who it was. The traffic warden.

"Mam, I really need to go. Emergency! Marianne, I have to run, darling! Back soon."

Sheena left her mother and Marianne singing, Two little dickybirds sitting on a wall. One called Peter and one called Paul. A dickybird called Sheena flew away.

* * * *

Walter Duns walked blindly towards the school railings. He was close to weeping. He had been on the telephone to his dear old friend who had been telling him of the vile way he had seen Lorraine behave with other men. That she behaved in this way brought Walter to a boiling rage, but also to the deepest sorrow. If it were not his lifelong friend giving him the sordid details, he would never have believed it.

Playing in the schoolyard at teatime had become popular. The cricket game had grown. Miss Kaplan had given them chalk to draw a wicket. Morris was batting in great style. Lorraine was sitting with three girls talking and laughing. The Head Teacher was always the first out of the building so the children were free of his unwelcome presence.

Walter appeared at the railing and called, "Lorraine!"

The child rose because she knew now what to say. She skipped down towards the railings. Ask for his telephone number so Mam can ring up. She saw no danger in what she was doing.

Arriving at the railing, Lorraine asked, "Me Mam says, can she have your telephone number so she can talk to Melanie's Mam, please?"

"Of course! What a good idea! Let me find you a pen."

He reached into his inside pocket and Lorraine instinctively came close. The wire noose slipped through the railing and around her neck before she could cry out. Walter pulled on the wire, forcing her face up against the railing.

"I only wanted to be loved!"

Lorraine was struggling for breath, trying to get a hand under the wire that tightened mercilessly, cutting her neck and hair. She knew she was dying. Walter was weeping, pulling on the noose that was cutting her neck. Her eyes turned upwards.

Morris struck him behind the knee with his cricket bat. Walter fell down. The boy had run from the game as soon as he spotted Walter Duns. The cricket bat beat upon his wrists, striving to break his grip on the noose. Somebody tore the man away from the railing and punched him in the face twice, in rapid succession. In the yard, Lorraine fell down and the boldest girl pulled away the noose.

Lorraine drew in a long, ragged breath. Morris recognised the traffic warden who stamped his boot into Walter's groin.

"I was niver here, son," he said and walked away.

Morris saw Miss Kaplan running from the school door. He turned to hear Sheena shout as she ran towards him.

"Where's Lorraine?"

Morris indicated and said, "He said he was niver here."

Sheena ran for the gate. Walter Duns groaned and stirred. Morris threatened him with his cricket bat.

* * * *

The dream began pleasantly. It was a lovely summer's day with the faintest breath of breeze from the river. She was kneeling on the quay beside a boy she knew immediately was Daniel Fallon. A fishing line ran through her hand. Daniel was fishing too. Between them there were dead fish on top of the shabby haversack. Looking down at herself, she saw she was perhaps eleven years old, wearing a dress she remembered from a photograph of somebody's wedding. She was pleased Daniel was no longer old. He smiled at her and she was happy. She was not keen on fishing, but they were together. Daniel laid down his fishing line and stood up.

"Are you alright?"

"Just cramp."

He swung his arms and legs about. Sheena started to rise to join him. The boy pushed her off the quay. As she fell, Sheena felt only surprise, the line tight in her hand. The tide took her when she entered the water and pulled the child under the quay. There the nightmare began. There was a host of bloated corpses caught among the weeds and broken cables. Their eyes were white as the flesh. They smiled at her, beckoning her into their company. As the cold grave-white arms began to draw her in, Sheena began to scream. When she awoke she was still screaming.

Faster than she might have expected, Mam and Morris appeared at the foot of the bed. The boy clutched his cricket bat. Mrs. Galloway wore a pink baby doll nightie.

"It was just a bad dream."

167

Morris said, "I didn't know you had bad dreams when yi were grown up."

Her mother offered, "Yi sounded like yi was murdered."

"Mam, have you seen yourself in that nightie? It must be fifty years old."

"Well, Brian Slater was modelling them on the Quay Sad-da!"

"We live in two different worlds."

Morris asked, "D'y'want me to stay with you, Sheen? Case it comes back? I've got me bat."

Sheena smiled to say, "That's very kind, but you'd only talk all night. Buzz off, the pair of you! Not that I'll sleep after seeing that nightie!"

Mother and son vanished. Sheena waited until the flat was silent and then dialled the hospital on her mobile. When she was put through to the ward she asked, "My sister. Lorraine Galloway. How is she?"

"Fast asleep," the unknown voice replied, "Eaten her supper. Had two goes of ice cream. You can have her back today. Driving us mad with her jokes."

Sheena returned to bed and lay sleepless. She knew now Daniel Fallon had murdered Eric Johnson.

CHAPTER NINETEEN

"Are you gona do that on Tuesday?"

Janet Kaplan let her husband get as far as the bedroom door with the Saturday breakfast tray before she said, "I'm not leaving Ribble Road, Peter. I'm sorry. I know how much you wanted to move to the Lakes."

Whether she expected him to drop the tray, scattering toast crumbs everywhere or continue on his way to the stairs, ruminating on what she'd said, she didn't expect him to say, "Then it's just as well I haven't resigned."

He put the tray down on the dressing table and came back to sit on the edge of the bed.

"You haven't resigned?"

"I thought I'd wait until I was sure you were sure. Sorry. But you have been known to change your mind. That's a woman's perambulator, isn't it?"

His wife smiled.

"Prerogative."

"Which doesn't have any wheels."

"Now you're just being silly."

Peter Kaplan sat looking at her.

"So?" said his wife.

"I'm waiting for you to tell me why we're not going to live the rest of our lives under constant threat of flooding."

"Sheena Galloway told me the children needed me."

"That's alright then if Sheena says so."

"She's right. The Head's useless. He doesn't want to do anything. He cares nothing for the children. He's just waiting out his pension. Waste of space."

"That sounds rehearsed."

"I suppose it is."

169

Peter Kaplan rose from the bed to gather the tray. He looked around the bedroom.

"I've always liked this house."

He vanished downstairs. Janet heard him whistling in the kitchen. As she was getting dressed, she heard the front door open. From the bedroom window, she watched her husband uproot the FOR SALE board.

* * * *

The WPC came the next evening to take a statement from Lorraine who seemed untroubled and told the simple truth. Sheena was amazed how mature she appeared. The constable examined her neck and prepared to leave. Lorraine vanished to her bedroom.

"None of my business, I suppose, but Walter Duns?"

"Went before the magistrate this morning. Pleaded guilty to assaulting your sister and bailed."

Sheena was shocked.

"Bailed?"

"Professional photographer. Out of character, both his principal employers say. Never so much as a parking ticket. Mother died two years ago. Solicitor said he'd never got over the tragedy. And, of course, he pleaded guilty."

"But he tried to kill a child!"

"But he didn't."

Sheena showed the constable to the lift. She fought to contain her anger.

"He'll do it again."

"Let's hope not. Least we know his face."

Sheena listened to the lift as it wheezed its way downward, halting as it always did between three and four to enjoy a good coughing fit, before stumbling on to make the usual crash landing in the lobby that rattled the dentures of the old.

She let herself into Daniel's flat and found it empty. She knew he was out hunting for Guillaume. Sheena struggled not to believe the man was dead.

Aloud, she said, "I really can't dump this on you, Daniel..."

Without forming the words, she had decided to pay Walter Duns a visit.

When the doors opened, Sheena found Daniel waiting for the lift. He looked tired and anxious. She resisted the temptation to hug him. Moliere's words echoed. Who comforts the guardian?

Daniel asked, "Where're you going?"

She didn't say, "Going to the chippie," which is what she should've said.

"That creature got bail. I'm going to pay him a visit."

Daniel stepped out of the lift and the doors closed.

"Don't do that, Sheena."

"He tried to kill Lorraine and they let him out to have another go!"

"Don't go tonight. Go tomorrow."

"I'm not afraid of him!"

"My concern is what you might do to him."

Sheena turned to go.

"I'll try not to."

Daniel decided, "I'm coming with you."

"I don't want you to."

I want you to.

"You're not going on your own."

"I wish I hadn't said anything."

"You should've said, going to the chippie. I'd still've gone with you because Friday is chippie night."

* * * *

Rosebank Crescent was quiet. Lights shone from windows and cars were parked neatly on drives or garaged. There were no lights visible in number five and the car was standing in the road. Sheena parked the Seat behind Walter Duns' car.

As they approached the house, they were greeted with the opening chords of the 1812 Overture. Daniel rang the bell, but there was no response. When they moved to look into the front window, the opening chords of the Overture repeated themselves. Daniel smiled at Sheena.

171

"More tasteful than the yellow rose of Texas?"

Daniel opened the front door while Sheena tried not to watch. He switched off the alarm system and the orchestra laid down their instruments.

Sheena asked, "Should we be doing this?"

"It was your idea."

Daniel switched on the light.

"Lights are normal at number five."

Someone had torn apart every downstairs room. The contents of every kitchen cabinet were on the floor. In the sitting room, the bookshelves had been pulled down and every book torn apart. Every chair had been cut open and the stuffing decorated the carpet. The framed photographs from the walls had been broken and photographs pulled out. In the corners, the carpet had been uprooted. Carpet on the hallway floor had suffered similar outrage. The dining room had been vandalised and the crockery and display china smashed. The delicate cabinets had been thrown down.

Sheena said, "What was he looking for?"

Daniel shook his head.

"Don't know, but he didn't find it."

"How'd you know?"

"Look at the china. He's angry."

Daniel started up the stairs and Sheena demurred.

"We've done this before."

"Then we're better prepared."

The bathroom was cold, clean and searched. Broken glass littered the floor. Both cabinets had been wrenched away. The second bedroom, the child's bedroom in pink, had been similarly outraged. They opened the master bedroom door to find Walter Duns and a girl child asleep in bed amid a sea of mindless destruction. When they approached the bed, they discovered the child was a doll and Walter Duns was dead. Sheena recoiled.

"The creature tore the house to pieces around him."

She was almost sorry for this pathetic corpse cuddling the doll.

"It was a man. Or men who did this."

"How'd you know?"

"He didn't search the bed. The demon wouldn't hesitate. The man or men couldn't desecrate the corpse. Some lingering human feeling that a demon doesn't have."

"How did he die?"

Daniel picked up a stray tablet and the bottle from the duvet.

"Walter still retained some human feeling. He knew what he had done. What did Lorraine say he said?"

"I only wanted to be loved,"

Daniel pulled back the duvet. Walter had soiled himself. Sheena stepped back. Daniel picked up the corpse.

"What're you doing?"

"Searching the bed."

Sheena said, "You're no better than that creature."

"Sadly, that's true."

Treading carefully, Daniel carried the corpse through to the bathroom and laid Walter in the bath. He took Melanie from Sheena and returned her to Walter. Then he reversed the mattress.

Sheena said, "This mattress has been opened before."

The stitching was fine and precise. Daniel cut the mattress open. The envelope of photographs wasn't difficult to find.

"Walter Duns' insurance policy. Out of evil cometh redemption."

Daniel began to lay them out on the mattress.

Repelled by the images, Sheena cried, "They're disgusting! Oh, poor children! I don't want to look at them!"

Daniel continued to lay out the photographs. Sheena could not tear her gaze from the hell these men had created.

"Oh, my God, how could they do this!"

She began to cry and turn away.

Daniel said, "Look at them!"

"No, I won't! I can't!"

"You must! Do you see anyone you recognise?"

Sheena stared at the array of obscenity.

"It can't be."

"It can't be who?"

"He's a Councillor. And him! And."

She stopped and continued very slowly, disbelievingly, "That's Chief Superintendent Gerald Taylor. He's the top copper in Gallin."

"Do you know the man with him?"

"Yes. Tony Buckle."

"The gangster?"

"Yes."

Daniel made no comment, but began to return the photographs to the envelope.

Daniel carried the corpse back to the bed and order was restored.

He checked the bedroom was as they had entered it. Sheena wished to be out of the house.

"Why are you bothering?"

"They didn't find the photographs. The demon will send them back. Or he'll come himself."

* * * *

They sat in the car because Sheena didn't trust herself to drive. She couldn't dispel the images she had seen: the smiling faces of the men, the hopeless eyes of the children.

"Shall I drive?" asked Daniel.

Sheena started the engine.

When she parked beneath the cliff of Hugh Gaitskill House, Sheena said, "I know you killed Eric Johnson. I had this nightmare."

Daniel was silent so long Sheena thought he wasn't going to respond.

"And so, I am eternally damned. But the creature was wrong. I loved Eric. I didn't envy him. I was proud to be the pygmy to his giant. Beware how powerful is this demon that could twist my mind so."

* * * *

At Tillingworth House, Sheena had barely greeted the horses when Mr. Fitzpatrick darkened the stable door.

"Ready to ride? Let's say half an hour?"

"Yes, sir."

As he turned away, Sheena asked, "Three or four to ride, sir?"

She remembered the last humiliation. Mr. Fitzpatrick looked at her with astonishment.

"Four, of course, girl! Can't have an idle mount!"

He shook his head and marched away.

"Dozy girl!"

"Your lucky day, Baldrick," she said to the older pony, "You must've done something right."

The horses and ponies were standing quietly in the stable yard. Sheena heard Mr. Fitzpatrick before she saw the riding party. Baldrick trembled. Sheena soothed him and held his leading rein. There were Mr. and Mrs. Fitzpatrick and the two silent daughters. There was also a stranger, dark suit, tie, scarf, mackintosh, an anonymous face. Mr. Fitzpatrick and the solemn girls were in riding gear. Mrs. Fitzpatrick and the stranger were not. No one said a word of greeting to Sheena, the invisible stable girl.

Mr. Fitzpatrick mounted the gelding. Sheena assisted the girls to mount the mare and younger pony. She could sense Baldrick tremble. As she passed Mrs. Fitzpatrick and the stranger, she smelt the unmistakable stink of evil. For a moment she faltered, but went on to stand at Baldrick's head,

She looked to Mr. Fitzpatrick for instructions.

"Come along, girl! Don't keep us waiting!"

Sheena was surprised.

"You want me to ride, sir?"

"You do ride?"

"Yes, sir."

Mr. Fitzpatrick looked to the stranger in exasperation. Sheena mounted Baldrick and felt him relax. She stroked his neck and whispered to him.

"On Tuesday," said the stranger, "Tillingworth House will receive a very important visitor. His daughter has expressed the wish to visit an English country house and to ride in the parkland. I believe there has been a popular television series recently which has inspired the child."

Mr. Fitzpatrick announced, "This morning we will reconnoitre the route we will take with the visitor. Mostly at a walk. No faster than a trot. Is that understood? We will progress down the hill and turn at the Farther Oak to follow the river. If all goes well, we will cross at the ford and return by Nether Point."

All present nodded obediently. Sheena wanted to ask a question, but was ignored.

"Line abreast! Walk on!"

Baldrick co-operated willingly and stepped forward. The ugly buzzing sound was as disturbing to Sheena as it was to Baldrick. The pony fought to throw its rider, bucking, kicking and turning to bite at Sheena's leg. She lay along the pony's neck, talking to him, stroking to him, allowing him to turn circles, each circle wider until slowly, she brought him under control. Astride the shivering, sweating beast, Sheena realised it was the stranger who had been whirling a length of rubber hose above his head to create a nerve-cracking drone.

Without thinking, Sheena shouted, "Why the hell did you do that? If it'd been your visitor, she would likely break her neck!"

"Standard Met noise-maker," the stranger stated.

"Are you gona do that on Tuesday?"

The stranger didn't reply. Sheena turned Baldrick back to the stable yard. No one said anything. No one moved to stop her. She sponged Baldrick down and curried him. Slowly, he became calm. She led him into his stall and stole him an apple from the bran box. Then she drove home.

* * * *

She was sitting in the Seat struggling with the problem when Branco tapped on the window and smiled. Sheena wound down the window.

"You look upset, Yvette!"

"How does everyone know that?"

"It's an easy face to read."

Sheena hesitated to say, "D'you know anything about horses, Branco?"

"Me? Horses? I know everything about horses. Once I was known as Branco the Bronco Buster!"

Sheena laughed.

"Have you time to listen to me?"

"Sure!"

They went to sit on the grass and Sheena told Branco what had happened at Tillingworth House.

CHAPTER TWENTY

"I'm not much given to thinking."

It was a pleasant room modestly furnished. There was a table and two chairs. There was a sofa in green. The view from the window was dismal; looking down into a yard furnished with variously coloured bins. The nurse ushered Tom Moore into the room and left, closing the door quietly behind him. The journalist instinctively moved towards the table, but Daniel Fallon said, "No, no! Let's share the couch."

He sat down and Tom Moore cautiously followed suit.

"Do I know you?"

"No."

"Are you a psychiatrist?"

"I have been in your situation. Does that qualify?"

"Why are you here?"

"I came to tell you the truth."

Tom Moore snorted.

"What is truth?"

"You are not guilty of attempting to murder your son. That's the truth."

"I cut the rope."

"You were manipulated by an evil entity. In simple terms, a demon took over your brain."

"If I believed you, I might ask why."

"To punish you. To silence you. You know the recent deaths of Gallin children are linked."

Daniel saw the change in the reporter's eyes.

"Who are you?"

"Listen carefully to what I say."

"Why would I do that?"

"I want to save your soul."

Tom Moore laughed.

"They won't hold you much longer. The child is unharmed. You have no memory of the tragedy. You are truly remorseful. You are willing to accept rehabilitation. You will be tagged and released. You will not be allowed within miles of your son. But be patient. And I will give you the evidence to destroy the demon's creatures. Do we have a deal?"

Tom Moore hesitated and then nodded. Daniel held out a card.

"Memorise this number. When you are free, talk to me."

He waited until the reporter nodded again. Tom Moore repeated the number. Daniel put away the card.

"If I don't answer, talk to Sheena Galloway. Hugh Gaitskill House."

* * * *

There were no lights showing at Tillingworth House. Closing the stable door, Sheena switched on the lights. There was an uncertain hesitation before the horses recognised her. Starting with the gelding, she petted all four, feeding them apples. Branco talked to Baldrick who responded eagerly. She waited patiently until they had finished their conversation and fed him the last apples while Branco spoke to the horses and the younger pony.

As she switched off the lights, Sheena sensed the positive atmosphere in the stable. Branco said goodnight and the stable mates responded. In the lampless dark, she smelt the stink of evil drifting from the House and repressed a shudder.

* * * *

An owl questioned the pair as they walked back to the car, but they ignored him. They drove until Sheena could bear the silence no longer.

"Well?"

"Yes. Thank you," Branco replied, "In the pink."

"I mean, did you learn anything?"

"The Fitzpatrick creature has beaten and abused the pony for a purpose."

Sheena interrupted to say, "Next Tuesday, the President of the People's Republic of China's daughter is visiting Tillingworth House while her father tours the country with the Prime Minister. They'll be in Newcastle. His daughter's a big fan of Downton Abbey and wants to visit a stately home."

"The child will die here. Thrown and trampled by Baldrick."

Sheena stalled the car.

"That doesn't bear thinking about."

The car behind overtook with a blast of horn and profanity.

Branco said, "That pony has killed three children. He doesn't understand the concept of murder. He's an animal. He reacts to stimuli."

Sheena sat silent. Cars overtook and added to the cacophony of horns.

Branco said, "Perhaps we should move?"

Sheena ignored him.

"What can I do to stop this?"

"Nothing but what you are supposed to do."

"Watch as the child dies?"

"I've had a word with him."

A confused Sheena repeated, "You've had a word with him?"

"On Tuesday, he won't react to any noise. A bomb exploding wouldn't disturb him. His real name is Goldfoot. He once belonged to a little girl whom he still remembers and loves."

Sheena couldn't think what to say.

"He believes he will be carrying that little girl. She is precious to him. He will make sure no harm comes to her."

Sheena complained, "Couldn't you tell me that first?"

"May we go home now? Before those blue lights arrive?"

When Sheena dropped Branco outside his favourite chippie, he said, "Could I have a lift on Tuesday, please? I've promised them I'm going to take them away from Tillingworth. To a safe place."

"Won't Mister Fitzgerald object?"

Branco smiled at her.

"Sure you don't want chips? I'm buying."

* * * *

Karla Schuster sipped her coffee and tried not to laugh. The midwife, Joan Reynolds said, "The nurses don't find it amusing. They haven't got time to play hide and seek."

"Is the boy, Joe, still in attendance?"

"He's a treasure. He'll do anything the nurses ask. Or before they ask. He'll feed anyone, spends hours talking to the old ladies, listens to the old men. Once he had seen it done, he can make a bed as good any nurse. And he'll clean up the most awful messes. There's competition between the wards for Joe. All he wants is to be within reach of Donna. The staff knows that so they leave him alone."

"But Donna's not Patient of the Year?"

"She hides things. Blankets, diapers, towels, shawls, baby food, anything. Bedside cabinets, lockers, day room, cleaner's cupboards. Anywhere and everywhere. It's irritating and time-wasting to retrieve."

Karla explained, "She doesn't believe such luxuries will continue. When the black Jews, the Lemba, were first admitted to Israel, they persisted in filling their water bottles. They didn't believe such a luxury as water was freely available."

"She's not making any friends."

"But the baby is thriving?"

"Yes. Next week they'll be moved to Eastwood. But Eastwood won't take Joe."

* * * *

Ginny Galloway and Hilda had gone clubbing, Marianne was safely abed and Sheena was reading to Lorraine and Morris when Daniel Fallon knocked on the flat door for the first time. Sheena answered the door. When she saw Daniel she said, "There's a surprise!"

Daniel said, "I need you, Sheena."

"Now?"

"Now."

"I'm baby-sitting the little ones."

"Isn't there someone?"

Sheena called into the flat, "Lorraine, go down to Jenny and see if she'll sit with you. An emergency."

Daniel gave Lorraine a twenty pound note before she ran down the stairs.

Sheena broke the silence to say, "It's Guillaume, isn't it?"

Daniel nodded.

"Why do you need me?"

"However bad it is, I know I can rely on you."

* * * *

Sheena drove down to the Quay where few lights burned. She followed his directions to the smoke houses and parked in the yard. Two women came to the car and Daniel spoke to them. Sheena was regarding with dread the open door of the second smoke house wherein lights showed and shadows moved. The women began to weep afresh. Daniel embraced them and said, "You've done well. Go home now."

They hesitated at the entrance to the smoke house. Taking a deep breath, Sheena stepped in with Daniel. There were two men Sheena didn't know. Hanging from a beam by his wrists was Guillaume Barousse. His corpse was naked. Countless bloody cuts stained the body. Next to him hung the naked body of Eileen Galbraith, the tutor of the Gallin girls who died on the motorway. Sheena recognised her as the woman she saw in the seaside bungalow.

Daniel cried out and fell to his knees. The two men present knelt likewise. Daniel proclaimed, "This is the Angel Gabriel. We shall not see him again in this lifetime."

Sheena knelt in awe. When the group rose, Daniel said, "Why haven't we a ladder?"

The taller man said, "It's coming."

Daniel stood as if expecting more information.

The man continued, "Jean noticed the light. The smoke house was empty when she first searched."

A lorry rumbled into the yard and two strangers entered carrying an industrial ladder. Once in position the man climbed to examine the wrist.

"He used a nail gun."

"He had accomplices."

A hacksaw was passed up to the worker. To Sheena it seemed an eternity as the saw grumbled on in the twilight. Then the wrist broke free and Guillaume's body abruptly hung by his left wrist. As they were moving the ladder, the left wrist tore away from the nails. The corpse fell to the smoke house floor. Sheena went out to weep in the darkness.

* * * *

In the car, Sheena offered, "You said angel."

"Did you think you were alone?"

"Don't know what you mean."

"Alone, with all the forces of evil arrayed against you?"

"Who's you?" Sheena interrupted.

"The sons and daughters of Adam. In this endless battle against evil, does it never occur to you that you are not alone? That you do not fight alone? Do not die alone?"

"I'm not much given to thinking," said Sheena.

The Seat obeyed the red light.

"So, Guillaume, Gabriel was an angel?"

"Gabriel is an angel. Taking on human form, he accepted human limitations. He will return. But when, I know not."

"And Branco?"

"His name is Raphael."

Sheena hesitated.

"And you?"

"I am Daniel Fallon."

"I need to think about this," Sheena Galloway decided.

The towers rose before them haphazardly illuminated; the beacon of the Galloways' giant television surmounted Hugh Gaitskill House. Sheena parked her car and switched off the engine.

"Why did they commit such obscenity upon his body?"

"Because Gabriel knows the Child they seek."

"He didn't tell them?"

"He didn't speak."

In the lift, Sheena said, "He's been here. I can smell him."

She resolved to wash out the lift tomorrow. She hesitated on the landing, but Daniel didn't invite her into his flat.

He said, "The Head of Risborough School didn't arrange this ambush. But it has to be a Head Teacher. There's only one school not co-operating with the Bright Star programme."

"Which is?"

"Ribble Road."

"But that's Lorraine and Morris's school."

* * * *

Sheena slipped into Lorraine's bedroom to find her sister still awake. The wound about her neck stood out clearly.

"I thought you were never coming home."

"I'll always come home."

Sheena sat on the bed and Lorraine cuddled up to her.

"Are you alright?"

"What does that mean? Yesterday I was dying."

"It's what people say when they mean, I'm so glad you're alive and please, don't let this terrible thing darken your life forever."

"Then I'm alright."

Sheena knew it wasn't true. That there were many dark days ahead for this child and the woman-she-was-to-be when the memory of the past would be overwhelming. She vowed to be there when Lorraine needed her.

"Have you got a riddle for me?"

"What is a vampire's favourite fruit?"

A blood orange?

"Don't know. What is a vampire's favourite fruit?"

"A blood orange. You knew, didn't you?"

"Tell you what! I'll get ready for bed. Then we'll take turns whatever you're reading. Okay?"

The book slipped from Lorraine's hands as she drowned in sleep. Sheena slipped the bookmark in the page, put out the light and went to bed. She lay sleepless for a long time listening to the chimes of the old Gallin clock. A kaleidoscope whirled in her head. Past events collided with one another. Everything seemed to be out of control galloping towards an inescapable collision. Suddenly, she was overtaken by fear for Marianne.

She slid into her mother's bedroom and tiptoed to the cot. The baby was wide-awake looking up at her.

"Sheena!" cried Marianne.

"Shush!" said Sheena and smiled.

"Shush!" cried Marianne and chuckled.

Mrs. Galloway began to snore and they both struggled not to laugh. Sheena went back to bed with Marianne's chuckle sounding in her head.

But her dreams were dark and drab. She walked among human shapes that did not speak to her. When she approached they turned away. She approached two women sitting at a café table because she wanted to question them, but the chairs were empty. She sat at the table and a man came to her. She knew him, but could not name him. The man began to lay out playing cards on the table top. When he stopped, she began to turn them over one by one. She knew she was searching for God. When she came to the last four cards, she turned them slowly because she knew God must be under one of these cards. Sheena turned all four and there was no God. The man began to laugh and she recognised him. He was the teacher who walked her around the school that dark Christmas evening to calm her nerves and assaulted her by the kitchen bins.

Sheena awoke struggling with hands that stank of tobacco. When she had collected herself, she rose once again to assure herself the house was secure. She leaned against the front door, locked and bolted, oddly content that Daniel Fallon slept across the hallway.

CHAPTER TWENTY-ONE

"Have you chosen a name for him yet?"

Karla Schuster settled the mother and baby into the ambulance. She was surprised how little Donna Gilbert possessed. There was one small haversack. Everything else was what the hospital had provided, including the baby's soft toys. Since leaving the postnatal floor, Donna said nothing.

Karla had noted none of the ward staff came forward to offer encouraging words to a mother and newborn. The porter helping Donna into the wheelchair clutching the baby seemed restrained. She had ignored the ambulance driver's cheery greeting, "All aboard for Santa Punchup!"

"Where we going?"

Karla replied, "We're going to Eastwood House. Much more suitable for you. You'll have your own room. They'll teach you how to look after baby."

Donna said nothing, but glowered at Karla.

"You're very young," Karla temporised, "It's a big job you've taken on. Raising a child."

She secured Donna's seat belt. Donna freed the belt.

"I'm not your mother. You don't have to fight with me. The ambulance crashes. You get badly hurt. Who cares for your baby?"

Karla checked the baby was secure and invited Donna to do the same.

"That's what a mother does. Baby comes first."

Donna reclaimed her seat and Karla secured the belt.

"My job is to see you're safe."

The driver answered the radiophone.

"I'm not a magician. Eastwood. Mebbes before dark?"

Karla called loudly, "We're waiting for her file."

"Hear that? Okay. Ten four!"

"Have you chosen a name for him yet?"

"Where's Joe?"

"Joe can't come."

"Why not?"

"He's not a mother with a newborn."

"We're not going without Joe."

Karla gathered her patience.

"Donna, I'm not going to argue with you. You are an NHS patient. Joe is not an NHS patient. He can't come with us."

"Then I'm not going."

The driver said, "Let's go, miss!"

"Can't without the file."

The driver left his seat and came around the ambulance to close the rear doors. As he did so a nurse ran across the parking bays waving a fat file.

"Thank God for that!" cried the driver. He snatched the file and thrust it through the closing doors to Karla.

Leaving the hospital grounds, Karla saw Joe on a bicycle pedalling after the ambulance. At the same moment, Donna threw off her belt, stood up and began to free the baby.

"We're leaving and you can't stop us! We're not prisoners!"

The ambulance stopped and the driver looked to Karla.

"Sit down and put your belt back on!"

Donna hesitated and sat down. Karla checked the baby's webbing straps.

"If you promise to behave, I'll let Joe travel with us. Promise?"

Donna nodded.

"But he can't come into the House."

"On your head be it, miss," warned the driver.

Joe cycled towards Karla and stopped.

"I look after her. Nobody else."

"You can't move into Eastwood House."

She saw a handsome young man, straddling the bike, whose devotion to the girl she would not doubt.

"God knows she needs a friend. If I let you travel with us, have I your promise not to try to enter Eastwood House? Unless you're invited? Is that a promise?"

"Yes," said the young man and Karla believed him.

"Come on!"

Karla opened the rear doors of the ambulance and Joe lifted up the bicycle before climbing in himself.

"Bloody hell!" said the driver.

Karla closed the rear doors and walked to the passenger entry.

"I was never here," said the driver, "It was somebody else."

"Will you drive this ambulance?"

"If I was here I would. Which I am not."

He started the engine and entered the traffic. Donna was at peace. Joe sat contentedly, a finger in the baby's grasp. Karla wrote up her notes. The ambulance proceeded to Eastwood House without incident.

* * * *

The guests were assembled on the terrace of Tillingworth House. The terrace was suitably decorated with uniforms, designer dresses and a floral display. The security officers of both countries struggled for invisibility. The air resounded with the pomp and pageantry of the Grenadier Guards regimental band. At the centre of this bouquet of beautiful people were the wife of the President of the People's Republic of China and Mrs. Fitzpatrick of Tillingworth House.

Sheena said, "You wouldn't believe they're here to watch a little girl ride a pony, would you?"

Branco disagreed.

"I would believe it. What is nicer than to see a little girl ride a pony?"

They were standing with the Fitzpatrick mounts in the stable yard. Their charges' coats were shining like the morning sun. Only to be outdone by the glitter of the brasswork. Sheena and Branco were modestly dressed in green overalls and wellingtons.

Mr. Fitzpatrick led the short procession, walking with an excited child of perhaps ten years. This dainty, fragile creature, full of smiles and chatter was dressed in new riding gear. Her nurse/tutor and interpreter followed. The Misses Fitzpatricks, lifeless as ever, followed behind. At some distance, Sheena noted the dark suited figure that had swung the noisemaker in the near-tragic rehearsal.

She nudged Branco who nodded.

"Shall we mount?" announced Mr. Fitzpatrick, as if he had just noticed the horses.

The child came willingly to Sheena.

"Hello, miss! Please stand on the mounting block and I will help you to seat yourself."

The interpreter turned Sheena's simple words into music.

"Left foot into the stirrup, please."

The interpreter chirruped and the child complied.

"Now I will steady you as you bring your right leg over the pony."

The child sat in the saddle, feet in the stirrups, clutching the reins, aglow with excitement.

Sheena said, "This is a very good pony. His name is Goldfoot."

She couldn't resist lying, "He was Lady Mary's pony when she was a child."

She saw the wonder in the child's eyes and considered the lie worthwhile.

"Seat yourself comfortably. Goldfoot will keep you safe. Trust to him. Please, enjoy the ride."

The child listened to the interpreter, smiled and said something to Sheena. The interpreter said, "The daughter says thank you! Now she is at Downton Abbey."

"Shall we proceed?" suggested Mr. Fitzpatrick.

Sheena took the leading rein of Goldfoot and the riding party moved out from the stable yard onto the open paddock. The band struck up The Galloping Major.

"Walk on!" called Mr. Fitzpatrick.

Out of sight within the yard an horrendous buzzing noise erupted. Sheena saw the Fitzpatricks' hands tighten on the reins. The horses and ponies ignored the bedlam and stepped forward together. Sheena saw the delight in the child's face and the dismay in Mr. Fitzpatrick's. Goldfoot bore his charge safely down the long slope towards the Farther Oak. Sheena tucked up the leading rein, called,

"Ride on, Lady Mary!" and stepped away. She saw the child understood what she said.

The company of horses walked down the slope and approaching the Farther Oak broke into a controlled trot. Sheena heard the applause of the onlookers and watched as they turned to walk the mounts along the river.

Sheena knew what the Fitzpatrick creature would do to Goldfoot when the captains and the kings had departed. To the two Chinese women, Sheena said, "Please tell the lady wife, Mister Fitzpatrick would like to make a gift of the pony to the daughter. If that is acceptable."

Sheena found Branco behind the milking sheds. The whole estate had deserted post to enjoy the party at the House. Branco held the man who had swung the hose to kill the child. He turned with pistol in hand as Sheena rustled through the long grass.

"Our friend is a dentist. There was a patient he lusted after who would have nothing to do with him. Therefore, he was easy to corrupt."

The dentist babbled, "You let me go, I promise I'll never do anything like that again. I promise. Please! My wife will be wondering where I am."

Branco said, "You don't understand. You have failed your infernal friend. He has no more use for you. He will find and kill you."

"Oh, my God! Oh, my God!"

"So, it's really a question of who kills you. The demon. Or me."

"Please, I have two little girls. Nine and eleven. I swear I'll do anything if you let me go."

"You were prepared to kill another little girl. With never a thought of what might follow."

He kicked something metallic in the grass.

"This is the holding tank for dairy waste. It's sprayed on the fields. It is an impressive size. Do I shoot you before you enter? Or do I invite you to dive in?"

The amorous dentist began to scream and struggle within Branco's grasp. Suddenly, he broke free and began to run, wailing loudly. Sheena began to chase and then stopped, as Branco hadn't moved.

"You let him go?"

"He can't run away from himself."

* * * *

Daniel heard Sheena cross the landing, but still pretended to be surprised when she walked into the flat.

"You're not doing my old heart any good,."

Sheena brought two lagers from the kitchen and cracked a can for Daniel.

"Whenever you're ready," Daniel suggested.

"Whenever I'm what?"

"Whenever you're ready to tell me why you're so angry."

Sheena was silent. Daniel waited.

"Why did you kill the Fitzpatricks? Those poor girls! It's in the Gazette. Fire Tragedy at Tillingworth."

"We didn't kill them."

The anger in Sheena began to fade.

"They failed and he killed them. You can have no sympathy for the Fitzpatrick creature. In the past twenty years, there have been three riding accidents in which Fitzpatrick has been involved and children have been killed. He sold his soul, but worse, he sold the souls of his wife and daughters."

"The horses? What about them?"

"Goldfoot has gone to Beijing. The gelding, mare and pony to a sanctuary."

"Thank you."

"The demon's power is waning, but he's still a very present danger. We must find and destroy him before he slips from this world."

* * * *

Nobody ever used the bell at the Galloways door.

Ginny said, "Who can that be?"

"Yi could find out if you opened the door."

As Marianne was nestled on Hilda's lap, Ginny rose to answer the repeated summons. A Salvation Army officer smiled at her and Ginny responded.

"If I could take a moment of your time?"

"I never discuss religion at the door."

"Quite right, madam! But I'd like to take a moment of your time to see if you would qualify for our new carpet cleaning service. Our new community project. Do you qualify for benefits?"

"Aye, wi do. Me narves."

"Then the service would be free. And depending upon the age of your carpeting, we would replace it free of charge."

"Well, it is looking a bit manky."

"Then may I step in for a moment and take some measurements?"

Ginny said, "Yi'll have ti take us as we are."

The officer found the door closed in his face by Hilda who said, "Not tonight, Napoleon."

"Why did yi do that?"

"Didn't yi think it a bit dodgy? This time of night?"

"But you knew his name!"

* * * *

The text buzzed as Karla Schuster slipped into her car. She looked at the screen and sighed deeply.

"I'm going home," she said aloud, "I'm tired. My feet ache. I'm hungry."

She switched on the engine and headed for Eastwood House.

The House Mother said, "I need to talk to you about Donna Gilbert."

They were sitting in the cramped office that was once perhaps the butler's pantry. Around them, the House rumbled on, voices, music, shouts, doors, babies.

"What has she done?"

"It's all very trivial."

"Which is even more annoying."

191

"We ask her to do something and she agrees. But she simply doesn't do it."

"She neglects the baby?"

"No, no! She's a very attentive mother. But we all have to share the housework. Girls complain they've done their share and Donna's playing with her baby."

Karla looked up from her notes to sympathise.

"Running a household of young mothers isn't easy. I know."

"She's always stealing and hiding things."

"From the others?"

"No! Diapers, clothes, blankets, baby food, bottles, anything and everything. Hiding her loot in any cupboard, under beds, behind furniture."

"We've met this before."

"Well, it's very irritating to put it all back where it belongs."

For the first time Karla thought, She's planning to run.

She decided not to share this thought with the House Mother.

"And then there's her boy. He's always in the garden."

"Does he leave if you ask him to?"

He's waiting to be invited in.

"Yes, but the staff doesn't like him being there. The girls, of course, being girls."

"He means no harm. He's not interested in any girls. He's devoted to Donna. You're fortunate! You have your own security man out there!"

The House Mother was not impressed.

"What're you going to do about Donna?"

"Give me two weeks and I'll find her a flat."

Karla carried out a cheese sandwich and a cup of coffee to Joe and they sat on a bench together while he ate and drank. Karla took time to look him over. He was dressed in tee shirt, jeans, anorak, and trainers. His hair was trim. He was clean and muscular. She resisted the temptation to ferret for more information.

"You love Donna?"

"Not like what you mean. She's a kid."

"But you have feelings for her?"

"I told you. Not like what you mean."

"But you care for her?"

"You know I do."

"So how did you come to care? Have you known her long?"

Joe fidgeted and sought the last crumbs of the sandwich. Karla waited.

"This like between you and me?"

"Just you and me."

"I was going up these stairs."

"Where?"

"In this house, like."

"You were burgling?"

"The window was open."

"Go on!"

"This voice said, like, 'Joe, I got a job for you.' I was scared so bad I couldn't speak. Then it showed me this girl sleeping in a green bin on its side. 'You have to look after this girl, Joe. It's a very important job.'"

"You remember all that?"

"I'll never forget it."

Karla said, "You spend all day here?"

"Why won't they let me in? I would help."

"Because the rules say no."

"What if we don't agree with the rules?"

"Stay out, Joe. You can't help her if you're locked up."

CHAPTER TWENTY-TWO

"We don't kill people. We punish them."

The clock in the hallway chimed midnight as Peter Kaplan came home drunk. His wife Janet heard a scratching at the front door and approached it cautiously. She gripped the baseball bat tighter and opened the door. Peter Kaplan, key in hand, said, "Keep the door still, damn you!"

Janet watched her husband struggling to fit his key into the keyhole.

"The door's open."

"I can see that, thank you."

Janet stood aside to allow him to enter.

"I've been worrying about you."

"No need. I'm a big boy."

Janet helped him off with his coat and hung it up. She took the key from his hand and put it on the hall table.

"Where've you been?"

Peter ignored his wife and wandered into the sitting room. He sat in his chair and switched on the television. Janet followed her husband and switched off the television.

"I could do with a drink."

"I've made coffee. Sit there and I'll bring you a cup."

Janet poured her husband a mug of coffee and switched off the percolator. She returned to find Peter pointing the wrong end of the tuner at the television set. She gave him the coffee and took away the tuner.

"Where've you been, Peter?"

"Out with friends."

"Never like this."

Her husband was silent and Janet said, "I rang your friend, Allan."

"The telly's not working."

"It's broken. He said you left the stamp club at nine."

"Which reminds me."

Peter sought something from his breast pocket while Janet struggled to keep patience.

"Can you imagine how that worried me?"

Peter took a plastic envelope from his pocket and offered it to Janet. It contained a single stamp.

"The Zeppelin orange. Michael found it in Luton of all places."

"How much did that cost?"

"Why would you want to know?"

Janet kept patience and said nothing.

"Put it in the bureau before I lose it."

Janet put the stamp away in the bureau drawer.

"Where have you been since nine?"

"Met an interesting chap at the club. John. Worked in the postal service when Nairobi was Nairobi."

"You've been missing three hours, Peter!"

"Hoping to become a member. Salvation Army chap. Never met one before."

"How did you know he was Salvation Army?"

Peter regarded his wife with amusement.

"How did I know he was Salvation Army? Because he was wearing the uniform!"

He shook his head at her ignorance.

"You've been drinking that dreadful wine Allan makes."

"It's getting better."

"It'll never get better."

"You've never thought much of Alan, have you? Could've been a professional magician. Ever seen him do that trick where he tugs a string and pulls your card out of his nose?"

"Unfortunately, yes. But you left Alan's at nine. It's after midnight."

The hall clock chimed to confirm her words.

"Where have you been, Peter?"

"Well, after we elected John to the club, he suggested we go on to a club he knows. So, we did. Just to talk."

"Where you got drunk. What did John think of that?"

"Oh, he can certainly put it away!"

"Salvationists don't drink, Peter."

"Must've been his night off then."

Janet Kaplan awoke to find her husband sitting on the end of the bed.

Confused, she asked, "What time is it?"

"This is not how I expected life to be, Janet. John agreed. Very understanding chap."

Janet sat up in bed.

"What're you talking about, Peter?"

Her husband turned to her as if he'd only just realised she was there.

"I'm talking about us."

"I'd gathered that much."

"We've worked hard all our lives. Now we should be starting to reap the rewards. See something of the world before it's too late. John said he understood completely. It's natural to seek freedom. Couldn't have phrased it better myself. To seek freedom."

"This is the Salvation Army man?"

"Wise man! Though I suppose you should expect it. Salvation Army. Solving people's problems."

"Do we have a problem?"

"Yes, actually! It's sleeping in the spare room with its baby."

Janet was shocked.

"You're talking about Ellie and Sean?"

"I'm talking about the parasites that have invaded our home."

"You're not serious?"

"I wanted to take you cruising. But, oh no, we can't go! Ellie and Sean! I would like to take you touring in Scotland, but, oh no! We can't go. Ellie and Sean. I would like us both to retire and buy a caravan, but, oh no! Ellie and Sean."

"I never thought you felt like this."

"Didn't you? Perhaps I'm too acquiescent. That's what John said. Too acquiescent. We don't have children because you didn't want to. I would've loved a son. A son and daughter? I could've taken that post in Germany, but you wouldn't leave that damn school. I wouldn't be stuck where I am now bored beyond tears."

Janet was silent. She found it difficult to speak. Her whole world was dissolving before her eyes.

"We're stuck with two cuckoos in the nest sucking the life out of us. That's what John said. Sucking the life out of us."

Janet found her tongue. She spoke slowly as if she were listening carefully to her own words. The pain in her breast was overwhelming.

"If things had been different. If we'd had children this is exactly what our life would be. Supporting a daughter or daughter in law in trouble. It wouldn't all have stopped at the church door. It would only have begun."

Peter Kaplan stood up.

"You stupid woman! This Ellie Martin isn't our daughter! Or our daughter in law. This baby isn't our grandson! You're living a fantasy! They're cuckoos! John's right. And it has to end!"

Peter Kaplan vanished from the bedroom. Janet rose slowly to find her dressing gown.

She was tying the dressing gown cord to follow her husband downstairs when she heard Ellie scream. The baby Sean began to cry. When she got to the bedroom door, she saw Ellie lying on the floor with blood pumping from her chest. The young woman was conscious. Peter was holding the baby down on the bed with a kitchen knife raised.

"Peter! For God's sake! What're you doing?"

Peter faltered and turned to his wife. His eyes were wild.

"He's a baby, Peter! A baby! Don't kill the baby!"

It always seemed to Janet that her husband woke up. He dropped the knife and stepped back from the bed.

"What've I done? My God, what've I done?"

Janet took a towel from the bathroom and got Ellie to press on the blood flow from the wound below her left breast. She didn't move her, but propped a pillow under her head. She calmed the baby Sean and gave him to his mother. He stopped crying. Parting with the child, she thought, *This may be the last time. Goodbye, darling.*

Peter was sitting on the single bed.

"Are you alright?"

He didn't answer.

"Stay there until I come back to you."

Janet Kaplan went downstairs to telephone police and ambulance. Then she phoned Sheena Galloway who awoke confused.

"Miss Kaplan?"

"Tell your man to look for a Salvation Army officer. Calls himself John."

"Has something happened?"

Janet closed the call.

Then she climbed the stairs to the room where her marriage ended.

* * * *

Daniel was standing by the Seat when Sheena, Lorraine and Morris came to the car.

Sheena said, "We don't give lifts to strange men."

"Daniel's not strange," defended Morris.

"Oh, yes, he is," said Sheena, "You don't know the half of it."

Lorraine asked, "What's round, aggressive and very bad tempered?"

Silence fell on the morning.

Daniel said, "A vicious circle."

Lorraine clapped and said, "Daniel deserves a lift."

Sheena opened the car doors.

"Get in, monkeys!"

Daniel sat in front with Sheena.

"Where to, milord?"

"Ribble Street school, please. I'm going to have a word with the Head Teacher."

Lorraine said, "He's not very nice."

She looked to Morris for support.

"Some call him Pig-guts."

Daniel looked for an explanation.

"Piggott."

"But not you and Lorraine?"

Lorraine shook her head.

Her brother said, "If he comes into the classroom you know somebody's in dead trouble."

"He never comes to watch any games. It's all down to Miss Kaplan that we have a team."

"Well, forewarned is forearmed," Daniel offered.

He looked to the children.

"Don't worry. I can look out for myself."

The children ran into the yard. Daniel and Sheena sat in the car.

"Mister Kaplan's been taken into custody under the Mental Health Act. Ellie's in the General. Wounds not life-threatening."

"Wounds?"

"He stabbed her three times. Baby Sean is with a foster mother."

"And Missis Kaplan is on duty at Ribble Road."

Janet Kaplan had appeared at the school door. She blew her whistle.

Daniel said, "That's where you'd expect her to be. At her post. Safeguarding the children."

"Keeping calm and carrying on," offered Sheena.

The yard was empty and the last latecomer had scurried through the doors into school.

Sheena said, "Lorraine and Morris are in there with a lot of other children."

"I merely wish to talk to him."

"I hope I can believe you."

"I was hoping you'd wait for me."

"Unless I hear gunfire."

Daniel stepped through the school doors into the empty corridor. To his right were doors marked GENTS and LADIES. To his left the door declared RECEPTION. Daniel opened the door onto an older lady seated at a desk. He entered and smiled at the top of her head as she continued tapping at the keyboard. He waited politely until she had completed her task.

"Yes?"

There was no warming smile.

"I'd like to see Mister Piggott, please."

"This is a busy time for him."

"I'll wait."

Daniel could hear the sounds from afar of a school at Morning Assembly.

"You can't wait in here."

Daniel said cheerfully, "I'll stand in the corridor and catch him when he's free. I used to be a salesman."

The receptionist looked at him soberly. Daniel smiled.

"It can't be easy being the guardian of the Gate."

"What did you want to see Mister Piggott about?"

"I have twin boys of about school age," Daniel lied, "and I was told this is a very good school. My first stop this morning."

He smiled again, the doting father looking for an honest school for his cherubim.

"Then perhaps you should talk to Missis Kaplan?"

"Is she the Deputy Head?"

"She deals with parents."

"I'm sorry, but my wife said to be sure to speak to the Head Teacher. He sets the tone for the school. Our new neighbours were very positive about Mister Piggott."

Daniel's smile was breaking his face.

"If I may say so, I'm the CEO of a substantial stationery firm. I'm sure I could solve any budgetary problems you may have concerning stationery, jotters, paper, paints, arts materials. That sort of thing."

The receptionist surrendered.

"What name should I say?"

"Daniel."

The receptionist hesitated.

"Daniel?"

"Yes. Daniel."

The lady vanished through the door beside her desk. Daniel listened to a murmur of voices from the inner office. From the middle distance, he heard the school break up from Assembly. There were feet and voices in the corridor. It was a considerable time before the receptionist returned.

"The Head Teacher will see you now, Mister Daniel."

"Thank you. Very kind."

"He's not been well."

Despite the scent of peppermint, Daniel could smell alcohol. He recognised the botched operation on his harelip.

"It's been a long time since last we met, Harelip."

Ronald Piggott half-rose from his chair in greeting, but sat down again.

"Do I know you?"

"We shared a classroom once. You were the boy with your odious mates who dragged that poor girl into the boys' toilet and pulled down her knickers. God knows what would have happened if Alec Skinner hadn't walked in. You turned that child from a bright happy girl to a miserable mouse who grew up cutting herself until the final cut."

"I don't know what you mean. But I'd like you to leave this office now!"

"You always hated Alec and when you saw him, skipper of Arbroath Lady, with a fine boy, Bobby, you couldn't bear it. Did you push him? Or offer a hand that wasn't there when it was needed?"

"That is an absolutely outrageous accusation!"

"Then when someone started taking an interest in Alec, he was murdered. Not by you. You wouldn't have the guts."

Ronald Piggott started to come around the desk, but changed his mind. He picked up the phone. When Daniel continued to speak, he put it down.

"You betrayed my Captain and my friend to the demon. Were you there? Did you take your turn to cut Guillaume as so many of your foul breed did? Were you there when they crucified my friend? Did you applaud?"

Ronald Piggott began to weep.

"You can't know how it's been."

Daniel interrupted, "You signed up with the demon. You made a good bargain as far as it went, but the day of reckoning is at hand."

Piggott wailed, "You can't kill me! You can't! That would be murder!"

Daniel came around the desk and the wretched man struggled to escape, but failed.

"Now where would it be?"

Daniel opened the top drawer of the desk.

"No. Second drawer? No."

He opened the bottom drawer and took out the whisky bottle. "Here we are!"

Before Piggott grasped what was happening, Daniel forced open his mouth, thrust the bottle neck down his throat and poured a substantial quantity into his stomach.

Daniel released him spluttering and coughing.

"Well, it's been a pleasure, Harelip, meeting again after all these years. To exchange memories, honour old friends. Happy days! What chums we were, eh?"

On his way through the office he said to the receptionist, "If you're a sensible woman, you'd know it's time to go home now."

* * * *

Sheena saw Daniel emerge from the school and gave a sigh of relief. No one rushed out after him with a pistol. The school didn't explode. Daniel walked past the Seat to a car parked farther down the pavement. He spoke to the driver and then returned to Sheena.

Sliding into the car, Daniel said, "That went well."

In the rear mirror, Sheena saw an older lady bustle out of the school and march away.

"If I knew what was happening, Daniel?"

Two men in neat suits carrying briefcases exited the farther car and walked to the school gate.

"Who are they?"

"Two of Her Majesty's Inspectors. They're going to inspect Mister Pollard."

"Tell me what you've done."

"Mister Pollard is an alcoholic. He is no longer Head of this school."

"So, you haven't killed him?"

"We don't kill people. We punish them."

CHAPTER TWENTY-THREE

*"Me Mam always has an eye out
for dodgy old men."*

A young woman answered the door to Klara Schuster who opened her mouth, but closed it when the young woman said, "I know who you are. You're Welfare. Eleanor's in her hidey-hole."

The House Mother was in her butler's pantry cum office.

Klara said, "This your hidey-hole?"

"When I want them to think they've upset me, I dodge in here. Works a treat. They always come to apologise."

"The continuing saga of Donna Gilbert?"

"All quiet on the Donna front, but last night two men attempted to break into the House."

"Anyone hurt?"

"No. They were trying to force a window when Joe found them.

"Meeting Joe in the dark must've been a surprise."

"A big surprise! He fought them both. Gave more than he got. When they ran for it, he caught the younger man, but the older man got away."

"He would've thought they were after Donna."

"The police weren't a big help. Released with a caution. And Joe was warned that charges might be brought against him."

"Why?"

"Apparently you mustn't hit burglars and make them cry."

"I must have a word with Joe. Is he out there?"

"You'll find him in the kitchen."

Klara looked at the House Mother.

"Oh, Eleanor, what've you done!"

"The girls insisted."

"You're such a stickler for the rules."

"I've hired him."

"You don't have the budget."

"He gets his meals. His hours are eight to eight. He's not allowed upstairs. He does any job he's asked. The girls say they feel safer. And Donna behaves herself."

Klara was silent.

"Are you putting this in your report?"

"The problem is Donna's so young."

"Joe doesn't behave like that. He's not her boy friend. He's not interested in the girls."

"How d'y'know?"

"Seen too many of them. If I thought otherwise, I wouldn't dream of letting him into the House. He behaves as her brother."

Klara said, "I must find a flat. Then she won't be your responsibility."

"And we won't have to hunt the House for diapers."

"Ring me if she stops stealing."

* * * *

A seagull had found Sheena's car in the lane behind Mr. Singh's mini-mart. From the rooftop, he shared a big laugh with his mates. Sheena, cleaning the droppings from her windscreen, water bottle in one hand, sponge in the other, ignored him. At the end of the lane, Kimberley appeared and ran towards her. She arrived breathless.

When she struggled to speak, Sheena said, "Slow down, Kimbo! Or you'll burst. How'd you find me?"

"Shop. Said you'd just left."

"Well, if it wasn't for a certain seagull, I'd be long gone. What's the damage?"

"He's coming with a bicycle. I said no, but he insisted."

"When did you see him?"

"I was coming out of school. He said it was a special prize. For me."

"He's coming to the house?"

"He said to be there. Half four."

Sheena glanced at her watch.

"I must get back."

"I'm coming with you."

Relief lit the child's face.

"I hoped you would."

"Get in the car."

Sheena phoned Daniel and reached voice mail. Branco answered and she explained the situation.

In the car, Kimberley said, "He's not from the Gazette. He's wearing a Salvation Army uniform."

As they drove, Sheena said, "How's things at home?"

"Dad's back, but he hasn't done anything bad. He gave me some money and said not to mention it to Mam. I don't know what to do."

"How much?"

"A hundred pounds."

"Buy your own bike. Take Dad with you."

* * * *

Mel McLeod went to answer the door. An older man and a younger with a shaven head stood outside. They both had bruised faces. Mel braced herself against the door.

"Yes?"

"Is it McLeod?"

"Yes. But he's not."

The older man threw her down and walked over her. The young man dragged her from the floor by the hair and slammed the front door. She had just enough breath to shout, "Jack!" before he muzzled her with a dirty hand. A surprised Jack McLeod arrived from the bedroom.

"What the hell's going on?"

When the young man dumped Mel on the couch, Jack came at him. The older man put a pistol to his head.

"Behave yourself!"

The older man pushed Jack towards a chair.

"Sit down."

"You touch my wife again."

The older man rapped his head with the pistol. Jack didn't blink. A trickle of blood ran down into his ear.

Mel said, "Who are these men?"

"Never seen them afore."

Mel asked, "Wha'd'y'want? There's no money here."

She glanced at the young man standing behind the couch.

"Best yi can do? Threaten a woman with a knife?"

The older man said, "Sit still and shut ya gob."

The silence was brief. When Mel heard the key in the door she shouted, "The bairn! That's what they're after!"

Regardless of the gun, Jack launched himself at the older man and they went to the floor together. The gun fired. Mel bounced up. The young man came over the couch at her. Mel stabbed him with the knife she'd taken from under the cushion. He stared at her with surprised eyes and fell back onto the couch.

Branco, Sheena and Kimberley burst into the room.

"Mam!" cried the child, but Sheena restrained her.

The older man sat astride Jack with the pistol in hand. Before Branco could interfere, Mel slashed at the hand holding the gun. The pistol fell away. Jack overcame his opponent, pounding his head on the floor.

"Whoa!" Branco advised, "That's enough."

Sheena released Kimberley to hug her mother. The young man lurched from the couch and fled, holding a cushion against his wound.

Jack McLeod dragged the unconscious man out onto the landing and bundled him down the stairs. He returned to hug his wife.

"You okay?"

Mel nodded.

"You did good, kiddar."

Jack sat comforting Mel on the couch. Kimberley hugged Sheena.

"Thank you, Sheena."

Branco said, "Jack, this is where your life changes, man! When your daughter was threatened, you ignored the gun. When you were about to die, your wife saved your life. Everything changes now."

There was blood on the stairs, but no sign of the older man. As they walked, Sheena asked, "D'y'think things will change?"

"The answer to most questions is," said Branco, "why not?"

* * * *

Klara climbed out of the old Ford Transit when Donna and Joe appeared. Donna was lugging a carrycot. Joe was loaded down with more of the House's baby supplies than he should carry.

Donna said, "Oh, no!"

She stepped back.

Klara asked, "How far d'y'think you're going to get?"

Joe stepped forward.

"We're not going back."

"I don't think they want Donna back."

Joe said, "What now?"

"Open the back and put the stuff in the van."

Joe baulked.

"I'm not going to repeat myself."

Joe dropped his burdens, opened the van doors and began to load their acquisitions as fast as he could.

Donna said, "Why're you doing this?"

"I don't know," Klara said, "But it feels right."

Joe closed the van doors. Klara led them to the passenger door.

"Can you drive?"

"Yes."

"Have you a licence?"

Joe shook his head.

"Not good enough."

Klara pulled the passenger door open.

"Hi!" said Branco at the wheel, "I used to drive the Mille Miglia 'til I crashed."

"This is Branco. He tells lies. He's going to drive you wherever you wish. But don't tell me. I don't need to know."

She looked into the carrycot and smiled at the child.

"This child needs hansling. An ancient custom."

With a coin, she stroked a cross on the baby's brow. She gave the coin to Donna, saying, "Your son is not penniless and never will be."

When the carrycot was safely strapped down to the rear of the bench seat, the runaways climbed aboard.

"Has this baby got a name yet?" asked Klara.

* * * *

Sheena and Marianne were enjoying blowing dandelion clocks when a shadow fell over them. Daniel sat down to join them. Marianne's court of sparrows fluttered away, but returned, having assessed Daniel as harmless.

"How are you?" Daniel asked.

"Considering the roller coaster I ride, I'm fine. I surprise myself. Normal life is abruptly displaced by the distinctly unpleasant. And I cope."

"War's like that. Ninety-five per cent boredom and five per cent sheer terror."

"I have no idea how the war is going."

"We don't issue bulletins."

"We're losing?"

"We are winning. We are better co-ordinated than ever. We have neutralised a number of attempts on children's lives and taken a number of dangerous people out of the game. But the more frustrated the demon is, the more dangerous he is."

Sheena looked to Marianne who had a mouthful of dandelion seeds.

"Come here, cuckoo!"

Marianne obediently complied and sat patiently as Sheena cleaned her face.

"I'm not sure of Hilda," Sheena offered.

"Just instinct?"

"Not sure. I cleaned the lift this morning and I walked the stairs. I could smell him. He comes here. He could be meeting Hilda."

Marianne stood up and said, "Daniel."

She lifted her arms to him. Daniel was as surprised as Sheena.

"Up!"

Daniel took the child into his arms. Sheena felt her anxieties dissolve as she saw the child's complete faith in Daniel. Marianne laughed.

"If only I had a cam'ra," said the familiar voice.

They looked up to find Ginny and Hilda had arrived. Sheena noted Hilda did take a photograph with her mobile phone.

"Afore yi start, I don't mean owt. Just Granda with the grandbairns. Right, Hilda?"

Hilda bent down and scooped up Marianne who didn't protest.

"Where've you been, Mam?"

"Down the Council."

"What're you pestering them for now?"

Hilda said, "Ya Mam's fed up with all them stairs."

"Mam, you're not an old woman!"

"She's asking mebbes cud she get an exchange. On account of her nervous condition."

Sheena felt threatened.

"There's nothing wrong with the lift, Mam. It's clean enough."

"What if it got stuck?"

"You pee in a carrier bag 'til they mend it."

Sheena wanted to say *I'm not leaving the flat because Daniel's across the landing and I feel safe.*

She said, "You wouldn't get as much room in one of the other flats. And the O'Hooligans would be dancing on your head."

Watching them wander across the grass towards the tower, Daniel said, "Was that a little dig about me being an old man?"

Sheena laughed, saying, "Yes. Me Mam always has an eye out for dodgy old fellers."

* * * *

A car stopped on the farther side of the green.

Daniel said, "Sorry. Got to go."

"Be careful," Sheena advised.

For a fleeting moment, she was tempted to kiss him.

"Be aware," replied Daniel.

She watched him walk across the grass and slip into the car without looking back.

* * * *

For laziness Sheena took the lift, but as soon as she stepped out onto the landing she knew everything was wrong. The flat door hung from one hinge. Hilda was dead in the sitting room under the smashed television set. It was obvious she had fought like a Bengal tiger. Her body was broken and mutilated.

The bedroom door was splintered. Ginny Galloway had fought to the death for her baby. The kitchen knife she had picked up as she retreated had been used upon her. There was blood everywhere, but Marianne had gone.

Sheena was too shocked to weep. She took blankets from the bedroom to cover the dead women. Then she went out onto the balcony to ring Daniel. The call went straight to voice mail. She rang Branco, but his phone was turned off. Then Sheena began to weep.

CHAPTER TWENTY-FOUR

Marianne's tiara was much admired.

Daniel had stated, "Don't argue. You and the children shall have my place. I'll be fine in Guillaume's van. We can't have them taken into Care."

They sat in the flat. They could hear the voices of the forensics team, passing on the landing. Daniel had made coffee, but neither could face breakfast. Lorraine and Morris were still sleeping, drained of tears. Sheena was numb, stripped of all emotion. Making the formal identifications, she felt herself to be performing in a television crime show.

Daniel offered, "There's nothing you could've done."

"I wonder if I'd've fought like them. Or run away. I was wrong about Mam. She was no coward. I was so wrong about Hilda. She could've stepped aside, but she loved Marianne. Poor lamb!"

"Don't let yourself believe Marianne is dead. If that's what he wanted, you would've found her there."

"Why would he keep her alive?"

"Because tonight, at midnight, he will return to Hell and take Marianne with him."

Sheena struggled with rising hysteria. She knew if she began to scream, she would never stop. She forced herself to ask, "How d'y'know?"

"Because it has happened before."

"What're you going to do?"

She didn't expect an answer, but struggled not to break down. She wished with all her heart she had gone up with Mam and Hilda. There would be no more pain. It would all be over now. But she had wanted to stay with Daniel on the grass.

"Tonight, we'll kill the monster and save Marianne."

Sheena heard herself laugh.

"How you gona to do that? You've no idea where she is!"

"No," Daniel agreed, "but the sparrows do."

"What did you say?"

"I want you to look to Lorraine and Morris today. If you can get them out of here and take them somewhere to distract them, do so. That's the most important job."

"What'll you be doing?"

"Tonight, we win or lose this battle."

"You're not going to answer my questions, are you?"

"This is no time for questions, Sheena."

* * * *

Karla locked the car and walked as far as the police tape. When she tried to lift the tape, the constable called, "Whoa there! You can't go in."

"I'm the Welfare Officer."

"There's nothing for you to do, miss."

"What happened?"

"Fire started in the kitchen. They did good saving what they did."

Karla stared at the smoke-blackened windows of Eastwood House. The bedrooms above the kitchen area had suffered most.

"Everyone out safely?"

The constable shook his head. Karla felt suddenly sick.

"Two of the girls."

Karla fought not to weep.

"They were dropping the bairns out the window. Got the bairns out, but got caught by the smoke."

Karla could bear no more. She turned away from the small crowd of sensation-seekers. On a quiet pavement, she wept silently into her scarf. She was joined by a Salvation Army officer who said, "All your fault, Karla."

Shocked, she asked, "Sorry? What did you say?"

"If you hadn't helped that girl run away, this wouldn't have been necessary."

Karla stared at him in disbelief.

"We would have acted with discretion. But you never learn, do you? So, you've been punished."

Karla looked about for help, but there was none.

"Where has our runaway gone?"

"I don't know. If I did know, I would never tell you."

"I thought that's what you'd say."

The car accelerated onto the pavement and killed Karla Schuster.

* * * *

"Marianne's with a proper nurse," Sheena lied, "I'll bring her back with me."

"You will come back, won't you?" pleaded Lorraine.

Sheena tried to laugh.

"Of course, I will! Why ever not?"

Morris said, "She's frightened something's going to happen to you."

The unspoken words; like what happened to Mam and Hilda.

Lorraine said, "If you don't come back, there'll be nobody."

Sheena struggled not weep.

"That's silly! I have Daniel with me. He has a big stick. I'll be back, don't you worry. We just have things we need to do."

The children were sitting up in Daniel's bed. The mention of his name seemed to mollify them.

"Jenny will be with you until I get back. She's coming in to read to you, but I expect you two not to be a bother and go to sleep."

Sheena kissed and hugged them both. She struggled to be bright and positive, but she saw desolation in the children's eyes.

She said, "It's time for us to be brave."

Sheena felt far from brave.

When she left them, she wondered if this was the last time she would see them.

Jenny was waiting in the sitting room. There was little to say. On the landing, Daniel said, "Take this."

He presented her with the pistol.

"What am I to do with this?"

"Point it and keep pulling the trigger until it stops."

"What about you?"

"I have my stick."

In the car, Sheena asked, "How did you find where he is?"

"We didn't."

"Then who did?"

"I told you. The sparrows did."

"I don't understand."

When they entered darkened Percy Street and approached the lights of the Paddle Steamer, Sheena cried out in wonderment. She stopped the car.

On every lighted windowsill there were sparrows. On the Victorian gargoyles there were sparrows. On the cast iron gutters there were sparrows. On the roof crest there were sparrows.

Sheena said, "I've never seen anything like this!"

"It's what we used to call a miracle. Until people stopped believing."

"The sparrows know where Marianne is," marvelled Sheena.

Daniel added, "And where the Child is, there is the demon."

They exited from the car onto the pavement. The sparrows were silent. The passing of an occasional car sounded very loud. There was no one in sight.

"We're on our own?" Sheena guessed.

"Guillaume and Karla are dead in this lifetime. I have no idea where Branco is. Are you afraid?"

"Yes. Absolutely terrified."

"This is between him and me. If you'd like to stay in the car?"

"You've said that before. You know the answer."

"Then God go with us."

Sheena found the pistol grip most comforting. They walked to the front door of the familiar Steamer. Inside there were lights, noise and voices. It was a most welcoming place on a dark night.

"Leave the talking to me."

* * * *

They entered into the warm aroma of alcohol and fried food, blinded by the lights, deafened by the voices and stood at the end of the bar. The regulars cheered at the sight of Sheena.

"I'm not working tonight!"

She laughed at the cry of disappointment. Billy came to serve them.

"What'll it be?"

Daniel lied, "My grandson's twenty-first. I'd like to take a shufti at the Function Room, please?"

Billy displayed disappointment and shook his head.

"Sorry to disappoint you. It's booked solid."

Daniel said, "Dei nuntius sum."

Silence fell and all movement stopped. The clock above the bar stopped in mid-chime. Sheena froze. She saw clearly that the habitués of the pub were long-dead, sunken-eyed, mummified spectres, holding glasses in clawed hands. When she looked at Billy, Jessie and Joyce, she saw they were not real; that they were shop window mannequins.

"What's happening?"

"He need not keep up the pantomime any longer. It must've been a tremendous strain."

The lights began to go out as the bulbs splintered. The Flags of All the Nations dangled or dropped rotten fabrics from the cracked ceiling. Billy, Jessie and Joyce fell over stiffly. With a chill creaking, the figures at the bar lost mouldering clothing and bones clattered to the floor. A skull rolled unto Sheena's shoes and she cried out. The window glass broke and the windows were boarded up from outside. The dust of ages settled upon the bar and a rat chittered from the top of the till. Something answered from the darkness. The air stank of decay. Daniel produced a torch.

"This can't be true!"

"The Paddle Steamer has been boarded up for years. It went under new management. Evil Unlimited."

"But I work here!"

"You were useful to them. You were able to come and go."

"How did I not know?"

215

"The night we ate here, Guillaume suspected something was not right. I saw nothing wrong. It was a superb performance."

"Why did I not smell it?"

"Fried food and alcohol? The stink of humanity?"

Daniel tried the door that led to the stairs. It was locked, but he pushed it open. The hallway was dark and the staircase foreboding.

Daniel commanded, "Stay close to me. Do not believe what you see."

Cautiously, they began to ascend the stairs, the torch lighting the steps. Suddenly, there was light on the landing above and Marianne appeared.

"Sheena!" she cried and tottered towards the stairs.

Sheena cried, "Stay there, darling! I'm coming!"

She fought fiercely to pass Daniel, crying, "What're you doing? Marianne's there!"

The child cried from the landing and Sheena punched Daniel.

He slapped her twice sharply. The creature on the landing laughed and disappeared. Sheena stood defeated, breathing heavily.

Daniel said, "What did I say?"

"I'm sorry. I just couldn't."

Five steps farther and a stair was missing. Daniel stepped over cautiously and offered a hand to Sheena. They stood on the landing in an uneasy silence. Three doors were labelled *LADIES, GENTS* and *PRIVATE*. A more ornate double door offered *FUNCTION ROOM*.

Daniel said, "If you are threatened, use the gun."

It was stated so casually, Sheena doubted reality. Daniel opened the door and Sheena followed him into the Function Room.

* * * *

It had once been an elegant ballroom where generations of families had enjoyed unforgettable occasions. The walls were empanelled in a wood that glowed with the patina of ages. Where the plasterwork remained it was elaborate, but most of it was on the floor. Two chandeliers had been laid on the floor undamaged. Others lay in a shower of broken brilliance. In the great fireplace someone had tried to burn paper. At the opposite end to the stage, there was a crude altar lit by candles.

A Salvation Army officer with an eye patch stood before the altar. Marianne, by his side, was dressed in white linen with a tinsel tiara. Sheena's instinct was to run to her sister, but Daniel imprisoned her wrist. They approached the odd couple.

Sheena said, "Don't worry, sweetheart. Sheena's here!"

The Salvation Army officer ignored her,

"Daniel that cometh out of the lions' den. I nearly had you then, old man."

"My God sent his angel and he shut the mouths of the lions."

The demon laughed.

"Or the lions were too well fed."

Daniel said, "You will not take that child to Hell."

"How will you stop me?"

"I will kill you. Here, you die forever."

The demon was silent.

"This is not the Child you have hunted. That child has gone and no one knows where. Leave this innocent child. Take me."

Sheena cried, "No! Take me! Take me! Leave Marianne!"

Sheena rushed forward. The demon reacted. Daniel drew the sword from its wooden sheath. It unfolded its deadly beauty. Sheena struggled and failed to untangle the pistol from her pocket.

The flame that leapt from the demon's hand wavered, but it was enough to sever Daniel's left arm. The ragged sleeve smouldered. The dying limb fell to the floor. Daniel cried out in agony and collapsed. The demon advanced to finish the killing. Sheena picked up the blazing sword and charged at the demon. He stumbled and Sheena drove the sword into his chest. So great was the impetus of her assault that she carried him backwards to impale the demon to the panelled wall where he screamed and wriggled like a broken insect. The scent of burning flesh stung her nostrils.

Sheena turned to find Marianne kneeling by Daniel who was semiconscious, groaning with pain. To her astonishment, she saw her sister touch the stump and the bleeding stopped. Marianne kissed the wounded man's brow. Daniel ceased to groan and his breathing became calmer. He fell into a regular sleep.

"Help me!" whimpered the Demon.

Sheena turned to watch him, writhing on the blade.

"Whatever you wish, I will give you! If you will pull out this sword."

Sheena approached the demon and seized the sword handle.

"Thank you, oh, thank you, my princess!"

Sheena put her full weight upon the sword and pushed until the sword handle grated upon the creature's breastbone. He screamed afresh and spat at her. The girl stepped back to watch the demon die.

The human guise fell away and she saw what seemed more a clawed lizard than a man. The mouth of broken teeth screamed and screamed again as the limbs clawed for escape and found no release. The eye looked upon her with venomous hatred and spittle burned where it struck the floor. Then the creature died. The spindly body hung upon the blade. There was silence.

Marianne tugged at her wrist. To Sheena's surprise, she said clearly, "Bandage his wound."

She gaped and Marianne said, "Do what I say."

Sheena tore linen from Marianne's dress and bound up the fresh amputation. She wept as she worked.

Bandaging complete, Sheena found herself turning to Marianne who commanded, "Light a fire."

In the great fireplace, Sheena created a fire from broken chairs.

"Burn the arm," said Marianne.

It took more than tears to pick up Daniel's severed arm. She could not bear to watch it burn.

"Free the demon," Marianne ordered.

Sheena strove fearfully to pull out the sword from the corpse that slithered to the floor. She feared it would rise against her, but it didn't.

"Cut off the head and burn it."

"I can't, I really can't!"

"It must be done."

Sheena cut off the head and shuddered with revulsion as she dragged it to the flames. In one terrifying moment, the mouth opened on broken teeth and she thought it was about to speak. At Marianne's orders, Sheena cut up and burnt every scrap of the demon's body. She wept and vomited as she worked.

Exhausted, Sheena asked, "Who am I speaking to?"

Marianne smiled and said, "Up!"

Sheena gathered her into befouled arms.

"Sheena good!"

"Has that person, whoever it was, has he-she gone now?"

Marianne chuckled, but said nothing.

"You know I'm going to have nightmares forever, don't you?" But she never did. Afterwards, Sheena struggled to believe what she had done on the orders of a year-old baby.

When Daniel awoke, they left the ruined building. Nothing barred their way. Nothing stirred in the desolation. Nothing living or dead arose within the ruined walls. When they came out into the street, there was a great rushing of wings as the sparrows took to the air. Marianne laughed and waved her arms. As she drove back to the tower, Sheena pondered whether Daniel was mistaken in saying Marianne was not the Singular Child.

When they entered the flat, Sheena and Marianne were overwhelmed by Lorraine and Morris who wept and laughed and danced. Marianne sat in Daniel's lap as they waited for the takeaway Sheena ordered. Nobody seemed to notice Daniel was lacking an arm. Marianne's tiara was much admired. Happiness is very simple. To be with those you love.

* * * *

EPILOGUE

"Why did the chicken cross the Tyne Bridge?"

It was a fine sunny morning as Chief Superintendent Gerald Taylor tapped in the code that gave him entry to the building. On the stairs, he was caught by his Chief Inspector.

"That reporter? Moore?"

"What about him?"

"He's in your office."

"The hell he is!"

"Spoiler alert! Solicitor type with him?"

"Who let them in?"

"No idea."

The Chief Inspector closed his ears to his chief's obscenities and hurried down the stairs.

Chief Superintendent Gerald Taylor entered the office at full steam, hurling his cap at the coat stand. It fell to the floor.

"This is the worst day of your life, Moore! I would advise you to leave now! This minute!"

The two men were unmoved.

"Stand up! I never gave you permission to sit down."

Tom Moore stood up. He placed a single photograph on the Chief Superintendent's blotter. Gerald Taylor glanced down and went white.

"These gentlemen," Tom Moore indicated, "will be very interested to hear your explanation of this photograph and others in which you appear. They are Deputy Commissioners Norman Wilson and John Tillet. From the Met. I won't intrude further. I have a scoop to write for the Gazette."

* * * *

Tom Moore read aloud, "Apart from the Chief Superintendent, fifty-seven men and twenty-three women were arrested this morning, on charges ranging from child abuse to murder. The elusive Tony Buckle was released from remand and was about to deliver a speech criticising the police only to be re-arrested on the steps of the Magistrates' Court. Those arrested include a former sergeant and constable of the Gallin force."

His editor and former father-in-law commented, "This is your ticket to the Mail, Express, maybe even the Sun, Tommy."

"Would you be sorry to lose me?"

"No," said his editor truthfully.

* * * *

Sheena hugged the steering wheel. Daniel, Lorraine and Morris sat behind, belted in, unable to escape. Marianne chuckled in her safety seat.

Daniel asked, "Have you ever driven one of these before, Sheena?"

"Heaps of times," lied Sheena.

"It's not a Seat. You have to remember the length of it."

"You have to remember," cautioned Morris, "That my sister is the best ever liar."

Daniel said, "So be it! The Tyne Bridge, please! Drive South."

Lorraine offered, "Why did the chicken cross the Tyne Bridge?"

They all agreed politely they didn't know.

"To get away from Ant and Dec."

Lorraine laughed, but everybody else groaned.

Sheena drove Guillaume's mobile home steadily South. The children had fallen asleep. Daniel said quietly, "Soon's you can, come off the motorway and drive North."

"Why?"

"That was a skirmish. The war's not over."

* * * *

221

Everywhere there are certain human beings who illuminate our world. They are not heroes and their actions are not noticeably noble. But by their very presence, they light up everyone they meet and dispel the darkness within them. Friend and stranger then carry that light out into the darkness of the world. One day the world will rejoice in light eternal. Conversely, there are those creatures that wish the world to remain in darkness and will seek to put out the light wherever they find it.

The End to this Narrative
Alex Ferguson